DONNA ROSE AND THE ROOTS OF EVIL

GALE
CENGAGE Learning

Set in 11 pt. Plantin.
Printed on permanent paper.

LIBRARY OF CONGRESS CATALOGING-IN-PUBLICATION DATA

Johnson, Norma Tadlock.
  Donna Rose and the roots of evil : a Cedar Harbor mystery / by Norma Tadlock Johnson. — 1st ed.
    p. cm.
  ISBN-13: 978-1-59414-727-2 (alk. paper)
  ISBN-10: 1-59414-727-2 (alk. paper)
  1. Retired teachers—Fiction. 2. Police—Crimes against—Fiction. 3. Washington (State)—Fiction. I. Title.
PS3560.O3819D65 2009
813'.54—dc22
                                        2008039748

First Edition. First Printing: January 2009.
Published in 2009 in conjunction with Tekno Books and Ed Gorman.

Printed in the United States of America
1 2 3 4 5 6 7 12 11 10 09 08

A CEDAR HARBOR MYSTERY

Donna Rose and the Roots of Evil

Norma Tadlock Johnson

FIVE STAR
A part of Gale, Cengage Learning

GALE
CENGAGE Learning

Detroit • New York • San Francisco • New Haven, Conn • Waterville, Maine • London

ACKNOWLEDGMENTS

Thanks to all who shared their knowledge and in so doing, made *Donna Rose and the Roots of Evil* a better book. These include: Drs. Deborah North and Geoffrey Spielmann, who helped mold Alvin's injuries; Attorney Robert Cole, who enlightened me on legal matters; Randy Watson, Washington State Patrol, who informed me about AFIS; and florist Barbara Pinney, who designed Alvin's bouquet.

Any errors can be attributed to me, either inadvertent ones or places where I bent the truth to strengthen the plot.

For all the members of the Skagit Valley Writers League, especially those of my critique group: Serena DuBois, Helen Gregory, Robin Heflin, Judy Kirscht, Chris Measamer and Pat Cowgill. Many thanks for your help, support and encouragement.

CHAPTER ONE

The first gray, whipping wind of winter swooped in with accompanying rain to demolish what remained of my garden. It was the first week in November, and earlier than I like to hear the weatherman on the evening news speaking of arctic air. The headline in the *Cedar Harbor Post,* however, was of matters other than the weather. POLICE CHIEF DONNIKER REHIRED, it said. I had no difficulty figuring out which event was the more depressing.

The day was so gloomy that I sat under my brightest lamp in the living room to read, even though it was morning. My eyes need all the help they can get at my age. I threw down the paper in disgust as a movement outside caught my eye. The retired navy man who lives next door, Cyrus Bates, was striding along the walk from his house. The fact that he turned in to my place was no surprise.

I sighed over events in general. Cyrus's arrival these days would rate a five, maybe even a six in the general scheme of things. In other words, more or less neutral. There was a time, of course, when we were actively feuding, that I'd have scored a visit from the sandy-haired man with the bushy eyebrows and a trim moustache at no more than two. I'd been forced to reevaluate him.

"Come in," I greeted him. "No doubt you've just finished reading the *Post?*"

"Not finished. Just started. That was enough." He waved the

offending newspaper in front of my nose. "How can they? Why haven't we heard anything about this?" Cyrus was as agitated as I'd ever seen him. Normally, he'd have calmly digested the information. I studied him. Wasn't his hair actually ruffled a bit? Astounding. I could understand his feelings, though. Anger seethed through my own digestive system.

"Sit down," I suggested, ignoring his questions as being rhetorical. I led the way, settling on the couch where I'd been before. He remained standing for a moment, then said, "Oh, hell," and plunked into my leather chair. Air swooshed out of its stuffing.

"Please be careful, Cyrus," I said. "That's an expensive chair. I'm not likely to replace it now that I'm living on retirement."

He started to say something, then frowned. "Sorry, Donna Rose," he muttered. "But this news . . ." He seldom uses my disliked middle name. His agitation, no doubt, was the cause this time. "You had no inkling either?" he continued.

"Absolutely not. Didn't Jake know?"

"Jake doesn't keep me informed about everything in his life, you know. Surely he'd have called one of us if he had, though."

Jake is the young police officer who my daughter Roberta nicknamed "the hope of Cedar Harbor." Chief William Donniker, known as Billy to me when he was the terror of my sixth-grade class, had to be one of the most inept protectors of society in the State of Washington. After he so bungled the investigation of the murder of Lyle Corrigan, several of us had formed a "Dump Donniker" committee. The aim had been to replace him as Chief with the redheaded Jake Santorini.

"Perhaps our committee became complacent," I suggested.

"Complacent!" Cyrus was still angry. "No way. It's obvious to anyone with an ounce of brains that Donniker's incompetent. Maybe our mistake was in assuming a certain level of intelligence for the members of the town council. And then this . . ."

He leaned forward and punched the paper. "A party, for God's sake. For him! To honor him for his years of service." A growl emanated from deep in his chest.

"A party?" I snatched up my discarded paper. "I didn't get that far." Sure enough, three paragraphs down the article announced that a gathering would be held in the library meeting room on Monday evening to honor Donniker and to congratulate him upon the renewal of his contract. With a raise yet. "Mayor Roland Oliver said, 'Chief Donniker was responsible for the apprehension of the murderer in Cedar Harbor's recent sad episode. We're lucky to have a man of his ability serving our community,' " reported the *Post*.

"That idiot," I snapped. "I knew I didn't like the man."

"I assume you mean idiot mayor rather than idiot police chief, which is a given. What's this Oliver's history?" Cyrus asked.

"He sells cars. Used, I suppose. In fact, I believe he owns the agency. I've never paid much attention. I abhor politics and politicians."

"That's a general feeling these days." He grimaced. "But politicians are a fact of life, and we have to learn to deal with them. Tell me more about this mayor."

"He's been around Cedar Harbor forever. Probably not really, since he wasn't one of my students, but I honestly don't remember when he arrived. He was on various committees, then ran for the town council. After a while there, he rotated into being mayor."

"Umph," Cyrus commented. "Well. We are, of course, going to this party?"

I shook my head in disbelief. "Whatever for? To flatter that nincompoop?"

"No, to counteract any lies he might be telling. You did catch that statement about him being responsible for the apprehension of the murderer? I seem to remember seeing you rolling around on the ground and struggling for that blasted knife when Jake and I arrived to the rescue."

"Yes. Although by the time you got there I had things under control, if you remember. I was sitting astride—"

"And looking quite triumphant. I stand corrected. Are you going to let Chief Donniker get away with taking credit?"

I shook my head. "Certainly not! We'll go, and maybe we can at least remind a few people of the true story. I wonder if it's too late to reactivate our Dump Donniker committee? And . . . I wonder how Jake is taking this?"

"Like a man, I assume," Cyrus said.

As forecast, the arctic air followed on the heels of the storm. The night must have been well below freezing, I realized the next morning when I stared out the window at the dismal sight of cold-blackened chrysanthemums. The geraniums in the baskets at the window hung limp and drained of color. I could feel the chill through the glass, in spite of the expensive double-paned windows I'd had installed not long ago. I pulled my terry-cloth robe closer and clutched the neckline to shut out the draft.

I'm getting old, I thought. The rainy weather typical of the Pacific Northwest I've always liked and still do, and the cold has never particularly bothered me. It's so rare here. Just last year, my geraniums lived through the winter. But when freezing weather comes in November, who knows? Sometimes it's nature teasing, saying, "See what I can do if I want to?" But sometimes it's an ominous portent of things to come.

I sighed. What on earth was I going to do today? My first year of retirement had seemed so fulfilling. I had wondered, often, at the occasional retiree who was bored. Not me, I'd assured anyone willing to listen. I have my garden and my books.

Only gardens in November aren't that rewarding, and a person can't read all day every day. At least I can't. My eyes simply aren't up to it. No one tells you when you're young and looking forward to the freedom from commitments of raising a family and earning a living that the old bod might let you down.

Stop it, I told myself. Your old bod is better than most and there's nothing wrong with your mind, which you ought to be grateful for. Perhaps if Roberta had settled closer, had children on whom I could dote, I wouldn't be feeling so—so down-hearted.

And perhaps, I admitted, my mood was caused by the news about Chief Donniker. The whole business we'd all been involved with had been sad, of course, but still, in a peculiar sort of way, invigorating. It's not often one has an opportunity to meet evil head on and win. How many women my age have had to fight for their lives, have bested inept bureaucratic forces, have had the opportunity to influence the outcome of a murderous situation?

And then? Then what? To return to tending a garden which would inevitably fade, to continue a now generally harmonious relationship with my next-door neighbor, a state of affairs I'd assumed would be desirable? On reflection, I missed feuding with Cyrus.

Worst of all, I realized, was finding out that inept bureaucracy was going to win after all. My lips clenched. I was frustrated. How much more so, must Jake be? He had so much at stake.

Well, the old adage says something about not being able to change others but only changing oneself. I, clearly, needed more to do. I turned my back on my garden and reached for the phone. The number was long memorized.

"Cedar Harbor School District," a familiar voice answered.

"Hello, Martha? This is Donna Galbreath."

"Donna, how good to hear from you. How are . . ." And we

13

went on to exchange the usual pleasantries of two women who'd been friends for years but not seen each other recently. She finished, "Is there something I can help you with?"

"Uh, I was wondering," I asked, "how's the substitute situation this year?"

"You're thinking of coming back? How wonderful. There'd always be room for you, you know that. Let me transfer you to Mr. Kapochi."

And so, my return to the working world was instituted. Not full-time, I explained to Charlie Kapochi. I simply had to keep my earnings under the limit established by Social Security.

"Of course, Donna," he said. "We have several substitutes in your circumstances. We all know that teachers' pensions are inadequate."

"Well, I've been getting along fine." Still, I thought, the money for extras would come in handy. Better to let everyone think that that was why I'd returned to work rather than that I might have—horrors!—been bored.

My spirits definitely lifted. Children still bloom in November. When Monday evening rolled around, I slid into my quilted coat and headed out to meet Cyrus. As predicted, the wind had shifted to the north, bringing clearing along with the frigid air. The stars twinkled like sequins on a glittery party dress, I noticed as I crunched across the frozen lawn to his driveway.

"Good evening, Cyrus," I said, still entranced with the heavens. "Beautiful night, isn't it?"

Cyrus noticed my improved mental state immediately. "Uncommonly cheerful tonight, aren't we?"

"Is it that obvious? Yes. I made a decision. I'm going back to work. Oh, not full-time," I explained when he began noises of commiseration. "I'm going to substitute teach occasionally. I miss the classroom." And so I did.

"Well, then, it's the right decision for you." Cyrus held the door of his ridiculous but fun little red car as I maneuvered my way into the passenger seat. He shut the door with an expensive-sounding clunk, then strolled around to the driver's side, climbed in and turned the key. The car ran much too noisily. Had it been I with sufficient money to purchase a luxury car, this would not have been my choice. A smooth, quiet purr was more to my taste.

"You'll need some of that cheerfulness tonight, I fear," Cyrus said, backing out of his driveway.

"Did you have to remind me?" I frowned. "I have thought out the evening, and it seems to me that pleasant honesty is the best approach. I supposed I'll even swallow my distaste and congratulate the man. Billy always did respond to flattery."

Cyrus raised that bushy eyebrow he uses so effectively to express a questioning attitude or disdain. Which was it this time? "Well, don't you agree?" I asked.

"Oh, absolutely. Congratulate him, then do your best to sabotage him."

Was he merely being honest or did he disapprove? I couldn't tell from his expression.

"Here we are," Cyrus said unnecessarily, swooping into the library parking lot in his inimitable manner and causing a couple of suddenly fast-moving pedestrians to frown and leap for the curb. He didn't even notice.

"Had any tickets recently?" I inquired in an innocent tone.

He shot me a quick glance before turning away. "I refuse to answer on the grounds of self-incrimination."

"You *have* had a ticket. The chief? Or Jake again?"

"The sheriff," he growled.

"You really should be careful," I warned. "Aren't you in danger of losing your license? But of course, if you do, I'd be happy to take over driving for you. I think driving your car would be quite fun."

Cyrus does, I've learned, have quite a well-developed sense of humor. Not this time. His lips tightened as he opened the door on his side. "Must have been recently," I commented, not waiting for him and opening my own door.

"Donna Rose, will you please dry up?"

I turned my head so he wouldn't see my smile, but let him take my arm to create peace between us as we joined the crowd strolling toward the library meeting room. I suddenly felt quite cheery but, with a touch of guilt as I glanced at his face, I realized that Cyrus no longer did. It's such a temptation to tease Cyrus, an action I abhorred in my students. I needed to control that impulse, too.

"Everyone in town seems to be here," I commented, glancing around. "Oh, look, there's Jake. Somehow I didn't think he'd come."

"I told you he'd take it like a man." Cyrus straightened unconsciously into a military posture.

That is a phrase I've never particularly liked, with all its connotations of unnecessary bravado and unwillingness to show sensitivity. Not to mention being sexist, as if women aren't capable of bearing adversity. Typical Cyrus. However, I exercised forbearance and instead said, "Let's speak to him before we go in. Oh. And Sue's with him. I wonder how she's making out?"

Sue Reilly is the young widowed mother who Jake had finally been astute enough to realize cared for him. I had high hopes, at least before this present disaster, that the two would soon be married. A look at her face indicated to me that she was bearing up now, yes, but with difficulty. She was pale under the obvious blush applied to her cheeks, and I saw her bite her lip as she glanced in the direction of the meeting-room door.

Jake, however, was another story. His expression was mutinous, and as we crossed the parking lot in their direction, I saw Sue clutch his sleeve and pull toward the library. Jake reminded me, I remembered with a sudden flash, of a burro my husband Bob and I had made the mistake of hiring for a week-long backpack in the Olympic Mountains shortly before I became pregnant with Roberta and only a couple of years before Bob died. The burro, deceptively named Honeybunch, had straightened all four legs and balked at crossing the first creek we came to. We got no farther with her. Honeybunch's expression had been remarkably like Jake's.

"Wait." I stopped in my tracks which, since he was attached to my arm, effectively stopped Cyrus, too.

"Come on, Jake," Sue, not seeing us, pleaded. "You have to go in. Even if . . ."

"I don't think I can face the bastard!" Jake's voice was much too loud and attracted glances from others heading toward the library.

"But you're managing to do it every day."

"Yeah, but nobody's honoring him around the department. Everybody there knows he's a son-of-a-bitch, even the janitor. Anyway, I keep going by picturing handing him my resignation."

Oh, dear, I thought. I should have known Jake would leave. I guess I would, too, under the circumstances. But, still, what would Cedar Harbor do without him? And where was he going?

"Can't you . . ." Sue began to plead.

"No, I can't. If I go in there," Jake said, "I may do something you'll regret. I won't."

"But . . ."

"Somebody's going to kill that bastard," Jake said, "and I don't much care whether it's me or somebody else."

Now his voice definitely was too loud. Cyrus evidently decided it was time to intervene. Dropping my arm, he strode toward Jake with his hand out. "Jake, I just want you to know how stunned I was to read about this." He shrugged one shoulder toward the library. "What happened? Is there anything any of us can do?"

Jake's features rearranged into the control he usually evidenced. "Thanks, Cyrus," he said, shaking his hand. "No, there's nothing you can do. It's all over."

"We thought we'd reactivate our committee . . ."

"Too late. The buddy system conquers all."

"Buddies?" I interjected. "You mean Billy and Roland are old friends?"

"You've got it. The chances of getting the chief out of here are kaput. I don't know why or how it happened, but somehow the chief wrapped that council around his fat finger."

Sue spoke for the first time. "We thought that Chief Donniker was all through and Jake would get the job. That new city councilwoman, Geri Sataro, even implied that it was a done deal."

"What on earth could have changed their minds?"

"I don't know!" Sue was definitely wailing. "Just when—just when things were going so well. Now Jake's sending resumes all over. Some really awful places. Anywhere away from here."

"Sue," Jake warned in an undertone.

"Well, I don't care if Cyrus and Donna know. At least they're friends, Jake, and they wouldn't sneak around behind your back and slit your throat."

A smile that almost looked like the old Jake flitted across his freckled face. "At least none of those awful places have offered me a job."

"Yet."

"Well, let's go in together," Cyrus suggested in a hearty voice. "Strength in numbers, and all that."

He sounded like a caricature of an old-time military officer. I half-expected some utterance along the lines of, "Keep a stiff upper lip, old man." But his attempt at diverting Jake succeeded.

18

Jake managed a real smile and turned toward the library, with Cyrus beside him.

Sue hung back to speak with me. "I'm so glad you two are here," she said. "It was actually Jake's idea to come. He only changed his mind when we got here. I'm so upset. He's so— Donna, what am I going to do?"

I sighed. The question women face much too often. Men, too, perhaps, but they usually are in a position to take action. Jake was able to busy himself with looking for a new job, while Sue could do nothing more than wring her hands. And be supportive.

"I don't know. I really don't," I told her. "Hope for the best. If you care enough, follow him to one of those awful places. But let's hope Jake is wrong. I'm a great believer in fate. Let's wait and see what happens." I squeezed her hand.

I should never have said it. Fate doesn't always proceed in the direction we mortals have in mind.

CHAPTER TWO

Not surprisingly, Police Chief William Donniker was already holding court. I mean in the regal sense, of course, not the judicial. He was a large, imposing man, if you ignored the paunch. Actually, that evidence of too many steaks and beers wasn't as obvious as when he was dressed in uniform shirt and pants and his belly hung over a sagging belt. Today he wore a well-cut suit. New, no doubt. Billy had plans for moving up in the world, I'd have been willing to bet.

The smile which never left his somewhat florid face was self-satisfied. I realized, suddenly, how very much I disliked the man. The twelve-year-old whom I had tolerated in the sixth grade was an irritant. The grown-up version could be a danger-ous man as well as a fool.

His wife presided next to him, a half-step behind as suited a consort of royalty. Lucille, a tall, thin woman with salt-and-pepper hair pulled into a knot at her nape, watched her husband without expression. That was normal. I'd never seen her smile or frown or grimace.

They were surrounded by sycophants. Mayor Oliver, a man with a car-salesman smile and thinning blond hair, stood in the circle, of course. He was an ex-athlete, I'd read somewhere, and it showed in the trim body build. Good looking, if you liked the type.

Geri Sataro was there, too. I'd never had an opportunity to talk to her, and now, in view of what I'd learned tonight, I studied her closely. A tall woman, with sleek dark hair encasing her head like a helmet, she was reputed to be a multi-millionaire after having been fortunate enough to be in on the ground floor at one of the software companies. The opinions I'd heard from those who had dealt with her were mixed. Some, obviously impressed by her financial acumen, raved. Others were less positive, and described her as haughty and above herself.

Sweet little Bessie Amherst had said, "Well, I do think she might be rather shy, don't you know? Those people can so often appear aloof when they really just don't know how to be friendly."

Shy? I thought. When she'd clearly held her own in the somewhat male-dominated technology field? I doubted it. Besides, one did have to take into account that Bessie never said ill of anyone. I'd reserve judgment.

More significant was whether she truly had reneged on a promise to replace Donniker with Jake. If so, why? Unlike the rest, at least she wasn't fawning over Billy, but appeared to be quietly observing. Millions could do wonders for one's confidence. She wouldn't need a small-town police chief. Why, then, would she have voted in favor of his being given a new contract?

The sound of a sneeze interrupted my train of thoughts. "Oh, hell," Jake said, taking a handkerchief from Sue and blowing loudly. "This damned cold!" I realized that his voice when he'd spoken outside hadn't sounded completely normal, but I'd assumed it had been the strain of the occasion.

Jake headed away from the convivial group. "Come on," he said, "let's get some coffee."

I could understand why he wouldn't want to be any closer to the chief than necessary. I felt the same. Was I really going to be able to congratulate the man? "Looks like good food," I said, glancing at the table for the first time and noting professionally prepared snacks waiting to be devoured. The side table was staffed by two bartenders.

"Ah!" Jake veered in that direction.

"Jake," Sue warned, "do you need . . ."

"I wonder who's paying for this shindig," Cyrus said.

I merely sighed. Alcohol, no doubt, was not the best thing for Jake at this moment, unless he was one of those who were sedated by it rather than excited. And Cyrus was entirely right to wonder. Who was paying for this obviously expensive affair? I shot a glance back at Geri, the first to come to mind. My glance caught hers and she smiled ironically. I could have sworn that she was reading my mind.

Not for the first time I reflected on how Cedar Harbor had changed in the years since I'd moved here. Once it was a quiet small town on Puget Sound, a vacation spot for many, a sanctuary for those who wanted peace. Now it was acquiring too much traffic, more crime, and millionaires who built extravagant and sometimes inappropriate houses. Geri Sataro wasn't the only person with immense wealth who'd moved here recently. Property values, particularly of waterfront or view pieces, were escalating out of sight. The day might come when retirees such as I would be forced away by high taxes.

I turned back toward the refreshments. Meatballs simmered with pineapple and green pepper in a chafing dish; puffs with various fillings; eggs stuffed with something green, probably avocado, all reached out and said, "Eat me." Cyrus, whose good humor had obviously been restored, was heaping a plate with smoked salmon, shrimp, cheese puffs and egg rolls.

"Your cholesterol will soar," I commented.

"Mine," he answered before popping a sausage surrounded by pastry into his mouth, "is one seventy-five. What's yours?"

"Not that good," I admitted, sounding more humble than I care to with Cyrus. Like everything else in his life, his cholesterol remained under control. Didn't anything around him rebel? *You did,* the little voice inside me asserted. Defiantly, I began to fill my own plate. If Geri—or someone else—was willing to contribute this sumptuous food, we might as well enjoy.

"Well, Chief, let's help ourselves to some of this delicious repast," a voice behind me said. Startled, I glanced over my shoulder to see that the cluster of people surrounding Donniker had moved toward the table. Roland Oliver's voice had a hint of the twang one associates with a poorly educated person. It didn't quite fit with a man who used words such as repast. Was the accent a down-home touch affected to lure customers?

"Let's get a refill on our drinks first, though. Bartender!" the mayor ordered peremptorily. One of the white-jacketed young men trotted obediently toward him. Had it been Oliver, instead, who had paid for the food? Possibly, the way the bartender had responded. Maybe, though, the man wanted to stay on Oliver's good side because he was expecting to negotiate the purchase of a new clunker soon.

Jake's brown eyes narrowed as he glared at the chief. He seemed unaware of anyone or anything else. His hand appeared to have a mind of its own as it reached for a second chicken wing, hesitated, then placed it on his plate.

Susan said brightly, "Let's go sit over there." She pointed to a group of chairs in a nearby corner.

"Sounds good to me," I answered in a tone just as fakey as hers. Cyrus led the way, and Jake followed without arguing. Fortunately, I felt. We all settled on the uncomfortable metal chairs. I'd suggest to the Library Guild that they raise money for new ones, I decided as I wiggled my behind in an unsuccessful attempt to find a comfortable position.

"I can't stand that woman now," Sue whispered, staring at Geri Sataro.

"I don't blame you," I answered, "if what you say is true. I mean," I amended as Susan began to bristle, "if she didn't have some reason we don't know about for changing her mind."

"Of course she had some reason we don't know about," Cyrus said sarcastically. "Donna, that's a remarkably off-the-wall statement for you."

Sue laughed. "I didn't mean to get you two arguing. I think I know what Donna's trying to say. That I should keep an open mind until we find out why the council all voted to retain Chief Donniker."

"*If* we find out," Jake muttered before swallowing about half of a rather tall glass full of amber liquid. Oh, dear.

"And if they all voted for him. Was it unanimous? I'm curious enough to check," Cyrus said.

"All those people buttering him up," Sue said. "Look, there's Al Parry."

"Umm," I said, noncommittally. I no longer had to contend with Al on the water board, thank God, but it was impossible to avoid the prominent pharmacist forever. Should I ignore him if we came face to face or speak pleasantly?

"Trust Al to be hanging around Donniker," Cyrus said wryly. "One crook knows another."

"Yes, but on reflection, I think this is new for Al," I said. "I really don't believe they were buddies back when we had to work with him." Cyrus, too, is a member of the water board. In fact, he is the reluctant president, becoming so after proving that Al had developed too cozy a relationship with the developer Mark Gasper. Which reminded me, was he here, too? Yes, indeed. Why wasn't I surprised? Mark stood across the room, his dark head bent in conversation with a woman I didn't recognize. At least he wasn't in the group following the chief, which was to his credit.

I bit into a cracker spread with a paste. "Oh, yuck," I said, swallowing valiantly but placing the rest of the cracker on the edge of my plate. "I do believe that's liver pâté. Why they foist it on us, I don't know."

Susan laughed as Cyrus eyed a second cracker on my plate. "Wonderful stuff," he said. "Want to get rid of that one?"

"Be my guest." I held out the plate. "No one eats liver, so why they all gush over pâté, I'll never know. And anchovies . . ."

"I'm with you on that," Sue agreed. "They're so fishy."

Jake had been quiet during this interchange. I noted that somehow he'd gained a refill of his glass. His plate, heaped with cheese puffs, asparagus rolls and, of course, the chicken wings, was mostly untouched. As I watched, he again drank from his glass, not sipping as the rest of us were doing, while never taking his eyes off Donniker. He was making me very nervous. I caught Cyrus's eye, and made frowning faces toward Jake.

Cyrus nodded slightly. "Shall I get everybody coffee?" he offered, standing.

Jake stood, too, holding his plate in front of him. Was he a trifle unsteady? I couldn't decide.

Suddenly, he let loose a monstrous sneeze, directly at his food. The chicken wings quivered. "I knew I didn't want to eat this stuff," he said, laughing with embarrassment as he pulled the handkerchief from his pocket and wiped his nose. "Excuse me, folks," he apologized. "I'll help you get the coffee, Cyrus." And the two of them headed toward the serving table.

"Tea for me," I called after them.

"I know, Donna," Cyrus answered, sounding long-suffering. Well, I suppose he did know by now that I only rarely indulge in coffee.

I watched as Jake, with Cyrus following, steered a wide circle around the chief and his group. Jake set his plate down on a side table and then helped Cyrus fill our orders. I was relieved to see that Jake did seem completely steady. At least so far. Two drinks, after all, shouldn't have much of an effect on him. What worried me was the possibility that he might have been drinking before he came.

"We should mingle," Cyrus said as he handed me my tea. "We aren't going to accomplish anything by talking only to each other."

"Accomplish anything?" Sue inquired.

"Oh, just a little damage control. It's not important to most people, I guess, but Donna and I resent the chief taking credit for solving the murder last year. We thought we'd just do a little reminding . . ."

"Oh, that's good," Sue said, springing to her feet. "I like that. Jake . . ."

Cyrus shook his head. "All things considered, I think Jake should stay out of it. He still has to work in the department, among other things. But if you want to slyly remind people . . ."

"I will. Jake, you stay here."

"We're hoping that it isn't really too late to get rid of the chief," I said. "How can everyone have forgotten what a poor job he did?"

"Well, most people don't know anything about local politics except for what they read in the paper," Cyrus said. "That reminds me. I wonder . . ."

He turned, his eyes searching the room. "Ah, yes. I thought he'd be here. There's Tim Borland, the new owner of the *Post*. I think I'll just sidle up to him and see what he knows."

Borland had recently come to Cedar Harbor and bought the paper. I knew very little about the gray-haired man except that he'd come here from some Midwestern big city. Cincinnati, maybe? "Be careful," I warned. "He printed that glowing statement the mayor made."

"He did, but that's just journalism."

"He could always write an editorial," Jake interjected. He began to rise. "I don't want to just sit here and do nothing."

"Sit," Sue ordered, pushing him down by his shoulders. "I don't think you could be tactful about this if somebody paid you."

Jake grinned unpleasantly. "You're right about that."

"There's Ann Pullen from my babysitting co-op," Sue said, nodding toward a blonde, one of those with bushels of unkempt hair. "I'll go talk to her."

"It won't do any good." Jake's words were clipped.

"Maybe nothing but make us feel better," I said firmly. "Sooner or later, though, we'll get that guy."

Cyrus, carrying his coffee, headed casually toward the editor. Sue, looking purposeful, charged toward her friend. I, after glancing around, chose Mark Gasper as my target. Mark was, if nothing else, influential in the community. He also, unless I missed my guess, always knew what was going on.

I left my empty plate on my chair and headed across the room, tea cup in hand. "Mark," I said feigning more enthusiasm than I felt, "how are you these days?"

A look of surprise flashed across his face, but he quickly suppressed it. I couldn't blame him. I had, after all, not exactly welcomed his attempt to bring a huge development called Shadybrook Meadows to Cedar Harbor. But that was in the past, and I'd heard somewhere that Mark was now involved with an expansion to the shopping center out by the freeway.

"Donna," he said effusively, shaking my hand. "I'm just fine. How goes it with you?"

"Oh," I said, "good, good. I'm going to return to substitute teaching, and . . ."

"That's wonderful," he interrupted. "I'm sure you've really been missed." The smile he flashed was one of the reasons the man was so successful, I concluded. His parents must have spent a fortune at the orthodontist, but it had been money well spent. "What grade will you be teaching?" he asked.

"Oh, elementary, I assume, because of my experience. I'm qualified, however, in English at the high school."

"I'm sure you'd handle it very well."

Enough of this nonsensical chatter, I decided. I'd get right to heart of the matter. "Mark," I asked, "do you know how the town council ever came to renew Chief Donniker's contract?"

"I've been wondering the same thing myself. Although," he said, smiling a trifle grimly, "the town council's decisions have often baffled me."

"I suppose they have," I agreed in sympathy. "I've never known anyone who didn't find their meetings extremely frustrating. But still, have you heard anything specific about . . ."

The screech of a defective sound system and an irritating burst of static interrupted me. The honeyed twang of the mayor followed. I turned to see Oliver standing at a microphone in the corner of the room. He fiddled with it for a moment, his lips pursed, then tried again. The sound system still prickled and complained, but he spoke louder to overcome it. "I'm glad to see such a good turnout to honor our esteemed guest of honor," he began.

Odd how he'd chosen a word I'd used so often to describe the chief disdainfully.

"Cedar Harbor wouldn't be the same without him."

Indeed it wouldn't. Roland was using decidedly ambiguous terms in his presentation. Billy, who laid the chicken wing he'd been about to stuff into his mouth back onto his plate to join its mate and a heap of other goodies, clearly didn't notice. He'd always been dense.

"Not that he needs any introduction," Roland went on. "We all know Cedar Harbor Police Chief William Donniker!" His voice rose at the end like an announcer at the county fair. The audience obediently clapped. Most of them. I didn't, and I noticed that Mark didn't either.

Billy grinned. I half-expected him to clasp his hands overhead like a winning prize-fighter. Let's hope, I thought, that this is only the end of the first round instead of the conclusion of the fight. He set his plate of food on the side table and took the microphone. "Thank you, thank you," he said. "I'm honored that you could all come tonight. I . . ."

To be honest, I tuned him out. I couldn't stand it. I'm afraid I muttered an opinion of the proceedings under my breath, because Mark grinned suddenly. People weren't being exactly quiet, and as the level of conversation rose, the chief realized he'd lost his audience.

". . . and so enjoy the food," he concluded, "which was so generously provided by our welcome newcomer, Tim Borland, the editor and publisher of the *Cedar Harbor Post.*" He waved his hand toward Borland and people again clapped, this time with more enthusiasm.

Then Mark surprised me. "Not a word about you or Cyrus."

"Or, more to the point, Jake," I added. "Surely, if people knew what really happened, they'd see that the council got rid of the man and offered the job to Jake. Mark, we need a good police chief."

"I couldn't agree more. I want a competent police department because I live here. I want Cedar Harbor to have a good reputation because it sells houses."

That was clear and remarkably honest. "Then, why do you think the council . . ."

"Why?" He sighed. "Donna, you're not that naive. Somebody got to somebody. Why else?" He tossed back the last of his drink.

"Who? Do you have any idea?"

"Of course I have ideas. Oh, there you are," he said, reaching an arm to pull the young blond woman I'd seen earlier to his side. "Have you met my sister-in-law Melissa Gasper? Melissa, this is Donna Galbreath. I'm sure you've remembered my mentioning her."

"Indeed I do." She took my hand and met my gaze with direct, hazel eyes as I gulped and wondered what Mark had told her. That I'd resented the way he'd approached the water board about Shadybrook Meadows? I shouldn't have cared, but I was relieved when she continued, "You were so brave when you captured that woman. I was really impressed."

"Thank you," I said.

"Melissa and Jim are in the process of moving to Cedar Harbor," Mark said. "Jim couldn't be here tonight. He's still finishing up tag ends back in Colorado, but Melissa came early so the kids could start the school year here. Jim's going to join me in Gasper Enterprises."

"How nice," I said. "How old are the children?"

"James Junior is twelve and his sister Carol's eight," Melissa said, beaming with pride. She turned toward her brother-in-law. "That reminds me. It is a school night, and I promised the babysitter we'd be home early."

"Of course," he answered. "Will you excuse us?"

"Certainly." We said good night, and then I scanned the crowd. Cyrus was still deep in conversation with the editor, and Sue had left her babysitting friend to speak with another young woman. Jake had picked up his plate of food again, but as I watched, he set it back down on the side table. He seemed to hover over it, but I couldn't quite see what he was doing since his back was to me. He then crossed the room and folded his arms. As I watched, an expression of satisfaction whisked across his face. He was up to something, but I didn't have a clue as to what. Jake obviously had dimensions that I'd never realized. He was bright and capable. But tonight he'd shown a temper and possibly a tendency to drink too much. Both, I told myself, were excusable given the circumstances. Nonetheless, I was relieved to see Sue heading in his direction.

Donniker's face was becoming more ruddy all the time as he glowed from pride and sweat. The mayor had drifted off and so had Geri, but they'd been replaced by other, no doubt ignorant, well-wishers. Lucille had finally managed to tear herself away from her husband.

Just then I noted Cyrus gesturing, obviously wanting me to come over. "Donna, Tim tells me that he hasn't met you," he said as I approached. He performed the introductions.

"I'm delighted." The editor took my hand in both of his.

He was in the same age bracket as Cyrus and I. His face was lined as are those of most of my generation who have spent too much time in the sun, but it was a pleasant face, with the spark of real intelligence.

I'm a sucker for gentle, brown eyes like the ones looking at me. So like the eyes my husband Bob had. So like those of my daughter Roberta. I found myself stuttering. "Me—me, too." Oh, dear, I was being so articulate. Beside me, Cyrus cleared his throat, and I feared that he knew exactly what I was thinking. I pulled myself together. "Cyrus has been bringing you up to date on our happenings of this summer?" I asked crisply.

He threw back his head and laughed, showing teeth almost as good as Mark Gasper's. Almost, but the slightly crooked incisor made his look more real. "I didn't write the article in the paper, by the way, but I can see why you might have thought so. I approved it, though. When someone says something insufferable," he said, shrugging, "that's the way we report it. It's up to the reader to form her own opinion," he said gently. I liked the feminine pronoun he used instead of some awkward gesture toward gender neutrality.

"Well, I suppose."

"Tim is interested in the question we've been raising," Cyrus interjected.

"Good," I said firmly.

"We'll need more time." Tim Borland glanced at his watch. "Perhaps we could meet for lunch? How about Thursday?"

We agreed that Thursday was good for all three of us. "You have met Jake Santorini?" I inquired.

"Actually, I haven't."

"Why don't we introduce you," I suggested. "He was involved in this from the beginning, and he's the man we're supporting to be the next police chief." Cyrus frowned. Oh, my. Perhaps he hadn't gotten that far in his conversation with Tim.

"I'd like to meet him," the editor said.

"Come along then. He's over there talking to his . . . friend, Sue Reilly."

As I pushed through the crowd, I noted that Jake was still watching the chief in the manner that made me so uncomfortable. Why on earth had he decided to come tonight, since it clearly upset him to be here? Lucille arrived back from the direction of the restroom just then, picked up the chief's plate and handed it to him, speaking a few words. If she was urging him to eat, the effort was unnecessary. He immediately began to stuff food into his mouth. Two chicken wings, minus the bones, of course, an asparagus roll and several cheese puffs disappeared so quickly it made me shudder.

I gritted my teeth as I turned back to greet Jake and Sue. "Hi, gang. I want you to meet Tim Borland, our new editor."

Jake did appear sober. The expression on his freckled face was genial. His red hair was a trifle mussed, but his brown eyes were sharp. The Jake we were used to. Sue shot me a relieved glance. She was, no doubt, grateful that the evening was drawing to a close with no disasters.

"I did meet you." Jake held his hand out. "At the station, about a month ago. You were just coming out of Donniker's office."

"Oh, yes." Tim blinked quickly. "I'd forgotten. Sorry. I was there to introduce myself to the chief and get acquainted."

He shook Jake's hand as they eyed each other. I've always thought it interesting the way men size each other up by a handshake. You'd think, under the circumstances, they'd practice when they were young, but one does meet an occasional man who should have.

"Cyrus has been telling me the details about the tragedy here last year," Tim went on. "I'd heard about it, of course. It was the first thing everyone wanted to talk about when I came to town. Any chance you can join Cyrus and Mrs. Galbreath and me for lunch on Thursday? Both of you, of course."

Jake shook his head. "Sorry. I'll be on duty. Susan?" He turned to her.

"I'm sorry, too, but it's my day for a shift at the baby-sitting coop."

Suddenly Jake's eyes widened as he took in something that was happening behind me. Then his mouth opened and his jaw dropped. I realized that voices in the direction he was looking had grown louder. I turned, to see everyone staring at a white-faced Chief Donniker.

"I . . . I feel awful," he said. "My hands. They tingle. They don't want to . . ." His gray-green eyes bulged.

Suddenly he dropped the coffee he was holding. The cup shattered, and brown liquid splashed all over his new suit. No one moved. No one except, I saw out of the corner of my eye, Stan Chung, the new young internist in town who had volunteered to be on our water board.

Before Stan could reach the chief, Billy suddenly vomited, spewing out the considerable contents of his stomach. And then he slumped to the floor, face down.

Everyone moved now. "Call 9-1-1!" Mayor Oliver hollered to no one in particular as he gestured wildly. Dr. Chung knelt

33

beside the prone Donniker, picking up a limp wrist. Lucille Donniker threw her hands over her mouth and moaned.

And I? I spun around and grabbed Jake by the arm. "Jake," I inquired breathlessly, "what have you done?"

CHAPTER THREE

Time is supposed to move relentlessly toward whatever end is in store for each of us and, for that matter, the universe itself. Occasionally, though, it doesn't work that way. A time-out occurs, and the moment is frozen forever. That's what happened, I can almost convince myself, that November day in the Cedar Harbor Public Library meeting room.

Jake stared, his face locked into a wide-eyed, open-mouthed expression of horror. Sue gaped at me. Cyrus clutched my arm in a tight grip. Even the sound from the commotion behind us faded from my consciousness. Tim's face was the only one that held any animation. The spark of interest in his eyes made me realize instantly that I'd made a mistake, even before Cyrus spoke.

His hand squeezed my arm even more tightly. "For God's sake, shut up!"

"Donna," Sue said, "you used to be our friend." Tears oozed down her pale cheeks.

"It isn't what you think," Jake muttered. "I only meant . . ."

"You shut up, too," Cyrus ordered, with a quick glance toward the avidly listening Tim, who stood, hands in pockets, rocking on his heels. "I'm not your attorney, but you of all people ought to know better than to talk in front of the press. I haven't a glimmer of an idea what Donna thinks she's imagining, but I'd suggest—"

"We don't even know what's wrong with the chief," Susan

interrupted. "Maybe it's his stomach, or his gallbladder, or . . ."

"You're right. You're all right. I'm sorry. I had no business blurting that out," I apologized. "No doubt Chief Donniker has a sudden illness that's perfectly innocent. We all know how he loves to eat."

Sirens approached outside, and Mayor Oliver ran over and threw open the front door of the meeting room. Around us, the buzz of voices subsided as the aide technicians hurried into the room.

I'm ashamed to say that just like everyone else, I turned and watched as the two men and a woman went about their business. One strapped a blood pressure cuff on Donniker's flaccid arm, another listened to his chest with a stethoscope, then peered into his eyes.

Al Parry was the one who took charge of the crowd at that point. "Folks," he said in a penetrating voice, "we're not helping the situation. The party's over. Let's go home."

I sighed, ashamed that I'd been gawking and not moving, just like everyone else. What is it about tragedy that can cause such a bizarre fascination? I shook myself and looked around for my coat. Cyrus no doubt agreed we should leave.

But then he surprised me by saying, "I'm not sure. Just in case . . . What do you think, Jake?"

I knew instantly what Cyrus had in mind, even though he was being inarticulate. Just in case. Just in case Chief William Donniker had been poisoned, as Marie Corrigan had been and the poisoned cookies had been meant to do to me. Shouldn't Jake at least make a list of who was there?

I heard Cyrus's quick intake of breath. I turned to see that Jake and Sue were no longer standing with our group. Sue was obviously hurrying a reluctant Jake out the door.

"Jake!" Cyrus called across the room, but he was too late. They slipped out of the side exit door even as he spoke. "Come on," he said, grabbing me by the arm again. "I want to know what you were talking about when you accused Jake."

"And so do I," said Tim, whom I'd forgotten all about.

Cyrus nodded. "Understandable. If it's pertinent, we'll get back to you. Okay? But in the meantime, I'd appreciate it if you'd keep quiet."

"Absolutely," Tim agreed. "I understand that Mrs. Galbreath spoke in the stress of the moment." His brown eyes were understanding, but his next words showed that his newsman's instincts would take precedent over any sympathy. "Of course, if Chief Donniker's illness turns out to be anything but natural, I'll expect to hear from you immediately."

"After the police."

"Naturally. But—Who are the police in this situation?"

"Jake. Until proven otherwise. If the situation should arise, I imagine the sheriff's department would be next in line. The others in the department are too new or inexperienced."

"Wait a minute." I extricated my arm from Cyrus's grasp. I would have to speak to him about his tendency to maul me when he wished to make a point. I've never cared for that particular gesture of male dominance. But, later. "We have no reason to assume that there's anything wrong with Billy but his usual gluttony."

"Has his 'usual gluttony' ever caused a scene like this before?" Tim asked.

"Well, no. But anyway," I said in haste, "it was such a little thing. I'm sure Jake has a reasonable explanation."

"Come on, Donna," Cyrus said, grabbing me again.

I shook my arm loose and smiled at Tim. "Thank you for being so understanding," I said.

"You're welcome. I trust our luncheon date for Thursday still stands." He gazed deep into my eyes and I almost giggled. But that, surely, was because of the stress of the situation and not because he was appearing to ignore Cyrus. I knew without looking how Cyrus would react to that.

He answered graciously though, apparently assuming that Tim was speaking to both of us. "We'll look forward to it. Now we'll join the others and leave."

When Al had spoken, most of the crowd had begun to depart, some with relieved expressions on their faces, others with reluctance as they glanced over their shoulders with avid curiosity.

I saw, glancing around, that only a few remained. The aide personnel were loading the chief onto a gurney as a stricken-appearing Mayor Oliver supported the ashen Lucille. Hastily I headed for the door, Cyrus right behind me.

The parking lot was nearly empty now except for the aide car with its ominous flashing lights. We hurried toward Cyrus's car without speaking, and both inserted ourselves into the low-slung seats. As he turned toward our houses, he said with raised eyebrow, "Your house or mine?"

"What are you talking about?" I asked.

"You did expect to explain your accusation to Jake, didn't you? We may be able to put Tim off temporarily, but I think you owe it to me to come clean."

"When did I ever not?" I asked, not surprised when he shot me a skeptical glance.

I was feeling even more guilty as I took off my coat and carefully hung it in the front closet. Cyrus was already ensconced in my leather chair when I turned around.

"Well?" he said. "Whatever inspired you to make a rash accusation like that, in front, I might add, of a representative of our local media?"

I grimaced and sank to the couch. "I'm wondering that myself. We all know Jake couldn't do anything like that. It isn't in him."

"Like what? And how do we know?" Cyrus probed. "There are many people in prison whose neighbors said couldn't possibly do 'that.' Come on. I'm waiting. Not very patiently, I might add."

"Are you ever?" I sighed. "Very well. Only it required such a jumping to conclusions. Not my usual manner."

"Donna!"

"Okay. I think Jake was up to some skullduggery with the plates. I mean, both his and the chief's were sitting on that side table near the door to the kitchen, you know the one—"

"It doesn't matter where," he said through gritted teeth. "Get on with it."

"He hovered. His back was turned to me. I didn't see anything, honestly. It was just . . . the look on his face when he turned around. He looked . . . satisfied. Almost happy. And you know what his expression has been like all evening."

"Yes, I do. But yes, you were jumping to conclusions." He stood up, reached for his coat, and said, "I can understand your unease. Let's hope that Donniker wasn't poisoned."

"Amen," I said softly as Cyrus went out the door.

The next morning I was unaccountably restless. I shouldn't say "unaccountably." I always am restless when events prevent me from knowledge. My husband Bob used to say, laughing, "You have ants in your pants. You can't change things. Simmer down, Donna." How I missed his sage advice on occasion.

The first thing I'd wondered upon awakening and remembering last night's fiasco, was how the chief was doing. He might after all be on his way to recovery, having had antibiotics, surgery or a nasty stomach pumping. I wasn't sure why we all jumped to the conclusion he was going to die. It was just that the sudden, violent incident was so reminiscent of Marie Corrigan's attack after the murder of her husband Lyle, combined with the very ill appearance of the chief.

I'd hear sooner or later, I surmised as I warmed my hands on my mug of tea. The thing to do now was get busy. And so I changed into my working clothes and went outside to whack away at the damaged plants in my garden.

I snipped off brown and curling flower heads, ruthlessly pruned the chrysanthemums and raked the fallen leaves beneath the flowering plum we'd planted when Roberta was born. I was glad I'd had the foresight to mulch generously. The annuals were shot, of course, but the perennials should all be okay. It would take a much deeper freeze of several days to do any real damage, and we don't get those often in the Northwest. I emptied my hanging baskets. Stuffing everything into garbage bags for pickup took the rest of the morning, and I ended up feeling satisfied that I'd accomplished something instead of sitting around moping.

A message on my answering machine brought me the news when I came in the door for lunch. "Donna," said the voice of Sue Reilly, "the chief passed away during the night. I thought you'd want to know. Jake called me, but he was in an awful hurry."

So that was that, I reflected as I spooned up some leftover casserole to heat in the microwave. It was just that . . . Well, the passing of anyone is sad. Someone would care, would feel the same way that I did when I had memories of my regrettably short marriage. Presumably, his wife Lucille was now going through that bewildered, spacey feeling that most every woman experiences upon the realization that the man she'd lived with and loved would no longer be there. I recalled changing a ceiling light bulb shortly after Bob's death, fumbling with the screws when it occurred to me that he'd always taken care of those jobs. Ashamed, I suddenly remembered my agitation as I dropped a screw to the floor and exclaimed, "Gol-darn, Bob!

What'd you die for? I need you!"

And my heart would jump as a car drove up in front of the house . . . and then pass on by. Even the times when we'd argued, fortunately rare, would seem good now if we could only have the opportunity again. And as everyone says, how difficult it is to reflect upon the unsaid things that never passed either of our lips because we didn't know there wouldn't be another chance.

Certainly neither the chief nor Lucille would have wanted the public display, the unpleasant scene that occurred last night. I wondered as I ate a lunch I didn't really taste how long it would be before we knew the cause of death. An unpleasant chill shuddered down my spine as I recalled the other unexpected deaths in the community.

I put my dishes in the dishwasher, then lay down for my usual nap. I woke with a start to find that I'd actually slept an hour and a half. Last night's sleep had been punctuated by nasty dreams, and obviously I was making up for it. I'd go to the post office next, I decided. Probably no one really had any scoop on last night's affair, but I hadn't picked up my mail for a couple of days. Maybe, just maybe, I could glean some tidbits from the usual informants who hung around there.

No one was about as I cleaned out my box and carried the contents over to the counter for sorting. Two-thirds of it went directly into the recycling bin. There were three bills—it was that time of month—and, oh, good! A letter from Roberta. I tucked it into my purse to read at home.

As I turned, I saw that my friend Carrie Sanderson was coming in the door. As usual, her immaculate attire made me regret I hadn't changed out of my work clothes. A lovely rose-colored shawl, probably comprised of wool and silk, was draped to one side over black slacks and a turtleneck. Her crisp white curls matched her personality, and her face was beautifully, if inconspicuously, made up, with lipstick exactly the same shade as the shawl. I sighed and rubbed my rough hands together. I should at least have remembered to cream them after gardening.

"Hi there," she said, and I was pleased when she suggested, "Give me a sec to get my mail and then let's have a hot drink over at the bakery. We haven't had a chance to chat recently. We certainly didn't last night, did we?"

"No, but don't you have to get back to work?" I asked as she headed toward her box. Carrie's sharp, and working downtown, she picks up lots more information than I. It's always fun to converse with her.

"Nah. Business is slow at this time of year, and I'm up to date on the bookkeeping. Just mailed out the bills. My time is flexible."

I had been instrumental in getting Carrie her position. Carrie'd had to close her small gift shop because of the machinations of some of the local businessmen and had been at loose ends, when it occurred to me that she'd be the perfect fit at the local hardware store. Her experience with her own business had given her knowledge of ordering and record keeping, and I knew she was a trained bookkeeper. She also was a great salesperson.

The unfortunate murder of the former owner, Lyle Corrigan, had left his son Will in charge, but he was still working part of the time as the controller of a Portland company. He was delighted at my recommendation of Carrie. Will had been a former student of mine, and I'd become very fond of him during the time we were sorting out who was responsible for his father's villainous murder. I'd thought he might return to Cedar Harbor permanently. For one thing, my soon-to-be divorced daughter Roberta and he had seemed to hit it off, and I'd selfishly hoped the relationship would develop and she'd give up her job in New York and return to the Northwest. Even Portland would be a big improvement as far as I was concerned.

However, so far nothing had happened. I knew they were corresponding, but both had been decidedly reticent concerning their thoughts about each other.

Well, either things would work out or they wouldn't.

Carrie had finished tossing out her junk mail as I mused. "Such a waste of trees," she said as she dumped the bulk of it into recycling. "Let's go."

We stepped out of the post office into the chill air, and I gathered my down coat around me. The waters of the Sound at the foot of Main Street were gray and flecked with whitecaps as the chill wind whipped up froth. Definitely the onset of winter.

"What's this I hear about you going back to the classroom?" she asked as we waited for the driver of a brown van to make up her mind which direction she wanted to turn.

I laughed. There were few secrets in a town the size of Cedar Harbor. "Where'd you hear that?" I asked.

"Well, let's see. Oh, yes, Ann Pullen stopped in after work the other day. She'd been talking to Martha—"

"Well, that's how the grapevine works! Yes, I'm making arrangements to return as a substitute. I'm qualified for both elementary and high school, and I'm finding that I miss the students."

"That's great, Donna. You're such a good teacher. Although I understand substitutes can get a lot of flak from the kids."

"Oh my, yes. But they won't put anything over on me."

The warm, wonderfully fragrant air from the bakery swelled out around us as she pulled open the door. Several of the tables were occupied, but we found a spot for two in a corner where we'd be able to converse without being overheard. We set our things down, then went over to the counter.

"Um, I do believe I'll have one of those maple bars with my

coffee," she said, pointing through the glass.

Well, of course, so did I. I mean, I normally eat healthfully, but once in a while it's great to sinfully splurge on calories. And fat. And sugar. We took our drinks and sweets to the table and settled in for a talk. I slid out of my coat, draping it over the chair back.

Carrie sipped her coffee as I stirred honey into my tea. She opened our conversation, bringing up the subject that we were bound to discuss. "What a disaster at the library last night."

"Oh, yes," I agreed. "And I just heard that Donniker is dead. I've found it difficult to think of anything else since I got the news."

"The word got around quickly as usual, didn't it? The whole thing was horrible! Of course, everyone's gossiping about the possibility of poison, considering, but odds are it was something natural."

We continued to nibble and sip, each of us engrossed in memories of the unpleasant ending to the party at the library.

"Mm, changing the subject, I hear Roberta's coming home for Christmas. Will said . . ."

I must have given a start, because she continued, "Oh, shoot. I hope I haven't spoken out of turn." Pink tinted her cheeks.

"No, she told me she was considering it. I have a letter in my purse I haven't read yet. Wait a minute. I'll take a look." Removing the envelope from my purse, I slit it open and quickly glanced at the first page. "Um, yes, she is coming. I'm so glad."

Carrie's and my glances intersected and we both laughed. "Interesting, isn't it?" I said. "Will knew before I did?"

"Wouldn't that be neat? Will and Roberta? Oh, hell, don't we sound like a couple of gossipy spinsters?" She grinned. "I think they'd be good for each other."

"So do I, but . . ."

"But you can't interfere."

"Right. I've learned that the hard way."

She reached for her purse, then pulled out her wallet. "I'd better get back to work. My treat."

I started to argue, but then shrugged. "Thanks. I'll get it next time."

The door opened as we reached it, and Jake walked in. He really was a fine-looking man, and I could certainly see why Sue was attracted to him. Especially on the occasions when his nose didn't almost match his red hair as it did today. Nevertheless, I hesitated before greeting him, and he noticed.

"Good morning, ladies," he said, holding the door for Carrie. "Donna, can you stay a minute longer? I'd like—I need to talk to you."

"Of course. I'll see you later, Carrie."

She raised one eyebrow, looking curious as she flicked a farewell with her hand and went out.

"Coffee?" Jake asked as he held a chair for me.

"No, thanks. I'm satiated. Had a maple bar with Carrie."

He went over to the counter and soon returned with an espresso and a large butterhorn. "Um, I need to explain," he said. "And apologize. My behavior last night was despicable."

"I agree. However, perhaps it was understandable. I mean, given the way someone has shafted you. But still, Jake, was it wise to show up at least partially under the weather, and what on earth were you up to with those plates, yours and the chief's?"

He hung his head. "I should have known you'd catch that. I wasn't thinking too clearly. You're right. I shouldn't have had anything to drink. I've got this awful cold that's going around, you know, and I drank the first one thinking it would make me feel better, but of course it just led to having another. Anyway, I sneezed all over my plate. You saw that. When I noticed his plate sitting there with almost the same food on it, on impulse I switched them. I was hoping to give him my beastly bug." He

45

smiled ruefully. "Childish, I know, but it seemed like a good idea at the time."

I considered his words momentarily. I could see it. Especially since his thinking was no doubt somewhat impaired by what he'd had to drink. Jake was really not that old, and in my experience, young men tend to be so much more impulsive than those in my age group.

"Okay," I said. "I accept that. And I'm truly sorry I spouted off like that. But it won't make any difference, will it? After all, there's no reason to think his death was anything but an illness. It's just that with all the poisoning that went on around here, one's mind does tend to leap to conclusions."

He didn't answer, but only sipped his espresso.

"Jake," I asked, suddenly apprehensive, "there isn't any reason to think otherwise, is there?"

He took a deep breath, then said, "I hope not. But . . . they've ordered an autopsy."

"Isn't that usual when they don't know the cause of death?"

"In my experience, when one's own doctor is involved, they usually have a pretty good idea what killed a person. Maybe it's just routine, but—but Donna," his voice quavered, "I have this feeling that it wasn't a normal death. They've been pretty reticent, and I'm guessing they're looking for something. I'll be very anxious to hear the results."

"So will I, Jake," I said, placing my hand on his, "so will I."

CHAPTER FOUR

In truth, I was a little miffed that I'd heard about Roberta's impending visit from the grapevine instead of from the horse's mouth, to employ two overused but apt idioms. I threw my coat on the couch and settled in the leather chair to read her letter.

"You are hard to reach," I read. "You're out so much and you forget to turn on your answering machine. Besides, I hate to talk to them. Yours always cuts me off in the middle of what I'm saying. Anyway, I have decided to come home for Christmas. It's been years since we spent it together and I think it would be fun to share it with you, as we talked about earlier.

"Last visit turned out to be so hectic," she continued. "It'll be fun to just lie back and decorate the tree together. I even think I'll do most of my shopping there. Just don't get involved in another murder, okay?"

Oh-oh, I thought. Well, there certainly wasn't any real reason to think another murder had made its horrible appearance in Cedar Harbor. And on the off chance it had, there wasn't any need for me to be involved. I was thrilled she was coming and somewhat mollified by her explanation for not telling me before she told Will.

"I've made my reservations," her letter continued. "Didn't dare wait any longer. Let's hope there aren't any disasters like terrorists or hurricanes."

How sad that a person had to have such thoughts these days. Would we ever be able to confidently make plans again? I doubted it. The state of the world was frightening and I didn't see what anyone could do about it except vote, hoping one was making the right choice, and conserve, recycle, write letters. I do all those things but sometimes I feel so ineffectual. Like so many friends my age, I wasn't worried for myself but for my child. All of the children of the world. I guess old fogies my age have always asked themselves what is the world coming to?

I shook off my unease. I should be joyful that Roberta was coming. And I was. It was only a momentary frisson, no doubt. The holidays this year would be so much more exciting than any I'd had for a long time. I made a note on my calendar as to her travel days and times and pinned her letter on my bulletin board so I could find the flight information when I needed it.

On Thursday, a little before noon, I answered the door to Cyrus's knock. As usual, he was punctual and immaculately dressed, with a navy sport coat, dark slacks, and a blue tie that almost matched his eyes. The tip of a white handkerchief showed in his breast pocket. His sandy-colored hair and moustache were, as usual, so perfectly trimmed it was hard to believe they ever grew.

"Good morning," I said. I peered over his shoulder and saw his red sporty car in my driveway. "Oh. I assumed we'd walk."

"It's chilly," he said. "You look dashing today. I wouldn't expect a lovely lady to subject herself to this inclemency."

I looked at him suspiciously. Lovely lady? Indeed. I knew I looked better than usual. I'd put some effort towards my appearance for the lunch with Tim Borland. I had on my muted teal knit dress, a scarf that incorporated the same color with soft lavenders and coral, and I wore pantyhose and pumps, something I normally avoided. Still, did he imply I usually didn't look good enough to waste his fancy transportation on? No, I'd just accept the compliment for what it was. After all, he'd decided to bring the car before he'd had a chance to look at me. I picked up my purse, then pulled my front door closed behind me.

He opened the door of the car for me, and I slid in. It was toasty; he must have warmed it ahead of time. How gracious!

"I'm looking forward to this occasion," I said.

"Obviously." He quirked an eyebrow in my direction.

"If you're talking about the fact that I dressed up a mite more than usual, it just seemed appropriate. Anyway, so did you."

"Of course. Tim Borland strikes me as a formidable man, and I prefer not to be put at a disadvantage."

"Hmm. Well, I'm not expecting him to be an adversary. What makes you think—"

"Donna, I always think of the press as being an adversary."

I looked at him, shocked. "You must have had some bad experiences to make you so cynical."

"I have. Anyway, I certainly haven't led the sheltered life that you have."

Sheltered, indeed. I fumed for a minute, but then decided to get to the point. "Do you think we should tell him Jake's explanation for the incident with the plates?"

"I don't see why not. It sounded reasonable, considering what appeared to be his state at the time."

"My thinking exactly. Anyway, we probably should assume Donniker's death was natural. But I do wish they'd hurry with the autopsy. What's taking so long, do you suppose?"

"They wouldn't be doing it in Cedar Harbor, and it undoubtedly had to get behind a backlog."

I shuddered at the vision of the chief's naked body in some drawer in a frigid room along with other unfortunate beings.

Cyrus drove relatively sedately, only passing one beat-up pickup whose young male driver saluted us with his middle finger. "Young people are so rude these days," I commented. "It was a perfectly safe pass, although perhaps a mite close."

He grunted, then swung into a parking place directly in front of the Cedar Harbor Inn. His usual fashion. I don't know how he does it, but things always work out for him.

Delicious smells wafted out the door as we walked in. Alissa, a former student of mine who was a waitress here, greeted us. "Mr. Borland is waiting for you," she said, leading us to a prime spot in front of the water. Tim, also dressed in a blazer and tie, rose and shook our hands. Cyrus seated me across from Tim and then settled beside me.

"Care for drinks?" Alissa asked as she handed us menus.

"I'll have a martini," Tim said. "How about you two?"

"Um, house white wine, please," I ordered as Cyrus shot me a glance. He knew I only drank on occasion. For some reason, this seemed like an appropriate one. Cyrus ordered the same.

"It's good to be able to have fine seafood," Tim said. "I've lived in the Midwest too long."

"Cincinnati, I've heard?" Cyrus inquired.

Tim nodded. "A fine city. But I was glad to have the opportunity to return to the West Coast. I graduated from Reed College in Portland, you know, too many years ago. Wrote for several West Coast papers before I settled in Cincinnati. But enough about me. I want to hear about this famous episode you were involved in. I've heard the chief's version."

I let out an unladylike snort, which I do much too often, I know. Still it seemed a reasonable reaction to what I knew must have been a vastly distorted tale. "Chief Donniker had so little to do with solving the case," I said. "I know one shouldn't speak ill of the dead, but he was inept, self-important, and a disgrace to the profession."

Tim smiled wryly. "I'm not surprised to hear you say that. Tell me about it."

Alissa brought our drinks just then. "Ready to order?" she asked.

I nodded. I knew the menu by heart and I suspected Cyrus did, too. "I'll have the fried clams today," I said, and the two men gave her their choices.

As she moved away, Cyrus took up the story. I was a little irritated, as I felt I'd had more to do with finding the solution, and certainly for apprehending the murderer than he, but I had to admit he reported the whole thing in a concise, clear fashion. Probably his lawyer training taught him to do that. I pride myself on being able to do the same. Still, I suspected the male ego had something to do with his taking over and I might as well let him have the satisfaction. Somehow I sensed that Cyrus looked upon his relationship with Tim as a rivalry, not a cooperative venture.

Tim took it all in, making appropriate remarks from time to time. Alissa brought our mixed green salads, which briefly interrupted the narration, but then Cyrus got to the part about my tackling the fleeing perpetrator.

"So Donna took off in hot pursuit. Fortunately, I'd found Jake and we were following—"

"Which I was very glad of," I interrupted. "Nevertheless, I did have the situation under control and was on top of her behind the Dumpster when you arrived."

Cyrus smiled jauntily. "And it was a sight I'll never forget. You, astride her, triumphant but red-faced and panting, with the knife lying there just inches from her fingertips."

"Thanks for the description," I said, grimacing. I suppose I hadn't been the picture of decorum.

"I am impressed, Donna," Tim said. "I don't know many women who would do what you did. Not to mention that your obviously acute intelligence led to the solution." And then he looked at me with those fabulous brown eyes, and I was sunk.

Brown eyes with lashes to covet. What an attractive man! It had been a long time since I'd seen one my age who made me feel like that.

We gazed into each other's eyes while beside me, Cyrus stirred uncomfortably. Alissa arrived just then with our entrées and the moment was broken.

As always, the food here was special, and we ate quietly for a few minutes. The Sound was definitely in its winter mode today, with whitecaps and even waves breaking against the shore and pilings of the dock. Beyond, a stately white-and-green Washington State ferry plied its way toward Seattle, tooting its horn occasionally when the captain thought another vessel was coming too close. The seagulls always seemed to savor this sort of weather, and swooped and swirled and floated over the surface of the water as they searched for tidbits, or just maybe because they were enjoying themselves. The hum of voices and clinking silverware around us was soothing.

Tim broke the silence. "Tell me a little about yourselves. I'd like to know more about you, since I hope we'll be seeing each other. I'm here because I heard of the opportunity to buy and publish my own newspaper, something I've always wanted to do. What brought you two to Cedar Harbor?"

I'm ashamed now, how long I took to tell a great deal about myself, explaining how I'd lived in Cedar Harbor ever since I was widowed and left with a small child, how I'd returned to college and then taught until I retired. Cyrus completed his story in about two minutes. I guess the duration of our recitals was related to the length of time we'd lived here, but I was a little uncomfortable with having been so garrulous. "And Tim," I asked, "are you married and do you have children?"

He smiled ruefully. "I'm divorced. Not her fault, I'm sure. I was so wrapped up in my job. And yes, my two kids are on their own. I don't see them as often as I'd like."

We chatted on about inconsequential things: the benefits and disadvantages of the gloriously dry and warm summer we'd had, what we might face in a so-called normal year. Then he asked, "Are you in a position to enlighten me about the situation the other night? I mean, of course, your accusation of the young policeman."

I let Cyrus take the lead again. He reported Jake's explanation, and then added, "He's a fine young man. He deserves to be the new police chief. He did even before the chief's death. If I were you, and wanted to do a little investigating, I'd be curious about why he wasn't chosen after Corrigan's murder. In my opinion, it's inexcusable that he wasn't."

Tim nodded gravely. "That's extremely interesting. I will look into it. Thanks for your candor." He paid the check, and we walked out together. "I hope I'll see you often." He was looking directly at me, but then he added, "Both of you."

"Thank you for the wonderful lunch."

We separated outside, Tim striding up the street in the direction of the *Cedar Harbor Post*'s facilities, Cyrus and I getting into his car. Neither of us spoke as we headed toward home. Finally I asked, "Well, what do you think of Tim?"

He took a deep breath, then answered, "As I said before, 'formidable.' "

"I don't understand why you persist in thinking of him in those terms. I mean, he seemed personable and intriguing, as well as interested in us and the town."

"You forgot to say 'charming.' "

"Oh? You find that objectionable?"

"Not at all. Here we are." He stopped in front of my house. In weather like this, I was very glad I'd painted it a rosy pink. So necessary to have something cheerful in view.

"I just . . . Well, never mind," Cyrus said, getting out and opening my door, something I've assured him over and over isn't necessary.

"Humph. Well, thanks for the ride. I enjoyed myself. See you subsequently, no doubt."

"No doubt." For the first time today, he grinned.

As I walked up my driveway and unlocked the door, I thought about Cyrus. The man was an enigma. I had found Tim charming, yes, but Cyrus clearly had other feelings. The vibes he'd emanated during the entire lunch, I realized now, had not been good. I wondered if Tim had felt them also.

It was the next day when my *Cedar Harbor Post* was delivered that I received the stunning news. The headlines were clear. POLICE CHIEF MURDERED was spread across the top of page one in large type. I gasped, then read quickly. The gist of the article was that the autopsy results clearly showed that Chief Donniker had been poisoned.

Worse yet, the poison had tentatively been identified as monkshood, the same poison that had been used against Marie Corrigan and had showed up in the lemon crisp cookies delivered to my door. How could that be? That perpetrator had been caught and was now awaiting trial. And how had my usual pipeline, mainly through Jake and Sue, failed to report the news before there was time for it to appear in the local paper?

For that matter, how had the news ended up in the *Post* so shortly after our luncheon with Tim? Did that mean he'd known when we had lunch yesterday and hadn't seen fit to tell us?

I crumpled the paper and headed for the phone.

CHAPTER FIVE

The most frustrating sound in the world has to be that of the busy signal on the telephone. Cyrus must be using his phone. So was Susan. And Jake. Grr. I'd have to assume that at least two of them were talking to each other.

I sat there and fumed, but then my phone rang. I answered after only one ring, something I normally don't do so as to foil telemarketers.

"My, we're anxious," Cyrus said into my ear.

"Of course! I assume you've been checking on the news? What have you found out?"

"Um, well . . ."

"Oh, stop teasing. I'm not in the mood! I assume the report in the *Post* is correct, but why didn't Jake let us know? Or Sue? And, I might add, did our luncheon companion know all the time and not see fit to share the fact that Donniker was murdered?"

"So, Mr. Smooth Talker isn't quite the paragon you thought, eh?"

Reluctantly, I admitted, "Perhaps you were right, Cyrus."

"Well, to be fair, if Borland did know, he could hardly tell us before the paper came out, could he? And blow his story?"

I sniffed. "He should have known he could trust us."

Cyrus ignored my comment. "To answer your other question, presumably Jake and Sue hadn't heard the news either. Or perhaps, they couldn't find Jake. The man does have a life."

"The man also has a pager and a cell phone, I assume. This seems ominous to me."

"To me, also," Cyrus said, his voice no longer teasing but rather grave. "It would appear that the powers that be have indeed chosen to bypass our local police department. I'm not sure yet, but I suspect Mayor Oliver's oily hand. But I also suspect that Jake's improvident remarks as we approached the library that evening might have something to do with it. Half the world probably heard him."

"Hmm, yes. But surely that's not enough to make him a suspect. There's motive, and opportunity, and—"

"Which Jake had."

"But still, aren't we innocent until proven guilty? Or we used to be anyway." Unfortunately, our government these days seemed to be eroding some of those long-held principles.

"Of course. But Donna, think about it. Impartially, if you can. No, no," he interrupted as I began a protest. "I didn't mean to be insulting. I feel the same way. But how about the onlookers who heard him spout off? How many of them know Jake as well as we do? How many would feel, quite rightly I'd agree, that it might be best for him to be uninvolved in the investigation? Mind you, I don't know that that's what's happened. I'm just guessing."

Reluctantly, I agreed. "But how are we going to find out what's going on?" I almost wailed.

"Why should we?" Cyrus asked. "Even if Jake has been bypassed, we're no longer coping with the ineptitude we had before. That's something to be grateful for. Surely the county sheriff's department can conduct a competent investigation. Normally, police do get their jobs done, you know."

"Um, maybe. But an outsider doesn't know the people involved like we do."

"Donna, I hope that just because you were successful once

doesn't mean you're going to intercede in business that isn't yours?"

"Of course not! Unless it becomes necessary."

"Well, count me out this time. I mean it! I'd sincerely urge you to mind your own business . . ."

He didn't need to finish. "For once," hung on the wire as surely as if he'd completed his sentence.

"Ahem! Changing the subject," Cyrus continued, "I'm scheduling a meeting of the water board for Monday. My house. Eight in the evening." The usual abrupt Cyrus.

"That'll work okay for me," I answered. "Thanks for asking." I hoped he'd notice my tinge of sarcasm. "But what's this about? We just met a couple of weeks ago."

"Oliver requested it," he said dryly. "Wants to meet with all of us and with Kirk Bentner." Kirk is the very capable manager of our water district.

"Hm. What business is it of his?"

"Donna, he is the mayor. You realize, of course, that Cedar Harbor has a unique arrangement in managing the water, but ultimately it's his responsibility."

"He's never been interested before, as long as the water pours out of his tap. And keeps his expansive lawn green, I might add."

"Well, we'll find out, won't we? Nothing good, I expect."

"You're—" I started to accuse him of his not unusual pessimism, but then snapped my mouth shut and sighed instead. "I expect you're right, Cyrus. Never expect anything good from a politician unless he wants something from you. I suppose one should add newspaper people to that category also."

So on Monday evening I stepped outside into a clear but very chilly night. Since going off daylight savings time in October, darkness seemed to arrive inordinately early, but the pale light of the almost full moon adequately lit the way across my lawn and then Cyrus's, to his front door.

Donna Two greeted me as soon as Cyrus opened the door. She's the once-tiny, but loud, white, fluffy cat that Cyrus, much to my amazement and amusement, adopted last summer. She's still a beautiful white fluffy cat, no longer tiny, and even louder. She bellowed a greeting as she rubbed against my ankles, scattering white hair up to my knees. "And how's my favorite pussy?" I baby-talked as I lifted her to my chest. She rubbed the top of her head against my chin. Fortunately my coat was relatively impervious to cat hair. Donna Two and I had become good friends in the past months.

Cyrus had claimed he'd named her because she reminded him of me. "Loud, and with a mind of her own," he'd insisted. But I've noticed that he's become extremely attached to her, so the resemblance couldn't be all bad.

Reluctantly, I put her down as Cyrus helped me from my coat and hung it in the closet. Turning, I saw Michael Jarvis rise from the couch, and I reached forward to shake his hand.

"Michael! Good to see you. It's been a while." Michael had finished his term on the water board and been replaced by Will Corrigan. However, when it became evident that Will wouldn't be able to make all the meetings because of his job in Portland, Michael had volunteered to substitute when necessary.

I'd always assumed that Michael was probably an accountant. He fit the stereotype. Pleasant features, nothing memorable, glasses, a deferential and serious manner. I blinked as I studied him in his sedate gray sweater and slacks, and for a moment I recollected the fantastic, tanned fit body that he'd shown last summer in the hot tub when the water board had met at the Parry home. I blinked again, and blushed slightly. I hoped he wasn't remembering my aging body in the hot tub at that same time, although Cyrus had indicated that I didn't look too bad for an old lady. I sat down beside Michael on the couch, and

Donna Two jumped into my lap.

"Michael," I said, "I just realized how little I know about you. Let's see, you work for Boeing, I think you've said?"

He laughed. "I did. As a planner. But like so many others a while back, I was laid off." As I started to make sympathetic noises, he interrupted. "No, you don't have to feel sorry for me. It was really an opportunity to pursue my dream. I bought a bike shop."

"Oh, near Green Lake?" I was remembering the droves of bicyclists that make their way through the crowds of skateboarders, joggers, mothers with strollers, waddling squawking geese, dogs with waving tails, and others enjoying the slightly over two-mile trek around the charming lake in Seattle's north end.

His head flipped back, and he laughed loudly. I didn't see what was funny until he broke off and said, "Not that kind of bike. Didn't you see my Harley out in front?"

"Harley? Oh, my. No, I didn't see it. I was too intent on not tripping over something on Cyrus's lawn." I was lying, because Cyrus's lawn never had anything on it to trip over. Nothing connected to him was ever out of place. Then I remembered. "Oh, I do believe I heard you arrive." Actually, I was startled at the time because one doesn't often hear that distinctive roar in our neighborhood.

He laughed again. "I'll show it to you, but maybe it'd be better in daylight when you won't freeze your buns . . ." He glanced sideways at me.

"I'd like that." Perhaps he was indicating he'd give me a ride. I hoped so, although I wondered if he drove it as ferociously as Cyrus does his red sports car. I could picture them side by side, eyeing each other the way men do, gunning their motors, and then racing down the highway. So much for forming an opinion of someone based only on appearance. "Congratulations. On your new business, I mean."

"Thanks."

Stan Chung was the next to arrive. Instead of sitting down, he gave a start, then headed to the wall to look at Cyrus's gun collection. "Remarkable," he said, peering more closely. "You didn't find that specimen in the local gun shop, did you?" And then he and Cyrus were off in a long-winded discourse on guns. I, for one, wouldn't have known what they were talking about even if I wanted to, since I detest guns, even historical ones.

"A friend's father got that from a German finance officer who'd surrendered in Italy at the end of World War II." The piece didn't look big enough to be lethal.

Cyrus's house is a mirror image of mine in layout, but the resemblance stops there. Mine I consider warm and relatively traditional, with a few family antiques and cherry cabinets in the kitchen. Cyrus's, however, was furnished with, in my opinion, rather stark modern pieces. However, I had to admit, glancing around, that they were the perfect foil for his remarkable collections from around the world.

After studying the Southeast Asia masks for a moment, Stan turned and apologized. "I'm sorry! I've been rude. I was just overwhelmed to see museum-quality pieces. I'd no idea."

Cyrus sounded almost embarrassed. "Just a few things I've picked up during my travels in the navy."

"Well, obviously you've seen the world, as the navy claims in its recruitment ads. Or used to. Not sure they do anymore. People are seeing parts of the world that they'd just as soon not, I imagine."

I studied his face as he sat down in a side chair and pulled a notebook out of his pocket. Ethnic strains interest me. Clearly, although he had the eyes typical of an Asian, he was a mixture. As many of us are. I knew my family tree was enough to make one wonder where some of my ancestors had met each other.

"Dr. Chung," I began, "where are you from? I mean," I added

as I saw Cyrus frown, "where did you live before you came to Cedar Harbor?"

"I'm strictly local," he said. "Grew up in the north end of Seattle, left to go to Cornell for my undergraduate work, but came back here to the U. for medical school. I decided that I'd like to live in this part of the country. I practiced with a partnership for a while in Yakima, but then when the opportunity came to buy into the practice here, I jumped on it. And, by the way, please call me Stan."

"Ahem." Cyrus made one of his disapproving noises yet again. "Donna seems to be collecting biographies tonight."

Stan smiled at me. "Perfectly natural. I can't imagine working with a group like this and not getting to know everyone."

I liked him.

Mayor Oliver and Kirk Bentner arrived together. Kirk looked a touch disgruntled, and I wondered why. Although, on reflection, I suspect too much time in the company of the mayor might do that to a person. Oliver was being his usual charming self tonight. I wasn't sure why I didn't respond as he obviously expected people to, but I'm quite sure I hid my antipathy. What was it Cyrus had called him? Oily? Yes, that was it. Oily Oliver. It fit. Unconsciously I broke into a grin.

Cyrus noticed. "Something funny, Donna?"

I shook my head in disclaimer. "No, just a thought that crossed my mind."

"Umph," he said, again glancing at his watch. "Well, we're all here except Sue Reilly. I wonder what's keeping her. Perhaps we should have our snack while we wait?"

This time he'd made lemon bars, and they weren't those packaged ones that I use all the time since they're so good and easy. These, however, were no doubt made with fresh lemons. He'd prepared coffee and tea for me in a chunky oriental tea pot.

61

He peered at his watch again. "It's getting late. Think I'll give Sue a ring and see what's keeping her." Which he did, but it was clear she wasn't home as he left a message on the answering machine.

We talked, sipped and ate for a few minutes more, and then Cyrus said, "I can't imagine where Sue is. I spoke with her just this morning."

"Perhaps one of the children became sick," I suggested.

"Well, regardless, I think we'd better continue with the meeting. Mayor?"

Oily—darn, I couldn't keep from thinking of him as that—waved a hand toward Kirk. "Bentner here will make the presentation," he said. "We've been having some discussions down at City Hall, and, well, the consensus is that it's time to form a regular water district." He held up a hand to forestall the murmurs that were arising. "Wait. Hear us out. Kirk?"

Kirk sighed. Clearly he was uncomfortable with being the presenter, maybe only because he had little experience in public speaking. Still, there were only five others in the room.

"There's no question," he began, "that the state requirements are making things more difficult. Not that I find them objectionable," he said, "but the paperwork alone is overwhelming. The bottom line is that we need to do a lot to upgrade our system. I've brought some figures . . ." He handed out a packet to each of us. ". . . for you to study at your leisure. You'll see that at the very least we'll be facing bond issues and construction with all its turmoil. Torn-up streets and traffic delays. I don't expect our customers to be very excited, especially when the bills go up as they'll have to."

Silently, we all thumbed through the papers in our packets. The issue was complicated, no question. But perhaps just hiring more help would do the trick. I asked if an assistant for him would solve the problem.

Kirk shook his head. " 'Fraid not. What worked when we were a small community is no longer doing the job with the expansion of Cedar Harbor. You guys have been wonderful to work with. Well, by and large," he added with a crooked grin, and I knew he was thinking of the infamous murdered Lyle Corrigan, not to mention Al Parry whose downfall Cyrus and I had engineered. "But something's going to have to be done."

The phone rang, and Cyrus answered. "Sue," he said. "We've been wondering—" We could hear Sue's excited voice in the background as she interrupted him. "Oh, my God," Cyrus said, clearly disturbed. "You can't mean it." Her voice continued on, high and shrill. "We'll be in touch tomorrow, I promise. I'll get right on it. Does he have an attorney?"

Oh-oh, I thought as my heart sank.

"Keep up your courage," Cyrus said, then hung up and raised his stressed face towards us. "They've arrested Jake," he said somberly. "It seems they've discovered that the monkshood that was stored in the evidence room at the police station is missing. They're assuming Jake took it."

Stricken, my eyes met Cyrus's. Could this be true? Could it be possible we'd been wrong about Jake? I shook my head in disbelief. Deep down, I didn't think so. Something was terribly wrong.

CHAPTER SIX

Disturbing news can affect me in different ways. This time, it was reflected by tormenting nightmares that kept me tossing most of the night. In all of them, I was chasing or being chased. I relived the episode where I was going after the murderer in the parking lot. Only in the dream, she suddenly grew fangs and great talons for fingernails and was closing ground on me. The fangs already dripped with blood.

I awoke soaking wet and tangled in the covers. It took me a while to fully extricate myself from the dream. I thought about that woman in jail. Was she somehow sending these thoughts in retaliation? I shivered. In the middle of the night almost anything seems possible, but that idea was totally fanciful, of course.

I finally turned on the light next to my bed and reached for the perilous stack of books on my night table. Not a mystery, I decided. Something soothing and humorous. I finally settled on *Eats, Shoots and Leaves,* that marvelous book written by a fellow stickler for the English language. I always laugh out loud at some of the errors the author had found, and eventually I settled down enough to turn out the light and try to sleep.

It was still difficult to let go of the news about Jake. I needed to keep my mind open to the possibility he actually had committed the crime. I could see it—maybe—if he'd done it in a fit of alcohol-induced anger, but stealing the monkshood showed a convincing premeditation.

No, I could not believe the young man had wanted to murder Chief Donniker enough to plan it ahead and, even more inexplicably, been dumb enough to put the finger on himself by stealing the monkshood. No way.

Obviously, many gardeners grew monkshood themselves or could have purchased it at a nursery. Someone planning murder had no reason to risk stealing that at the station—except to put a finger on Jake.

How I wished he'd controlled what he said at the festivities for Billy at the library! I smiled wryly. No doubt Jake was having the same thoughts. And how about Sue? Her mind must really be in turmoil.

Who could have had access to that monkshood at the police station? Not many people, surely, but I did remember Jake once questioning Donniker's security measures, one of the things he'd planned to fix if he was named chief.

Bleary-eyed in the morning, I found myself continuing those thoughts over my first cup of tea. Stop it, I told myself. I sincerely hoped that whoever was taking charge at the police station was as competent as Cyrus assumed he'd be.

There were other officers in the department, of course, even though I'd had little contact with any of them. I did know that to a man (no women of course, since Donniker was in charge) they were relatively new and inexperienced. They weren't qualified to manage even a department as small as Cedar Harbor's. Low salaries had kept the positions rotating, typical of small towns, I understand. When young people proved they were capable, they ended up moving to a larger city. Probably more exciting, too, in the normal course of events if one likes that sort of thing.

That was why we'd had such hopes for Jake. He seemed to have settled in and become part of the community in the way none of the others had.

It was senseless to sit here stewing. There was nothing I could do. Or was there? I mused over possibilities. Previously, I'd have called Cyrus, but he'd made it totally, emphatically clear that he wanted nothing to do with this investigation.

Why would anyone want to kill Donniker, other than because he was arrogant and obnoxious? If that was sufficient motive, possibly ten percent of Cedar Harbor would be dead. He'd been retained as chief of our local police department. But why? Mark Gasper had implied that there definitely had to have been shenanigans in this decision, and this led back to the town council. Who was on it?

Geri Sataro, Roland Oliver, and let's see. Who else? I should know, but it was too early in the morning to think clearly, especially after my unusually disturbed night. I scrabbled through my stack of papers ready for recycling and found the latest edition of the *Post,* where I should be able to find the information.

Sure enough. There on the editorial page was a listing. Oh, yes, Ben Flannigan, the local broker. Sal Hansen, my very own lawyer. I should have remembered him. Geri and Roland, of course, and Ross Diego, the manager of the local country club. The usual wheelers and dealers in a community such as ours.

Geri had replaced Katherine Shaffer, who'd been a business-woman in Seattle but moved to Hawaii from Cedar Harbor after she retired. Our token woman, no doubt. Katherine had traveled a great deal, as I remembered, and had not always been available. I grinned. I had a hunch Geri might surprise a few who perhaps thought she'd keep the minutes. Maybe I'd have to go to an occasional meeting. There might be interesting fireworks instead of the deadly squabbling that usually occurred. Oh, dear. Perhaps "deadly" wasn't the best choice of words.

First of all, it would be informative to know how the group had voted on the retention of Donniker. There must be minutes somewhere. Wait a minute. Hadn't Cyrus said he'd look into how the vote went? Well, yes, but that was before the question had been made moot by Donniker's demise. Well, we're supposed to have freedom of information. I'd check with City Hall and see where the records were kept. Such a nuisance that Cyrus wasn't available to help. His snooping expertise had indeed been invaluable when we were trying to uncover Lyle Corrigan's murderer.

I reached for the pad I keep near the telephone and began to make notes. First I wrote down the five names, one to a page, then tossed the newspaper on the stack waiting to go out to the garage.

The phone rang, and I grabbed it and said hello. I recognized the voice even if she hadn't said, "This is Martha. Short notice, but could you come in tomorrow? Our sixth-grade teacher at the elementary school, Ruth Palmer—don't think you know her, she's new—has to leave for a funeral. She'll likely be gone three days."

"Why, certainly, Martha," I answered. "I'll look forward to it."

I bustled around, showering quickly. I'd only have today to catch up on things, and perhaps make a few inquiries along the way.

I went to the grocery and picked out a few necessary items. As I was standing in the checkout line, long for this hour, I had a sudden thought. What was happening at the police department these days? Someone was going to have to step in and take charge. Had it happened yet? I stowed my handy L.L.Bean shopping bag in my trunk and then drove to the post office. Before I went in for my mail, since it was a little early, I'd mosey on over to the department and see what I could ferret out.

Sheryl Adams, who efficiently handled the nitty-gritty of the department, was at her desk. Her rueful smile said it all. At the larger desk behind her sat a man I'd never seen before, dressed in the gray uniform of a deputy sheriff. His broad-brimmed hat lay firmly on one side of his desk top. His eyes remained focused on the stack of papers in his large, capable-appearing hands.

"Good morning, Sheryl," I said, wondering why I hadn't thought this out before I came in. "Um, we were all sorry, I mean dumbfounded, to hear about Jake." I spoke to her, but kept the sheriff in my peripheral vision. The twitch to his lips indicated he was eavesdropping. "I'm sure there must have been a mistake . . ."

The figure rising from his chair was imposing. Well over six feet, broad shoulders, trim abdomen and none of the gut I was used to seeing behind that desk. He fixed his cold gray eyes on mine. He would be a difficult person to lie to, I concluded.

"May I help you, ma'am," he said, not asked, coming over to the counter.

"Oh, perhaps not," I said, holding out my hand. "I only was wondering . . . I'm Donna Galbreath."

He gave no indication that he'd ever heard of me, which was perhaps just as well. He ignored my hand. Instead, dipping his head slightly, he did introduce himself. "Deputy Sheriff Calligan. Was there something on your mind?"

"Well, only . . ." I floundered. "It's just that I am concerned about Jake. Everyone in the community has a great deal of respect for him."

"Officer Santorini is incarcerated in the county facilities," he said.

"But—it must be a mistake."

"We seldom make errors, ma'am," he said. "If you'll excuse me?"

As before, it wasn't really a question. He was already turning away. I'd been dismissed, brushed off, whatever.

I was fuming. I stuck out my tongue in a childish gesture that was probably an error as he was certainly the sort who had eyes in the back of his head. I didn't care. Sheryl hid a snicker behind her hand and we shared sympathetic smiles.

"We'll see," I mumbled as I departed, not really caring whether that cold machine wearing a badge heard me or not. I hoped Jake had a lawyer by now, and a good one. Police, I understand, don't deal kindly toward one of their own who offends. Not to mention that Jake could be in real danger from the others behind bars. I surely hoped they'd been smart enough to put him in a cell by himself, even if the county jail was as overcrowded as it was reputed to be.

Carrie Sanderson was coming out of the post office as I walked up the sidewalk. How often we ran into each other there. We obviously had the same habits. "Good morning," she said. "Have to dash. But I was wondering what you and Cyrus are doing for Thanksgiving. Have you heard about that dinner the Boys' and Girls' Club is putting on at the Lutheran Church Hall for anyone who wants to come? It's aimed at people like us who might be alone otherwise."

"Oh, I remember last year," I said. "Didn't Phil and Gretchen Larson cater it?"

Carrie nodded. "Can you imagine volunteering for such an immense job? But after all, they did have a catering business before they retired and must actually enjoy cooking for a crowd."

"No, I hadn't heard they're doing it again," I answered. "I certainly can't speak for Cyrus." I was wondering why anyone would start linking us as a couple. "But I'll think about it. Thanks."

"Sorry, I'm in a hurry." She dropped a magazine and muttered something that was surely a swear word, which wasn't like her. Although I could empathize. How often hurrying made a person do that sort of thing. I pictured my mother saying, "Haste makes waste."

The rest of the day was filled with laundry, necessary correspondence, and gathering materials to take to the classroom. Walking in cold can be intimidating, I understand from substitutes I've talked to. Not only are the children primed to test an unfamiliar teacher and to take every advantage they can, but I was quite sure many classroom teachers aren't as organized as I had been. I needed to be prepared, just in case. I'd seen harried substitutes in the teachers' room, hair ruffled, clothing in disarray, who were clearly wondering why they'd ever taken on the job. Sixth-graders could be more rambunctious than the younger ages.

I, however, was anticipating the day with enthusiasm. I'd gone into teaching because I expected to enjoy it, and I'd rarely been disappointed. Even the troubled kids who were challenges provided gratification as they made progress, as incremental as it might be.

Administrators, however, could be a source of real frustration. Fortunately, I'd taught recently enough to have a handle on how to deal with most of the difficult ones in our system, and how to avoid the others. That's not to say that there weren't many competent people at the upper levels.

It wasn't easy to rise while it was still dark, even though it had been part of my routine for so many winters. My tires hissed and slick, wet streets glistened in the lights from my car as I drove to the school. The rain clouds had moved in during the night. I checked in at the office and found out which classroom housed the sixth-graders.

I was pleased when I opened the door. One look told me that Ruth Palmer was probably a good teacher. Her classroom had colorful displays on bulletin boards, maps and children's art work, and a large collection of books on a long bookshelf under the window. From experience, I knew that it was likely Mrs. Palmer had contributed her own books or perhaps regularly checked some out from the county library to supplement the system's meager collection.

A green-striped garter snake resided in a glass cage atop the bookshelf, and a Thanksgiving cactus in one corner was festooned with graceful orange-red blooms. Four computers sat along the wall on the other side of the room.

Best of all, I found the well-filled lesson-plan book centered in the middle drawer of the desk. How much more difficult it would be to have one partially filled in or, horrors, missing entirely. Most classrooms have a routine, and the children don't respond well to change. Unless, of course, the change involves something new and exciting. I had a couple of things in my bag that might accomplish this.

I was well settled in when the bell rang, and the sixth-graders poured through the door. With a certain amount of noise and a few shoves, they sat at their desks. I studied them. As usual, some of the girls were twelve going on sixteen, or trying to look as if they were, and some of the boys could have been in a fourth-grade classroom without looking out of place. It's an interesting age as the hormones hit, usually the girls first. Some of the boys, however, had begun lengthening out and obviously were attempting to cope with deepening voices.

"Good morning." I quelled a small disturbance between two boys with a glance. Good. I still had that magical look that had worked so well for me in the past. "My name is Mrs. Galbreath, and I'll be your teacher for the next few days." I wrote my name on the board. I'd already ascertained that the class had twenty-seven members, pushing the number that I thought desirable for this age level. Not surprisingly, several had familiar surnames, either because I knew the father now or had had him as a student.

A robust boy, one whose somewhat soft body build and features would likely mature into a rugged good looks, was waving his hand.

I checked the seating chart quickly. Oh. Jim Gasper. The son of the woman I talked to the other night, and thus, Mark Gasper's nephew. "Yes?" I inquired.

"Are you the lady who caught that murderer?"

Oh, dear. Not the way I'd planned on beginning the day. "Well, I suppose so, but that's not what we're—"

"My uncle said you were very brave. He said maybe you're going to find the murderer again."

I blinked, momentarily nonplused. Twenty-four avid faces stared at me. Two others were engaged in what appeared to be a face-making contest and one was already reading.

I chuckled weakly. "That's the business of the police and not ours. Ours is to get on with class work. But first, can someone tell me about the snake in the cage? What's its name? And how did it get here?"

"That's Sylvester," several shouted out at once.

I held my finger to my lips in a shushing gesture and waited for them to quiet down. "One at a time. Who'd like to tell me?"

Hands went up, and I glanced at the seating chart on my desk. Oh. I seemed to have children of two families I knew in this class. "Let's see. Luke. Perhaps you can tell me." Luke Jarvis, a bookish-looking boy with glasses, had to be the son of the previous water-board member, Mike Jarvis.

"It belongs to Amy. She likes snakes." His voice squeaked. "And she's a girl."

"The snake is?" I asked. "How can you tell?"

Everyone laughed. "We don't know," said Luke. "Amy's the girl!" His tone indicated that he would have liked to add, "Dummy," but he'd managed to restrain himself.

"Amy, perhaps you can tell me how you came to have such an unusual pet?"

She shrugged. "I've always liked snakes. Mom made me turn

my last one loose when we moved, so I caught another one right away in the woods behind our new house. Mrs. Palmer said we could keep it here for a while, as long as it doesn't get out." Her eyes flickered in Jim's direction. "Mrs. Palmer doesn't like snakes much."

"Did you know that snakes are beneficial in your garden? They eat slugs, among other things." I didn't add that true as that was, encountering one unexpectedly always gave me an unpleasant start. I sincerely hoped that this one did not escape on my watch.

Silly me. We'd barely come in from recess when a shriek sounded in the back corner of the room. A blond girl, Susan I determined with a quick look at the seating chart, had leaped from her desk.

"What . . . ?" I began.

"The snake," she whispered from behind the two hands now covering her mouth. "The snake's in my desk!"

Some of the class were laughing and some looked fearful. "Amy," I said calmly, "will you please take care of Sylvester?"

She was already on her way, sighing. She picked the snake up and petted it with soothing noises. "Sylvester's more scared than she is," Amy said, as she returned him to the tank.

I frowned at the class. "I understand Mrs. Palmer said the snake would have to go if it got out," I pointed out.

Several students protested. "We like having him here," they said.

Thoughtfully, I studied the faces in front of me. All looked innocent. Was Jim's demeanor a trifle overdone? If I'd had to bet, I'd have said he was the culprit.

"All right," I said. "I'll report this incident to Mrs. Palmer, though, and Sylvester's fate will be up to her when she gets back. She's at a funeral, you know, and we really don't want to have a list of things for her to deal with when she returns, do we?" The latter I said firmly, looking around at the chastened faces.

"No, Mrs. Galbreath," they all said.

The rest of the day was uneventful. We studied long division and Civil War history. For English I had them write a short essay on the subject, "The Best or Worst Thing That Ever Happened to Me," and when the bell rang for departure and the students hurriedly departed, I gathered up the papers to read tonight.

The message light on my phone was blinking impatiently when I set my things down on the small desk in my kitchen. Three messages. They were all from Cyrus.

"Where are you?" he asked imperiously when I punched the play button. "I have news. Call me." Typical Cyrus, assuming I had nothing more important on my agenda than conversing with him. I was half-tempted to feign not being home, but that would be difficult when he'd undoubtedly been aware of the arrival of my noisy old green car. Besides, I had to admit his tone sounded urgent enough that my curiosity was piqued.

I settled in the desk chair and punched in his number.

CHAPTER SEVEN

"Where have you been?" Cyrus's voice was gruff.

"Hello, yourself," I answered in saccharine tones. "Did you have a nice day?" Sometimes the man was insufferable.

An exaggerated sigh drifted across the line between our two houses. "You don't need to be sarcastic. As usual," he added.

"You do bring it out in me," I said. "Am I supposed to report my whereabouts at all times?"

"No, of course not. I apologize." A pause. "But I have been trying to reach you."

"I told you I was going to begin substituting. This was my first stint."

"Oh. And did it go well?"

"Actually, yes," I said. "Except that they'd have liked to discuss murder and the snake escaped."

"I seem to remember having aided such an episode myself in grammar school. Except it was a frog. I recall being put on detention."

"That sounds excessive," I commented.

"Well, that was the fourth offense. But I didn't call to discuss my youthful transgressions," he said over my chuckle. "I checked on Jake's situation and also located the minutes of the recent city council meetings. I thought you'd be interested in what I ascertained."

"Of course," I answered, surprised. "First tell me about Jake. How is he?"

"Hanging in there, as I said he would. But the things I found out about the council should also interest you."

"I understood you to say with a good deal of force, in fact, that you weren't willing to investigate the murder."

"I'm not. I said I'd look into anything that relates to why Chief Donniker was promoted instead of fired."

"Well, yes, you did. But I assumed the question was moot now that the man is dead."

"Not moot," he said. "Jake's name must be cleared so that he can get out of jail and assume the position."

"What's the difference between investigating the murder and investigating old politics?"

"Donna," he said, "let's not quibble over semantics. Do you or do you not want to know what I found out?"

"Of course I do. And I have a question for you also."

"I'd rather have the discussion in person if it's not too late for you. As you so quaintly put it the other day, 'Your house or mine?' "

We settled that question, and fifteen minutes later we were seated at my kitchen table over tea. As I poured from my lovely bone china pot with—what else?—roses on it, he began.

"Jake, unfortunately, appeared at his hearing in front of Judge McCreary, otherwise known as Hanging Mike. You may not be aware of the fact that one thing a good lawyer does for a client is try to arrange what court he appears in. Hanging Mike, among other things, is planning on running for prosecutor next year on a tough-on-crime slate. Jake, in all his innocence, called a buddy recently out of law school, one not familiar with the local courts, to represent him. The case was made to order for Hanging Mike. He set an enormous bail."

"But . . . but, that's not fair. What can be done about it?"

"Fair or not, that's the way it is. But it's only temporary. He has to be arraigned within two weeks, usually sooner, and we'll make sure he has adequate representation who'll see this won't happen again. I'm confident we can at least get Jake out on bail."

"That would be wonderful," I said, "but expensive. Can he afford it?" I asked, momentarily but futilely considering the state of my bank account.

"Don't worry," Cyrus said. "It'll be taken care of. I've talked to Sue and explained my strategy." He frowned. "Donna, you're obviously agitated. Drink your tea, and relax from your stressful day. I'll explain. It appears that the evidence is not strong. Jake says—"

Surprised, I interrupted. "You've talked to him?"

"Naturally. He can make phone calls. I've also talked to his present lawyer. Anyway, Jake presented another avenue for us to explore. The security at the police station was incredibly lax. He's mentioned that before, as you know. It was one of the things he intended to remedy when in charge. However, I had no idea how lax. The key to the evidence room was kept on the door frame above the entrance of the room. Can you imagine? How many people must have known that? It shouldn't be difficult to prove that virtually anyone could have had access, which certainly should provide some reasonable doubt."

Appalled, I said, "I would think so."

"Now as to my research on the city council." He reached into a briefcase he'd set beside him, extracted some papers and spread them on the table. "Not a lot of surprises," he said. "There are five people on the council, as you know, I'm sure. Geri Sataro, Roland Oliver, Ross Diego, Ben Flannigan, and Sal Hansen. The vote was four to one."

"Let me guess," I said. "Well, at least two of them. Oily Oliver and Geri. She was acting too enthusiastic at the event not to have been pro."

"I won't keep you in suspense. The only negative vote was from Sal."

"Oh, I'm glad to hear that. He's my attorney, and I've always had a lot of respect for him. I'd hate to have been disappointed. But was there any debate?"

"Surprisingly little. Sal expressed some concerns, but in the usual careful manner of an attorney, if I may say so myself before you point out the fact that I am one, also. However it became clear quickly that he was a minority. Geri had particularly flattering things to say about Donniker, as did Oliver. The other two were reticent, but when a vote was taken, they went along.

"Naturally, I was curious. Nothing was said about his deficiencies, even though they were apparent to everyone in the community. So . . ."

In usual Cyrus fashion, he took a sip of tea and reached for one of the cookies I had put out before he continued. I've never been sure when he does this whether the man's gathering his thoughts together or pausing deliberately to annoy me. A bit of both, perhaps. I held my tongue, just in case it was the latter.

He ate the cookie, then took another sip of tea. "So?" I finally couldn't resist nudging.

"So I invited Sal to lunch today. We're acquainted through some Bar Association meetings. I was honest about what I was after. He was quite open with me."

"And?"

"He was puzzled over the whole procedure also. Said that early on they'd had some informal discussions and he'd also, of course, talked to people in the community. As he put it, he was dumbfounded when Geri made the motion and it went through with almost no discussion."

"Well, Mark Gasper did feel that there was something nefarious going on. As he put it, 'Someone got to someone.' "

"I suggested the possibility to Sal. His answer was that he'd been suspicious, too, but short of making accusations, there didn't seem to be much he could do."

"So, it boils down to us—me, doing some investigating?"

He frowned. "We have to remember that someone murdered Donniker. You almost lost your life investigating before. As I futilely urged you then, we should let the police do their job first."

"Huh!" I said. "Have you met the deputy who's running our police department yet?"

"I'm sure he didn't confide in you, Donna," he said in a patronizing tone.

"The man's a jerk," I answered.

He raised an eyebrow in that infuriating manner. "Were you not predisposed to that opinion?"

"Probably. But just wait. You'll see. He's cold, unfriendly—"

"Which of course makes a person conclude that he's inefficient."

"—and, if you hadn't interrupted me, he's not interested in looking elsewhere for the murderer. He has his mind made up."

"Hmm, yes, that would indicate problems."

He put his chin on his hand and proceeded to rub it. He was clearly cogitating on the subject.

I refrained from prompting him.

"All right. I'm convinced. If we're to succeed in having Jake as our chief, we'll have to start investigating right now."

"The murder may have had nothing to do with the police chief situation," I said, hoping to mollify him a little. "In fact, I doubt it does." This I wasn't at all sure of, but I was delighted at his joining the investigation. The man does have some uses. "But—what do we do next?"

"That's the question," he said. "I'll have to ponder on it. Obviously, talk to people," he continued. "Perhaps cultivate more than a passing acquaintance with the council members. But you said that you had something else to ask me about. What was that?"

"Totally unrelated. Except that it might be a good place to do our inquiring. Carrie reminded me that there is going to be a community Thanksgiving dinner." I didn't add that she had assumed we might be interested in coming together. "It's for people who don't have anywhere else. Well, like us. No family nearby. And I know it will be a feast."

His face brightened. "A good idea." Cyrus does enjoy his food. "We'll plan on it. Let's—is it next week already? Time does sneak by, doesn't it?"

"Yes, it does. Roberta will be here in about three weeks and I'm going to be thrilled to see her. I do wish she'd move closer. It's so nice to be able to get together with family."

A shadow crossed his face, and I immediately regretted my comment. With the death of his son from AIDS and his wife's abandonment, he had no family nearby. At least he'd never mentioned other relatives.

"Well," he said, standing, "I'll let you get on with your dinner."

"I'd suggest you join me except that I'm eating leftovers."

"I've already eaten," he said.

As the door closed behind him, I shuffled through the remnants in my refrigerator. One container had my salad of beans, cheese, apple, celery and onion. That would make a good basis for dinner. I was hungry, though, so I pulled a teriyaki chicken breast out of my Costco stash. Three minutes later I was ready to eat. I might as well start on the essays I'd assigned today in class while I ate, I decided, and I took them out of my bag.

I'd used this subject as an assignment before, and I'd sometimes had intriguing results. Fortunately, everyone could remember outstanding events in life, so it was easy for the class from that standpoint. Very occasionally I'd encountered a situation that required action. I remembered in particular one in which a well-behaved youngster who was a good student and had showed no problems reported the beatings he received from his dad. He seemed almost to accept them as routine. I'd seen that the authorities heard about that one.

This bunch, on the other hand, were on the normal side, although as usual they provided insight into family background. The best thing for many had been a visit from their grandmothers (who'd obviously spoiled them) or a trip. These varied from one to the Seattle zoo to Yellowstone and even a cruise, and perhaps were reflections of the families' economic status. Getting a pet was high on the positive side. Losing one, as one boy had with the recent death of his dog in front of a speeding driver, was the worst thing several could think of. Amy chose to write about her recent move to Cedar Harbor. Not only had she had to release her snake, but the family dog, who was a dedicated roamer, had been given to neighbors with acreage. Besides, of course, she'd had to leave behind a cherished best friend. Moving is so often traumatic for kids.

The level of writing also varied. Jim's was vivid as he'd described the Hawaii cruise he'd taken with his parents. Most had punctuation and grammatical errors, and I cheerfully pointed them out with my red pen. There is debate on the wisdom of doing this. Some think it hampers creativity, but in my opinion it's necessary to make it possible for young people to write competently in later life.

As I finished the last essay, I was startled to see that it was already ten o'clock. I put the papers in my bag to return tomorrow to Mrs. Palmer's sixth-grade class.

Fortunately I slept better that night and, while I hadn't had a chance to do much thinking about Cyrus's and my investigation, I was ready to return to the classroom in the morning.

When I handed out the papers, there was grumbling. "You didn't say we were supposed to be perfect," one girl complained.

"I didn't expect you to be. You had no chance to revise, which is very important in successful writing. I just wanted to make suggestions for you to look at. I was impressed with your papers," I added. "You did a good job."

It *was* a good class. Some, obviously, would never make their livings as journalists, but that was okay. We wouldn't want the field to be any more overcrowded than it is.

"I'll leave them for Mrs. Palmer to read. If any of you have questions about the changes I suggested, ask me and I'll explain."

The rest of the day went on uneventfully, and after the students noisily departed, I prepared to go.

My eyes scanned the room, checking to be sure I hadn't overlooked anything, and stopped with a jerk. Sylvester was not in his cage. I'm sorry to admit I swore. I set my things down on my desk and gingerly walked around the room in search of the snake.

Fortunately, I found him quickly. He was coiled in a corner, watching me with evil, but probably scared, eyes. I gathered my courage to capture him, and as I bent down, his head thrust forward and he stuck out his tongue.

I jumped back. My little talk about the benefits of having a snake in one's garden was true, but a little incomplete. I don't know if it's innate or learned, but I have the classic run impulse when I see one. I reached for my desk phone.

"Uh," I told the office secretary, "I seem to have a little problem. Is there a custodian around?"

"Sure, he just walked out. I'll catch Sylvester and tell him to come down to your room, okay? Anything I can help with?"

Sylvester? Oh. That explained the rather unusual name attached to the thing in the corner. "No, it's small," I told her. "Here he comes already. Bye." I was grateful for having an excuse to hang up without explaining.

Sylvester didn't look at all snake-like, I was relieved to see when the kindly, older man came in the door. "You have a problem?" he asked.

"I'm sorry to bother you, but . . ." I pointed at the snake.

He laughed. "Sylvester and I are old friends." He picked him up, petted him and put him in his tank. He dusted his hands together. "Mrs. Palmer doesn't much like handling him either. I'm rather fond of the fellow."

I thanked him profusely and as he started out the door, he turned to say, with a twinkle in his eye, "I assume you'd rather this was just between the two of us like Mrs. Palmer always asks?"

Gratefully, I nodded. He really was a nice gentleman.

Again, I picked up my belongings from my desk and headed home. As I pulled up to my garage, I was startled to notice that my side gate was open. I knew it had been closed that morning when I left. Had Cyrus been wandering around in there?

CHAPTER EIGHT

Puzzled, I shut my garage door and walked around the side of my house. I pushed open the gate, now silent since Cyrus had treated it, and cautiously stepped forward.

A man was sitting on my bench, his back toward me. I must have exclaimed, and my heart thumped as I put my hand to my mouth. His head turned. I'd never seen him before.

He stood, his face creased with worry. "Oh, my," he said. "Did I scare you? I'm so sorry." His suppliant hands were shaking.

Studying him, I decided he didn't really appear frightening. He was slight of build, thin and pale, as if he might have been ill. He removed his red-brimmed cap, revealing light-brown hair that had been combed sideways to hide the fact that it was thinning. He was dressed in worn jeans, a faded black jacket, and boots that needed slicking up.

"What are you doing in my yard?" I asked, now more curious than scared.

"I'll—I'll leave," he said, his green eyes skittery. "It was only that—that your yard is so lovely. I haven't seen a garden like this for so many years. The front was enticing, and I just intended to peek at the back."

"Lovely?" I said, glancing around at the empty ground where my annuals had stood, at the pruned remnants of perennials with mulch round them, at the bare tree limbs.

"Oh, yes. Look at the curls of cinnamon bark on that twisted branch. Harry Lauder's walking stick, is it not? And that vine with silver-veined leaves. Hard to believe it must be an evergreen. And the graceful fronds of that Japanese deer fern, the arbors hinting at summer's glorious color, the red berries on that shrub. And so well tended."

I blinked. He clearly knew his plants. And, yes, there was a certain charm to his manner. "You must be a gardener." I stated the obvious.

"Not anymore. I used to be. Please forgive me for trespassing. I'll leave now. I truly regret that I gave you a turn." He headed toward the gate, and I stepped aside to let him pass.

"Wait," I said. "I don't know you. Do you live around here?"

"You might say that. At least temporarily."

"What's your name?"

"Alvin."

"Well, Alvin, you might get shot wandering into some people's yards, but I do appreciate the nice things you said about mine. Just—be careful."

He twisted his cap like a character in a Dickens novel.

"Ahem."

We both started as Cyrus appeared behind us.

"Is everything all right?" He frowned at Alvin. "I saw you going into Donna Rose's yard. I don't believe I know you and I thought I should check."

"Cyrus," I said quickly before my visitor had a heart attack as it appeared he might, "meet Alvin. He's a gardener."

"How do you do?" Alvin said. "I was just leaving." He scurried out of the yard as Cyrus and I stared at his retreating back.

"How strange," I said. "There must be a story . . ."

"You know him? Or you don't?"

"No, I've never seen him before. But he's clearly harmless. Said he admired my garden so much he wandered in without thinking."

Norma Tadlock Johnson

"And you believed him? Donna, when are you ever going to learn some of the basic rules of self-preservation?"

I snapped, "I think I've shown that I do know how to take care of myself. You're not my custodian. But," I continued as he bristled, "I do appreciate your concern. And I know it is important for all of us to be aware of anything out of the ordinary in the neighborhood. He was just—strange. And forlorn. I feel sorry for him."

"How can you, when you don't know anything about him?"

"Let's just say some of us have a natural empathy for anyone who's obviously troubled."

"And you're saying I don't?"

I put my hand on the sleeve of his blue knit shirt. "You must be freezing," I said. "And, no I didn't mean that." Actually, it sometimes seems that lack of empathy is a common characteristic of people who've spent their lifetimes in the military, but I didn't dare say that. Cyrus would be offended, justifiably. Besides, reluctantly, I had to admit that I'd tended to stereotype this group based on only a few individuals I'd encountered.

"Thank you," I said instead. "Would you like to come in for tea or coffee?"

"No, I realize you just got home from the school. How did it go today?"

"Fine. Well, except for that darned snake. Can you believe its name is Sylvester? The same as the custodian who, I regret to say, rescued me."

He soon had the whole story out of me. A snort and a snuffle showed an attempt to conceal laughter, but he failed. As he finally let it loose, I had to laugh, too. The situation actually had been funny.

"And you, who confront murderers with knives, let a garter snake cow you?"

"Well, yes, when you put it that way."

86

I thanked him again as we separated and went to our own houses.

After dinner, it occurred to me that it was past time to check on Sue. A subdued voice answered my dialing, but when I identified myself and asked how she was doing, her voice perked up.

"Better than I was," she said. "That Cyrus of yours has been unbelievable. He found a new lawyer who has arranged for an arraignment next week in a different court. Cyrus has insisted that I not worry about how he's going to be paid."

"Oh," I said, feeling very guilty about some of the unkind thoughts I'd had about him.

"And, Donna. I want you to know that I understand why you said what you did at the library. Jake explained to me what he'd done, and I don't blame you. It was—so unlike the usual Jake."

"I know that, Sue, but I sincerely wish I hadn't said it." I sighed. "But we have to deal with the situation as it is, not how we wish it were."

"You're right, of course. The new lawyer talked to Jake in great detail, and he thinks there's a chance he can at least get Jake released on his own recognizance. This business about the evidence room being so easy to get into makes a real difference, he says. That was one of the main things they thought they had on Jake. Oh, Donna, I'll be so glad to see him." A half sob indicated the strain she was under.

"Well, Cyrus and I have agreed to put our heads together on this."

"Oh, would you?" Her voice exuded gratitude. "No one else seems to care, to believe in Jake the way you two and I do."

"Cyrus has talked to Jake too, but the minute he's available, I think we should have a meeting and discuss who could have gotten into the room. In the meantime, Cyrus and I are looking into why the City Council voted to practically sanctify the chief."

Now she really cried, and after uttering a few words of re-assurance, I cut the conversation short so she could collect herself.

On the way to the school the next morning, Friday, I thought about how I was going to handle the snake situation. As the students filed in, I watched their faces carefully. Only that of one, Jim, turned first toward the snake tank. He then looked at me, and blushed. I remained silent.

At recess time, I stopped him at the door. "Jim," I said, "would you stay for a moment? I'd like to speak with you."

"Yes, Mrs. Galbreath." His face paled.

"Here. Let's sit down." We settled at the two nearest student desks, and I stared at him.

It wasn't long until he broke. "How'dja know it was me?" he asked plaintively.

"You do mean the snake, don't you?" I wondered what other mischievous stunts he might have been up to.

He hung his head. "I just wanted someone . . ."

He obviously couldn't get the words out. I'll bet he was think-ing he wanted Amy to notice him, but in the pre-adolescent state he was in, his prank had perhaps seemed to make sense—to him.

I let him sweat for a minute. "Jim," I said, looking him in the eye, "how about you come in early at lunch after you've eaten and rearrange the books for me? They really are out of order."

He looked at me hopefully.

"And we'll forget about it," I promised.

"Gee, thanks Mrs. Galbreath!" And he turned to leave. Then, clearly having a thought, he asked, "How'd you catch him?"

I smiled benignly. "You'll never know, Jim. Run along now."

Later Jim came in as promised and bustled around with the books. When he finished, he looked at me speculatively. "Are you going to solve Chief Donniker's murder?" he blurted out.

"Me? What makes you think that? My solution of that first murder was just an accident. I don't intend to have anything to do with this one."

"Well, that's good," he said. "I guess. My uncle says the chief was a jerk. He said he didn't care if the murderer was caught."

"Jim!" I sounded shocked. I was. "Uh—I happen to think that murder is evil, no matter who the victim was."

"Uncle Mark says Donniker wasn't very smart. And he says he got the best of the chief in some business deal, but he was glad because he deserved it."

"Well, Jim, as I said earlier, I truly believe the murder is the business of the police, not mine. Not yours. Certainly not something to be discussed in school."

"Oh." His mouth twisted as he thought that over. "Well, am I done here?"

"You did a good job, Jim," I complimented him and gave him a quick hug. Sadly, hugs are discouraged these days, but I felt comfortable with it in this case. "Thanks so much."

When the afternoon dismissal bell rang, I was almost sorry to see my stint with this class end. But I wasn't through with them yet. I sighed as I spotted Luke headed in my direction. Surely he didn't want to talk murder too? I'd squelch that in a hurry.

"Mrs. Galbreath," he said. "My dad said I ought to ask you. I think I want to be a detective when I grow up. What do you have to do to become one? My mother thinks it's a dumb idea, but Dad said, 'Go for it,' and when he heard you were my substitute he said I should ask you about it."

"Your Dad said that? But I'm not a detective. He knows that. I don't understand why everyone thinks I am. I just happened to be drawn into that other situation by circumstances. But, Luke, I agree that you should reach for your own goals. I think your best bet, if you still want to do this in a few years, would be to major in criminology or criminal justice in college. There may be such things as internships when you're old enough. So many fields have them these days. But a good education is the first step."

"Um. Thanks!" Luke said. And he left.

My, I'd become really fond of this class in short order. Perhaps I'd end up substituting with them again.

I hoped so.

CHAPTER NINE

"Donna! It's been so long. When can we get together?"

It was Sunday morning. I'd forgotten my friend's propensity for early rising. "Alice! It has been ages!" I hurriedly poured my steeping tea. It was likely to be an extended telephone conversation.

"When did you get back from . . ." I had to think a bit to remember where my friend had gone on this occasion. ". . . was it South Africa? I'm sorry. You take so many trips I had to think where you'd been."

"Yes, South Africa. I have so much to tell you about the trip. I met a fascinating man, among other things."

"You're kidding!"

"No, I am not. But I'll save that for when we see each other. I was so disappointed to find that my house plants had all died! The neighbor who was supposed to take care of them was called away when her sister became deathly ill and she completely forgot about my plants. But, how about you? Any more murders for you to solve?"

"Well, I definitely don't have plans to solve this one, but . . ."

She squealed. "There *has* been another! How do you do it?"

"Alice," I reproached, "it has nothing to do with me. Just pure chance. The police chief—"

"That awful one you're always complaining about? What's he doing about it?"

"No, no. He's the one who got murdered. But can we talk

about something else? At least until I see you. When can that be? Let's see, this week's Thanksgiving. I have an idea. There's a community gathering here, catered by someone who loves doing it, can you imagine? We make a donation, that's all, and it goes to the Boys' and Girls' Club. Cyrus and I plan to attend. Why don't you join us?"

"Cyrus? That sexy next-door neighbor of yours?"

"Don't be silly. He's a stuffed shirt. But he has turned out to be a better neighbor than I thought he would. Do you or don't you want to join us?"

Alice had been a fellow teacher at Cedar Harbor Elementary. When she inherited money, she retired early, selling her house here and moving to a condo in Edmonds.

"Well, I think that sounds just jolly. Sure he won't mind?"

"Why would he?" I asked a trifle huffily. Actually, I wasn't totally sure, but didn't see any reason he should. I gave her the information as to time, etc., and we agreed she'd come to my house first.

Then I called Cyrus to tell him I'd invited her. "Her name's Alice Pierce, and she has no family nearby, and I haven't seen her in ages. She's always traveling. Just got back from South Africa. Have you ever been there?"

"Yes," he said.

"I know you'll enjoy her and I didn't think you'd object to my inviting her." A sigh across the phone line between our houses was almost loud enough that I wasn't sure I wouldn't have heard it without amplification. "I've been burbling, haven't I?" I asked.

"Yes, you have. Did you really think I'd have objections to your including your dear friend Alice who has no nearby family, whom you haven't seen in ages?"

"Well, no. I'm sorry. Guess I just felt I should have asked you first."

"That's fine, Donna. I'll look forward to meeting her."

"By the way, I talked to Sue Friday night. I should have called her sooner. Cyrus, how good of you to help her. She was extremely grateful."

"How could I not? And if Jake truly is let out on bail next week, we must have a meeting with him. We can no longer call it the Dump Donniker committee, of course, but I think a chance to sound him out should be our first step. This business about the key to the evidence room being so easily available certainly is a starting point. Who among the people who were at the party would have had an opportunity to get at it? And who would know better than Jake?"

"A good idea. Inspired, I might say. Surely not that many people would have had an opportunity."

"I'm not so sure. The place must have been incredibly unsecure."

"I wonder," I mused, "about Sheryl Adams . . ."

"Who?"

"The secretary in the department. I wonder how she feels about the situation? She's always seemed pleasant, but I've never really gotten to know her."

"First thing. Was she at the party?"

"I don't think so. Which might mean something, since she had to work with the chief."

"And it might not. But a good idea. Donna, would you be in a position to sound her out?"

"Well, I'm not sure how, but I'll see what I can do."

With that, we closed the conversation, to be renewed as soon as we had word about Jake.

I talked with Roberta a couple of times. "I'm really looking forward to spending Christmas with you, Mom," she said. "Does Molbak Gardens in Woodinville still have that wonderful Christmas display? And downtown Seattle?"

"They do," I assured her. "And if you like, I'll get tickets for the *Messiah*. I remember when the group from the high school here went, and I thought it might be fun."

"How grand! Uh—any news about your latest murder? You're not getting involved?"

I crossed my fingers. "Of course not! Let's see. You'll be here on the twelfth?"

"With bells on!" She giggled. "I think you were changing the subject, but just stay out of trouble, Mom."

Yeah, sure, I thought.

I was just as glad to have the three days free before Thanksgiving. I planned to order the tickets to the *Messiah*, buy my Christmas cards and begin addressing them. Obviously, life was going to be full after Roberta arrived and I'd better get as much done as I could. I made a Christmas list. Let's see, small gifts for Carrie, Meg and Alice. Should I get something for Cyrus? I mulled this over for a moment, then added him to the list. And Susan. Oh, dear. What was Christmas going to be like with her beloved in jeopardy? Would it be better to get her something, or not? I wrote down her name as well as those of her boys. Surely the celebration would go on for their benefit. And Roberta. I'd love to begin shopping for her, but I wasn't sure how her life had changed since her divorce and what would be appropriate. Perhaps I'd best wait until she got here and I could feel her out.

Tuesday morning, Cyrus phoned. "I found out something pertinent today." I could tell he was grinning from the tone of his voice. "Did you know Donniker spent some time in Cincinnati? Brief, but he was there not long ago."

"You have to be kidding!"

"No, I'm not. I checked it out today."

"And how did you do that?" I mulled the thought aloud. "I've always wondered how you get your information."

"Donna, you can find anything on the Internet. I keep telling you that you should get with it and learn to use a computer."

"And I keep telling you I used them at school. I just don't choose to spend my time in retirement hunched over a machine. Anyway, I don't have a place for one. Are you stalling?"

"I wouldn't do that, would I? But, well, ahem, this time I came about my information almost accidentally. You remember the strange character who showed up in your backyard?"

"Of course. Alvin. But what on earth does he have to do with Cincinnati?"

"Well, I saw him one day down on the waterfront. He was sitting on that bench in front of the dock, feeding seagulls with bread chunks. You were right. There's something forlorn about the man. Anyway, I was curious. And I wasn't in a hurry. I wandered over and sat beside him."

"And?" I prompted when he seemed to hesitate.

"He's quite a complex character. Very bright, I'm sure. And, as we might have guessed, an Iraq veteran. I was probing a little, I guess, just trying to be friendly."

"I thought you disapproved of my being friendly to him."

"Donna, he was trespassing in your yard. I met him in, I might say, a very public place. But do you want to hear what he had to say?"

"Of course. What did you find out?"

"I'd asked where he'd lived, and he rattled off a string of places. When he mentioned Cincinnati, I glommed on to it. I commented on the coincidence and I asked if he'd been aware of Borland writing for the local paper, and he said that he had. Then I said, 'Another coincidence. I heard recently that Chief Donniker, who was just murdered, spent some time there recently, also.' A really odd look crossed his face, and he clamped his lips together and would say no more."

"How strange! But where did you get that little tidbit?"

"It was mostly a hunch. I've found that Donniker has always

been a politician. He belonged to several professional groups, one of which sponsored training sessions in various cities. I checked, and one of them had been Cincinnati.

"Do you ever get one of those . . . I can only describe it as a rising, warm feeling in the gut, when you think you might be on the right track?"

"Well, yes, I guess I do, although I'd never thought about it. And I certainly wouldn't have expected it of you."

Sounding abashed, he said, "Well, whatever. I got on the 'Net today and checked it out. He was there ten days. It had seemed a possibility, and I threw it out to Alvin on impulse.

"Then, because . . . well, the man does evoke sympathy, does he not? He was clearly clean and well-groomed, in spite of the shabby clothes, so I suggested he join us all at the Thanksgiving festivities."

Cyrus was obviously embarrassed. Just a little, but enough to let me know he was aware of the irony of his change in position regarding the man. I decided not to push it. I was seeing a side to Cyrus that I wouldn't have dreamed existed.

"That was a nice thought," I said. "Where does he live now?"

"I was unable to find out."

"I sincerely hope it's not under a bridge somewhere."

"It could be. But at least he'll be warm and have a good meal that day. And Donna, it occurred to me that you might be in a better position than I to get him to open up a little. No," he said, interrupting me as I started to protest, "I did not have ulterior motives when I invited him. It occurred to me later."

I was silent a moment. Then I said, "All right. I hate to be nosy." There was definitely a snort on the other end of the line. I ignored it. "But the cause justifies a little subterfuge. Why on earth would he be evasive about something as simple as the subject of the three men having connections to the same city?"

"Good question. I hope you'll be more adept than I in eliciting answers from him."

To my surprise, when my phone rang a short time later, it was Cyrus again. "Jake just called," he said, "and he's out. As I surmised, the judge released him on his recognizance, with some rather pointed comments to the prosecution about evidence. Anyway, he and Sue have agreed to come to my house tomorrow evening at seven-thirty. I hope your friend isn't there yet and you'll be free so that we can have a council of war?"

"She isn't, and anyway, I'd make myself free for that. How did he sound?"

"Tired, but embarrassingly pleased that you and I are going to take on his cause."

"Oh, I sincerely hope we can help."

It was hard to concentrate on my activities on Wednesday, but I was in Cyrus's living room cuddling Donna Two when Jake and Sue arrived. I dislodged the cat and jumped up to hug each of them.

They both looked as if they'd aged about ten years, with extra lines on their faces. Sue's hair had even lost its luster.

"I hope it wasn't too bad," I said to Jake.

They sat down on the couch, holding hands and, to my surprise, the cat jumped onto Jake's lap.

"Well," I said in mock dismay, "I've been abandoned." Actually, I thought it was an example of how sensitive cats can be to people's feelings. Jake needed comforting more than I did. He smiled at Donna Two and began stroking her.

"You wouldn't believe that place," Jake said. "I won't go into details, but I'll think twice about sending some young kid there for something like pot, I'll tell you. Some of the guards—"

Sue interrupted. "Let's try to put the whole thing behind us, shall we? And see what Cyrus and Donna have in mind?"

I inwardly winced. They had a lot of faith in two old amateurs; that was evident. I surely hoped it wasn't misplaced.

My resolve grew.

Cyrus served coffee, tea, and some delicious brownies, and then we got down to business. "It seems to us," he said, "that this business about who could have gotten their hands on the monkshood is our most important avenue of investigation." He had a notebook and pen, as did I.

"We need to know who could have somehow managed to get in there, and then cross check as to who was at the party."

"It would be helpful if we had a list," I said.

Jake sighed. "I sure wish I'd done my duty and checked everybody out. But we'll remember a lot of them."

"Let's each write down who we remember," I suggested. "We can also cross check with a list of those we know didn't like him. It seems to me a person with a motive would be among those."

"That's a given," Cyrus said. "And there are plenty of them. It might almost be easier to find anyone who did. We also," he explained to Jake, "have been focusing on why the city council members voted for him, and they could be on the list."

Jake rubbed his hand over his forehead and grimaced. It appeared that he might have a headache in reality as well as metaphorically. "I've been thinking, too. One who comes to mind is Geri Sataro."

I perked up. "That's interesting. Why else, besides the fact she does fit into two categories? She voted for him, and she was at the party?"

"I can't be sure of this, mind you. It will have to be confidential."

"As will all our activities," I said. "But do go on."

"I don't know if many people know this, but her son has recently come to live with her. He'd been with his father, but I suspect Daddy'd had enough. We've been, shall I say, aware of him almost since he got in town. He's in his early twenties, old enough to know better, but not too long ago, he got drunk down at Dan's Tavern, got in a fight, and was arrested by one of our men."

"Oh? I think I see what's coming," Cyrus commented.

He nodded. "I know there were several phone conversations, and he was never charged."

"You mean conversations with Donniker?" Sue asked, looking appalled.

"Don't look so surprised, Sue," Cyrus said. "I imagine it happens all the time."

My, that man was cynical, I thought. But obviously, I'd been naïve.

"The Sataro kid's one who might benefit from a little time— Oh, hell, I can't wish that on anyone."

"Hmm," Cyrus said, making notes. "I think we can put Geri in one of the suspect columns, although murdering him over an issue like that might be a bit drastic."

"Yeah," Jake said, "but there may have been more to it than I know. I didn't actually hear the conversations, mind you."

"Was she ever in the office?"

"That I don't know. I'm really not there a lot. It was just chance that I found out about this."

"Well, if we're talking about confidential conversations, one of my students said something the other day. I really don't like to repeat it, but—Well, Mark Gasper's nephew referred to how his uncle hated the chief, even though there was some business deal between the two which came out in Mark's favor. Also, I wanted to ask you, Jake, about Sheryl Adams."

"Sheryl? She's great. What about her?"

"I'm thinking as a source of information. How does she stand on all this? I was at the station the other day, and she appeared rather obviously to be disenchanted with the chief's replacement. It seems to me that she'd have good information on who had had access to the office."

"Yeah, she would," Jake said, perking up. "And I'm sure she hated working for the chief, as we all did. But I don't know. I can't actually approach her. I'm not about to go near the place, for one thing. One of the other officers called me this morning, and he didn't have much good to say about Calligan, except that he's totally different from Donniker. At least he's disciplined, but rigid and of the old school. Also, he's convinced, according to my source, of my guilt."

I nodded. "I already found that out. I took an instant dislike to him which, I might say, was obviously mutual."

Jake laughed. "The proverbial fire and ice."

The expression was apt.

"Well," Cyrus said, "you two ought to go home and get some rest. It seems that we should explore the issue of who truly would benefit from Donniker's death. Let's all try to remember exactly who was at the party. Donna, if you can find a way to approach Sheryl, it would be appropriate. And I'll continue to search out deals involving the good citizens of Cedar Harbor. Fortunately, there are records of most of them, if you know where to look. And," he added, "I think I do."

He closed his notebook.

Chapter Ten

Thursday morning was one of those typical Seattle-area winter days when everything is gray. I swear that colors are absorbed by the atmosphere so that one would think there weren't any there. The Christmas-tree shaped fir in the Moores' yard across the street appeared black, as did the leafless deciduous plants in the neighborhood, and only a passing red truck enhanced the palette.

But that was okay. Days like this were likely to be windless, and the overhead fog might even disappear later in the day. I purposefully chose colorful clothes to wear: plain brown slacks, but a blouse that featured autumn colors at their finest in oranges and gold. I had to hunt for the jewelry I wore, since I so seldom bother with much, but I located the gold chain with a tiger's eye pendant and matching earrings that Bob had given me the last Christmas before he died. I studied myself in the mirror as I brushed my short, mostly gray hair. Not too bad, I decided.

The doorbell rang, and I opened it to Alice. Her auburn hair looked almost natural and her skin was radiant for a woman our age. Her coat was a bright cherry red. We were soon enveloped in each other's arms. "I'm so glad you came," I said. "It's been too long."

"I know, and so much has happened!"

And we were off, comparing notes about our lives in the intervening months. Actually, it had been over a year since I'd seen her. She was in the middle of describing her adventures with the fascinating Jeremy when the bell rang again.

"This'll be Cyrus." I opened the door. He also looked nice, with a camel's hair overcoat over his trim suit. A paisley tie brightened his outfit. "Come in and meet Alice."

He stepped inside and I introduced them. "My pleasure." He held out his hand.

"I've heard so much about you," Alice said, and Cyrus answered, "And I, you."

I thought he held her hand a trifle long, but maybe I was just a tiny bit miffed at Alice's response to him. Not that I should have been surprised. I don't think she even knows how she always responds to a good-looking man's pheromones, or whatever it is they exude.

"Obviously, we can't all go in my car," Cyrus said.

"Oh, we'll use mine." Alice pointed to the silvery Mercedes parked in front. I knew she'd inherited money, but it must have been more than I realized. "Would you like to drive it?" Her hazel eyes were warm and speculative when she looked up at him. Did I mention how tiny she is? One of those creatures people refer to as doll-like.

That was like asking a bear if he wanted honey, as you could tell from the look on his face. So we bustled out and climbed into the Mercedes. This was a car more to my liking than the little one Cyrus owned, no matter how spirited his was. The doors on this one shut smoothly and silently, the seats were comfortable enough to sit in for a long journey, and good speakers let us listen to soft jazz as we headed for the dinner. The motor hummed quietly after starting with no difficulty, unlike my old, I'm sorry to say, clunker.

Cyrus's expression was that of a delighted small boy. What is it about men and cars? I had to admit, though, that riding in this one was a joy. He even drove sedately—relatively, that is—

and we parked well away from other cars in the parking lot of the Community Center. "Wouldn't want to get a ding on this one," he said.

Alice answered, "How thoughtful."

The delicious smells of Thanksgiving greeted us even as we walked across the parking lot: turkey, apples, squash, whatever, all blended. My stomach gurgled at the prospect. When we got inside, Cyrus politely holding the door, I saw that there were a surprising number of people I didn't know. For a moment I felt a pang that my own family had dwindled to few enough that we had no one to share holidays with. If Roberta—Well, there was no point in going there.

I was somewhat surprised to see Geri Sataro. As I studied her, I noticed her put a proprietary hand on the elbow of a young man standing next to her. Must be the infamous son. He looked like Geri, with dark hair and eyes. His face was ingenuous, one that would carry him a long ways if he chose to straighten out. Only his mouth, slightly weak, hinted at his possibly troubled nature.

I hoped I could get a chance to speak to her even if she wasn't by herself, as I couldn't exactly make an appointment to sound her out about what her position had been regarding rehiring the police chief.

We said hello to Bessie Amherst and her husband, who now used a walker but otherwise looked as if he had recovered reasonably well from his broken hip, especially considering he was in his late eighties. "Isn't this nice?" Bessie said. "We usually go to our daughter's, but they've gone to Spokane to celebrate with her in-laws. Obviously, I wouldn't cook one of these big dinners for just the two of us. Have you met my husband Stewart?" she peered at Alice. "And I don't believe I've met you."

We introduced ourselves, and chatted for a moment. Cyrus

seemed preoccupied, and kept glancing around. He relaxed when he saw Alvin slither through the door. "Ah, there you are," his voice boomed out, and the poor man shuddered. He'd so obviously been trying to be unobtrusive. But in the next moment, Cyrus collared him, ignoring the curious glances around him, and led him over to our group.

"Glad you could come, Alvin," I said, and I began to introduce him. "This is Alvin—Uh, I don't know your last name," I said, "but he's a gardener like I am." Alvin still wore the shabby brown outfit, but he'd managed to find a crisp shirt and tie.

"Alvin . . . Jones," he said, holding out his hand. I was quite sure that Jones wasn't really his last name, but Cyrus was the only other who'd noticed the hesitation, as evidenced by his lifted eyebrow.

"Shall we find seats?" I suggested, seeing that others were choosing their places. Bessie and Stewart were already joining friends when I noticed Tim Borland waving at us to come over to the table where he was seated. I hesitated. Cyrus looked less than pleased, but then he straightened up. "Maybe we'll have a chance to ask a few pertinent questions," he said, sotto voce. Alvin appeared even more reluctant than before, but Cyrus shepherded him along so that the poor man really didn't have a choice.

Alice looked amused and bemused. "Oh, my," she said when she saw Tim. Had she always been quite this interested in men? I didn't remember so, but then, there hadn't been much opportunity in our usual school circles. Somehow she maneuvered it so that she was seated between Cyrus and Tim. I sat on the right of Cyrus, with Alvin next to me.

Will Corrigan and his mother Marie spotted us, and headed in our direction. Will, who'd begun using his middle name after his father Lyle was murdered, was the young man who'd more or less taken over the family hardware store and who'd been showing an interest in my daughter. He appeared pleased to join us. I wasn't so sure about Marie. After all, my interference at that horrible time had not been appreciated. She'd said I was forgiven, but I wondered if deep down she might still blame me for her daughter's death. They seated themselves and we'd completed introductions when Phil Larson banged a spoon on a pan for attention.

"Ladies and gentlemen," he said in a booming voice that needed no amplification, "it's time for dinner. But first, since we all won't be starting to eat at the same time, I've asked Pastor Grimley of my church to say the blessing. When he finishes, please come up one table at a time, starting in that corner and going clockwise, and serve yourselves."

Good-natured groans sounded from the tables that would be last. We, however, would be about in the middle. Just then, the door opened and Carrie, looking unusually harried, hustled through. Spotting the empty chair at our table, she hurried over and sat between Tim and Will.

"You wouldn't believe my day," she said as Will helped her with her chair. Again we went through introductions, and then I turned toward Alvin, who was nervously fiddling with his napkin. "Alvin," I said. "Cyrus tells me you've lived in Cincinnati." My peripheral vision noted that Tim's hand, which had picked up a napkin, stopped dead.

"There and other places."

"Oh? Like where?" I knew I was being as nosy as Cyrus always accused me of being, but what else could a person do with a reticent individual like Alvin?

"Many others. I've been . . . a rolling wheel. I . . . well, after the army, my life changed and . . . I don't talk about it much."

"Oh. I'm so sorry." We both fell silent, but next to me I sensed that Cyrus had stirred, and I glimpsed a strange flicker in Tim's eyes. He really was listening to us instead of Alice, who seemed to be prattling about her latest trip. What was it about Cincinnati? No wonder Alvin had piqued Cyrus's attention.

I, however, felt guilty for reminding Alvin of what was obviously an unpleasant part of his life. Finally, after several moments of not talking, I thought of the one subject Alvin had shown enthusiasm for.

"I'm glad you enjoyed my garden the other day," I said. "You're welcome to come again, although of course this isn't its best season."

"Better than it is now in the Midwest," he replied. "So many plants thrive here. The excessive cold in the northern tier is very difficult for a horticulturist."

Ah, I thought. Definitely a safe subject. But I'd better tread carefully. "Did you have a specialty?" I asked.

"I was particularly interested in hybridizing new varieties of perennials," he said. "The possibilities are so endless. New techniques, since I left the field." He paused and gulped. "I don't want to bore you."

"You ought to know you won't," I said. "I've read that Washington State University is doing a great deal of work along those lines, although I imagine most of it is in regard to edibles. I understand that they have a demonstration garden in Mount Vernon. Perhaps I could take you there someday? I'd be interested, too."

"How kind of you." He smiled. He was much better looking when he did. And he was clearly well educated and bright. I sometimes wonder if nature lovers like him don't suffer the most from the incredible harshness of war.

The others at our table began to rise, and I realized that it was our turn in the serving line. Marie Corrigan was first, followed by Will, and I was next. "Marie," I began. There were so many people around from whom I needed to guard my speech.

But Will had suggested that I approach his mother. I'd procrastinated and hadn't, but now I couldn't avoid it. "How have you been?" I asked, speaking around Will.

"Much better," she answered, smiling. "It's good to see you."

I breathed a sigh of relief, and reached for a plate.

As expected, a feast awaited us. How delightful to have such a wondrous meal with none of the arduous preparation. I must be sure to thank Phil and Gretchen. There are good people in this world. I hummed along with the soft music playing in the background as I began filling my plate.

While I'd chatted with Alvin at the table, I'd tuned out the conversation to my left. I wondered if Cyrus had been able to slip in any pointed questions to Tim. Probably not, with the garrulous Alice between them. But we'd have a chance later, as people usually lingered over their coffee and drinks at functions such as these.

"I can hardly wait until Roberta gets here," I said to Will. "We haven't spent Christmas together for some time."

"I know," he said, "and I'm looking forward to seeing her, too." He grinned. His mother smiled at him, then winked at me. Good. She evidently had been informed of their relationship and was as pleased as I. Parents' approval certainly smoothed the path of romance.

Then Marie surprised me by asking, "Are you and Cyrus going to find this murderer also?" I'd have thought she'd be reluctant to think about something so akin to her own previous problems. But, she was obviously so much happier than she had been. Losing her daughter had been traumatically difficult, but she'd also lost Lyle, and that, as it had turned out, was undoubtedly an improvement in her life.

"Oh, no," I answered quickly, feeling guilty about lying, "we only became involved before because we were inadvertently drawn into it. But . . ." I hesitated. ". . . I have to admit we're curious as to why Chief Donniker was so enthusiastically retained when he'd been so incompetent."

"So am I. I heard . . . Well never mind now," she said, forking some turkey onto her plate. "There is a lot of gossip and you two were so good at ferreting out the truth. Go for it!"

Just what had she heard? She'd never mixed much socially in the past, but presumably that had changed. I resolved to follow Will's suggestion and reach out to his mother, in spite of the niggling feeling that my snooping would be taking advantage of her. I sighed, and pushed the sweet potatoes on my plate to make room for the asparagus. Why was I taking so much food? I thought about pursuing the subject gossip that might pertain to Donniker after we sat down. Most of those at our table would be interested in any information she had.

"Hmm!" I said. "That's a provocative statement. We've heard rumors, too. Let's face it. Billy—Excuse me. Chief Donniker was not generally liked, we all know that. So why did all those people on the council vote for him?"

Marie glanced nervously over her shoulder. I tried to follow her gaze, but couldn't tell whether she was looking at some specific person or just checking out who was nearby.

"I'd—rather not repeat gossip," she said. "At least, not here. Perhaps we can have tea some day? I have a feeling we should get to know each other better."

Will glanced suspiciously at his mother, and his cheeks definitely acquired a rosy tint.

After we settled at the table, our conversation became more general, and soon I was ready to choose dessert. I joined the line to the goodies, and as I hesitated over the excruciating choice between pumpkin or pecan pie, or perhaps that chocolate cake, my problem was solved. A hand reached out from next to me and neatly sliced a piece of pecan pie in half. "What a good idea," I said, turning to find that Geri Sataro was deftly transferring the pie to her plate.

She chuckled as she did the same to the pumpkin, and then scooped some apple crisp. "I usually adhere to a strict diet, but that's what Thanksgiving is for, is it not?"

Well, not exactly, I thought, but said, "We can really be thankful for the opportunity."

As we moved over to pick up coffee, my impulses tangled with my judgment. Did I dare ask her about her vote for Chief Donniker? Impulse won. What was there to lose? "Geri," I said, "some of us have been curious as to how the chief was re-elected. He was . . . well, one can only say, not qualified."

Geri didn't get where she was in business by giving away her feelings. With a face devoid of emotion, she answered, "So I've heard, but," she said, shrugging, "it doesn't really matter now, does it? So sad for his wife to have people rehash the whole thing, don't you think?"

What else could I do but agree. "You're right, of course. I must pay a visit to Lucille. I've been remiss." I noticed Geri's son beyond her. He wasn't worrying about whether he was taking more than his share of dessert. His dark eyes turned toward me, and a sardonic expression crossed his face. What was that about? Geri, almost pointedly, hadn't bothered to introduce us.

We did linger when we were finished, but the general conversation was that of satiated people. Cyrus had done well on dessert also, but I didn't dare poke fun at him after he'd pointed out previously that he had much better cholesterol than I.

I did have an opportunity to ask Carrie if something was the matter, a question I couldn't exactly ask at the main table.

"You're perceptive," she said, not looking me in the eye. "I'll explain later."

People were beginning to gather their things to depart, so I limited myself to a quick hug, and agreed.

"Thank you so much for inviting me," Alvin said, shaking my hand and then Cyrus's. Then, before we could reply, he slipped quickly out the door.

As I was putting on my coat, Tim beat Cyrus to helping me on with it. "I'm sorry we didn't get more chance to talk," he said, patting my shoulder. "I enjoyed your friend Alice, of course," he said politely as Cyrus did the honors with her coat, "but I'd like to—"

Cyrus interrupted, rather rudely, I thought. "Shall we go, Donna? Alice has quite a ways to drive home."

"One thing before you go," Tim interjected. "Cyrus tells me you were both annoyed with me for not sharing my knowledge the day we had lunch. I am so sorry. But surely you realize that, as a journalist, I couldn't? But I do apologize. Forgiven?"

"Of course," I answered.

Tim's brown eyes really were compelling. He smiled wryly, and said, "I'll call you."

CHAPTER ELEVEN

When we arrived at my house, I invited Alice in, but she demurred. "I'd like to get home, but thanks so much for including me. You know such interesting people. It was good to meet you, Cyrus."

"And I, too. I did enjoy driving your car."

She slid into the Mercedes driver's seat and then, purring softly, waved goodbye. The car was purring as well. You can't possibly be jealous of your old friend, I told myself.

When Cyrus walked me to the door, I wasn't surprised that he accepted my invitation to step inside. "I won't stay," he said, "but did you find out anything?"

"Well, Marie hinted strongly that she'd heard stories, gossip, probably, but she did invite me to tea, implying that she'd say more then. She obviously didn't want to be overheard."

I hung my coat in the closet. "Do sit down. Shall I take your coat?"

He shook his head, but settled in my leather chair that he favors.

"I had a chance to speak to Geri Sataro in the dessert line about her vote," I continued, sitting on the couch, "but got nowhere at all, except for unpleasant vibes. I do want to pursue that question. It occurred to me that she might have been the one Marie saw nearby who caused her not to share her knowledge.

"I also found out that Alvin was evidently a trained horticulturist in his previous life, and we're planning a trip to the Mt. Vernon demonstration garden, so I'll have a chance to at least get to know him better. Obviously, one has to tread carefully. I so wish there were more things we could do as a society to help people like him."

"Your friendship is a good start on both matters, Donna," Cyrus said. "Maybe you'll be able to help him and also learn what it is about Cincinnati he doesn't want to talk about."

"That reminds me. Did you notice Tim's expression when I brought up the subject of Cincinnati? Did you learn anything from him?"

Cyrus grimaced. "As I've noted before, he has the characteristics of a politician. It won't be easy to pry anything out of him. He clearly has the talent to direct conversations. Speaking of which, I don't much care for his interest in you."

"Me?"

"Didn't you notice how he watched you? And he asked questions about you. You need to be careful around that man, Donna Rose."

He normally doesn't use my disliked middle name unless he wants to tease me. Or sometimes when he's distressed. "Cyrus," I exploded. "What business is it of yours? You're not my keeper, you know, as I've been forced to tell you many times before. In case you haven't noticed, I abhor someone attempting to manage me."

"Managing you and protecting you are two different things."

I sprang to my feet. "Protecting me? Protecting me? I am quite capable of taking care of myself, in case you haven't noticed. You'd better get over that if we're going to work together."

His face stiffened, and he rose to his feet. "I know that. But a little friendly advice . . ."

"Good night, Cyrus," I said, fuming and opening the front door.

He wasn't happy as he stalked through it and down the front walk with rigid shoulders and not even a backward glance.

I didn't see Cyrus for nearly a week. Unusual these days, for us. But my anger level remained high. I suppose nature has given men this need to protect women, dating back perhaps to the cavemen. But there are no saber-tooth tigers hanging around these days. One would think that this instinctive reaction would have been replaced by reason as women have clearly showed their ability to fend for themselves.

But, no. Only some women have learned this, I had to admit. Certainly many still depend on the other sex for sustenance and protection. Anyway, enough time wouldn't have passed for natural selection to have had an effect on the species. Perhaps I'd been unnecessarily harsh.

I was busy again anyway, working on my Christmas preparations and another two-day substituting session. These students were third-graders, such a charming age. They're able to work independently, are easy to control, and still think their teachers are infallible.

When I got home, perhaps feeling mellow from my successful two days, I decided to be the first one to make a concession. If Cyrus and I were going to save Jake, it was necessary for me to swallow my pride. The man wasn't going to change. He'd always be self-confident, fastidious, intelligent and bossy. When I thought about it, perhaps three of those characteristics could describe me, also. Not fastidious, but I did so often want to manage affairs because I thought I was more capable than others. I've tried to temper the tendency to take over as I've learned through the years how little it's appreciated.

I dialed the familiar number. "Cyrus," I said, "I want to apologize. Perhaps I was unnecessarily annoyed the other day.

After all, your intentions were good. I imagine."

After a brief pause, one of his rare guffaws came across the line. "Donna Rose, thank you. I never thought I'd hear you . . . ahem. Well, I, too, will humble myself and apologize. My intentions were the best. A woman living alone—"

"Why don't you stop right there?" I interrupted. "Your instinct to be protective is obvious, and I'll just have to bear it, I suppose. Um, may I ask, have you found out anything else pertinent regarding Billy's murder?"

"I wish I could say I had. However, I'm working on the Cincinnati connection."

"Actually, why?" I asked. "You're so fixated on Tim Borland that you're not looking at other possibilities."

"Oh, I will. I am. You know I don't like to talk about my research until I'm reasonably positive of my data. Changing the subject, do you drive a stick shift?"

"Of course. That's what my car has. Bob always liked them best, thought he had better control and got better mileage. Though, sometimes I think—"

"Smart man. He was right. I guess I've never ridden in your vehicle and didn't notice that's what you had. Anyway, are you busy tomorrow? Would you like to go for a spin in my car?"

"You mean—you'd actually let me drive it?"

"Humph. I said I would sometime. The weather forecast's good and I thought you might like to."

I realized that Cyrus was actually trying to make amends. I never thought I'd say it about him, but how sweet! "I'd like that very much," I said. "What time?"

I started out hesitantly, getting a feel for the clutch. Beside me, Cyrus was as tense as a humming telephone wire. I could almost feel the vibrations. "Where shall we go?" I asked.

"Oh, just around town at first. How about along Beach

Drive?" We passed the Corrigan home, which reminded me of Marie's suggestion that we have tea. Should I suggest we stop now? No. Cyrus's presence would probably intimidate her. I shifted into a higher gear and sped up. The car certainly was responsive. And once I was inside, it wasn't nearly as cramped behind the wheel as I had expected. "Vroom, vroom," I said under my breath.

The tension beside me abated slightly as he chuckled. "Do you want to try the Pipeline?"

"Really? Sure." I turned and headed for the twisty road that led over the hills behind Cedar Harbor. I still thought Alice's Mercedes was more to my taste, but perhaps it was time I considered getting a new car. The old green Chevy was well past its youth, and after all, I was earning money substituting. "Here we go!"

The car responded to my touch like an extension of my arms. Wow! I could get used to this. I zipped around a slow-moving truck on the straight stretch between two curves, then managed, barely, to overtake a beat-up old car before entering the tight curves leading uphill. I was beginning to get a hint of why Cyrus drives the way he does.

And then something went wrong. The car was not reacting to my directions. "Oh, my God, Cyrus!" I turned my head in his direction. "What's going . . . ?"

The next instant, we'd crossed the center line and bounced off the outcropping to my left. I twisted the wheel uselessly as we ricocheted across the road toward the guard rail. Cyrus moaned and tried to grab the wheel, but it was too late. Fortunately the rail held, as the drop on the other side was formidable, with nothing below but a brush-filled ravine. The sound of metal crunching was something I never want to hear again.

"What have you done?" Cyrus wailed as he futilely tried to

open his door. Finally, he managed to shove it open a crack, and he squeezed out, hurrying to inspect the damage.

"Thanks for asking if I'm okay," I muttered, putting my hand to my forehead, which had encountered the visor.

Behind us I heard the short burst of a siren.

Outside Cyrus hurried around the entire car, making noises that sounded suspiciously like whimpering. I shuddered and laid my head on my folded arms on the useless steering wheel. A knock sounded on my window.

Oh, no! I raised my head to see the cold, gray eyes of that insufferable Sheriff Calligan peering in at me. He made a gesture indicating that he wanted me to roll the window down.

"Ma'am," he said, scrutinizing me and apparently deciding that I wasn't injured, "may I see your license and insurance card?"

Still breathing hard, I fumbled for my purse and extricated my wallet. Wordlessly, I pulled them out, glad that I'd renewed the license not long before.

He studied it, looking back and forth between the photo and my face, as if he hadn't met me before. Probably trying to decide if I really wasn't older than the age indicated. Or maybe that I'd cheated on the weight.

Only a little, I thought.

"Please step out of the car."

I might not be injured, but I was shaking like an aspen leaf in the wind. Pushing the handle down and then grasping it with the other hand for stability, I complied, thinking it wouldn't have killed him to open it for me.

"Put your finger on your nose, shut your eyes, and step forward." I did, glad that I was able to control my shakiness.

I opened my eyes to see him scribbling in his notebook.

"Now count backward from one hundred in sevens."

What was he doing? Well, at least I'd surprise him on that.

"Ninety-three, eighty-six, seventy-nine, seventy-two, sixty-five—"

"All right." Again, he made a notation.

Then it hit me. "You thought I was drunk!" I spouted. "In the morning!"

Now behind him, Cyrus shook his head in warning. I knew he was reminding me that it wasn't smart to argue with a cop. Boiling, I clamped my lips together.

"Just checking routinely."

Knowing deep down that Cyrus was probably right about restraining myself, I gave in to the pressure boiling inside me. "It was the car! Why won't you listen? You, too, Cyrus. Something was wrong with the steering!"

Calligan wrote something else, then ripped the page out of his notebook. "I'll have to give you a citation, however. Negligent driving."

"But—but—" I knew I was sputtering, spit probably flying.

"Ma-am, I was right behind you. You were exceeding the speed limit considerably."

Un-oh! Cyrus's vehicle apparently had considerably more gumption than I realized.

"Your pass of that car didn't get you back in your lane before the yellow line."

Well, that might have been possible, I had to admit.

"And you weren't paying attention. Your head was turned toward this gentleman in conversation instead of looking at the road."

"But I was trying to tell him that the car—"

He interrupted. "Tell it to the judge. Sir," he said to Cyrus, "I assume it's your car. I'll call for the tow truck. You'll want to wait, no doubt. But, ma'am, you can ride back to town with me."

"I—don't—think—so!" It wasn't that I was anxious to sit

there waiting with the angry Cyrus, but it beat riding in a patrol car with the cop who had to be the most obnoxious lawman in western Washington. Worse yet, having the neighbors see me arrive in that manner.

Turning my back on both of them and trying to regain some dignity, I walked over to the guard rail and stared toward a spectacular view I wasn't even seeing.

Chapter Twelve

The wait was as interminable as a session in the dentist's chair, and not a word was spoken. Peripherally, I was aware of Cyrus checking the damage, stooping as he inspected the chassis. He ruffled his normally smooth hair as he moved his hand through it in anguish. His shirttail hung out. Motorists honked as they swung around us, whether in sympathy or annoyance because of the delay, I didn't know.

Eventually I heard the powerful motor of the tow truck. It pulled up, then reversed to be in position before the driver hopped out.

"Oh, man," said the driver, a burly fellow with one of those unshaven faces that seem to be popular these days. "Wow!" he repeated. "A classic. What happened?"

"My friend was driving," Cyrus informed him coldly.

"Oh, man. Well, these days they can bring it back to its glory, but it'll cost. I haven't seen a beauty like this since that car show in Seattle last year. And it's—was in great shape!"

"I'm aware of that." Cyrus frowned. "Shall we be going?"

He was perhaps unnecessarily curt, but I was glad. I didn't care to hear any more about the wonders of that dratted car. The driver bustled around, whistling annoyingly through his teeth, until he completed the hook-up with a series of bangs.

"Hop in." He opened the passenger-side door and gestured to me.

"Perhaps we can drop Mrs. Galbreath at her home on the

119

way," Cyrus suggested without looking at me. "She seems rather shaken."

Grr! I was in better shape than he was. Still, I was grateful that I wouldn't have to listen to all the ensuing shop talk that inevitably would occur. I climbed up into the vehicle with Cyrus next to me.

The driver rattled on about cars, with Cyrus making noncommittal answers. I was silent. That is, until we reached my house.

As Cyrus opened the door, I said to the driver, "There was definitely something wrong with the steering. Would you be sure to tell the repair people to look specifically at that?"

With raised eyebrows, he answered, "Sure, ma'am. Those things do happen more than you'd think. Especially on a car as old as this, even if it has been restored."

"Thank you for believing me," I said as I slid across the seat. Perhaps I should tip the man. No, I decided. I'd let Cyrus take care of that.

I was exhausted. After a light lunch, I took a nap, then got up with renewed determination. Obviously Cyrus's and my cooperative venture to clear Jake was over. Okay, there was no choice. I had to step into action. Quickly. The arraignment was coming up, as well as Roberta's arrival, and it was essential that I accomplish as much as I could now.

I put tea into a pot to steep and settled down to make one of my to-do lists. I must take Marie up on the suggestion she'd made at the Thanksgiving dinner that we visit. I hoped she had information that would provide leads. And I certainly should call on Lucille Donniker, even though we'd never been more than acquaintances. She attended Cedar Harbor functions but was always reserved, almost haughty. Still, I knew her well enough that a condolence visit would be in order.

And Sheryl Adams. How was I going to approach her? Lurk outside the police department until I was sure the sheriff wasn't there? That didn't seem too practical. Instead, I decided to call and suggest we get together at the bakery on her break. It seemed reasonable that she'd want to help Jake. I mean, who wouldn't prefer working for him to Donniker or Calligan?

I hoped I wouldn't be called to substitute during the next week or so, but that was unlikely. Teachers have a habit of becoming sick during the holidays. Only occasionally had I found it necessary to take time off during that period, but it's a stressful time at best, and the seasonal colds and flu begin making their sneaky appearances.

I mustn't waste time. With that in mind, I reached for the phone and dialed the police department number. To my relief, a feminine voice answered.

"Sheryl?" I inquired. She answered affirmatively, and I identified myself and went into my spiel. "I wonder if you'd like to have coffee with me some morning over at the bakery? Some of us, well, we want to help Jake, and I wondered—"

She interrupted. "Indeed, ma'am." In the background I could hear the rumble of voices, one of which likely emanated from the sheriff, which explained her formality. "Would tomorrow morning be satisfactory? At, uh, ten-thirty?"

"Great."

"I'll put it on my calendar." Her manner was businesslike. Good. It appeared she was as anxious to talk to me as I, to her.

Next I called Lucille. When she answered, I began the requisite speech to a recently widowed acquaintance. "This is Donna Galbreath. I've been wondering how you're doing? I'm so sorry about your husband. It's so difficult when it's sudden, isn't it?" Then I added, "Especially under the circumstances."

"Oh, my, yes," she answered. "It's been . . . devastating. But I'm doing just fine. He wasn't home much, you know, with the responsibilities he had and such a demanding job."

Why did her speech, which was about as lengthy as anything

she'd ever said to me, sound a touch insincere? Perhaps I was letting my feelings about the man color my impressions. "I remember him as Billy," I said. "I had him as a student in my sixth-grade class the very first year I taught."

"Yes, he often mentioned that."

Humph. What had his version of the proceedings been? "May I stop by for a short visit? Perhaps we could reminisce a bit. I so remember how alone I felt after my husband's death."

"Why, that would be nice." She sounded surprised, and I couldn't blame her considering our limited contact in the past. "Did you have a time in mind?"

"How about tomorrow afternoon? Say about three?"

We agreed on that and I hung up, satisfied that I'd made a start on my investigating. How could anyone truly miss the man? Not to mention put up with him for long years of marriage? I sighed, remembering my own very happy but short tenure as a wife. Everybody's different, I reminded myself. With different needs and expectations.

I didn't have any idea how talking with Lucille could advance the investigation. However, she'd said he was home so little. I truly doubted that he'd put in extra time at the station house. Perhaps—There had to be a side to the man I'd never seen.

Satisfied, I glanced at my list. The next person to tackle would be Marie Corrigan, but I'd wait until tomorrow evening to call her. I wanted first to see what I learned during the two contacts tomorrow. It was possible something more imperative would develop.

For a moment I felt a pang that I could no longer discuss proceedings with Cyrus. We'd been sounding boards for each other in the past and, I had to admit, given valuable advice to each other. He approached investigating slowly and methodically, whereas I admittedly tended to be impetuous. No question we'd complemented each other. I shrugged and reminded myself that our collaboration was over and I'd just have to do what was needed in my own manner. I was surprised at how glum that made me feel. I pictured him tweaking his moustache as his blue eyes looked at me, and I swallowed.

So the next morning at 10:20 I was at the bakery, having picked a table as far away from others as possible. Sheryl wasn't on time, and I began to fear she'd changed her mind, but then she hustled in full of apologies.

"I'm so sorry to be late. When Sheriff Calligan wants something, he wants it now," she explained.

"No problem. I'm just glad you're here. Shall we order? My treat."

"You don't need to do that," she demurred, but I settled the matter firmly. Sheryl was a forty-ish widow, tall and wiry, and I watched her choose a sugar bun dripping with frosting. I sighed. She was the type who could ingest ten of them without an extra ounce settling on her tummy. I rationalized that we were more likely to stay a while if we were eating as well as drinking, so I picked out a similar temptation. I hoped she dared be away from her job long enough for a real chat.

As if reading my mind, Sheryl said, "I told the sheriff I'd need a little extra time, that I had business to take care of. He didn't look happy, but then, he never does."

We settled down, placing our choices on the table. "Well," I said, pouring tea from the pot in front of me, "I'll get right to the point. Some of us, earlier, had formed a Dump Donniker committee, but of course that's moot now. However, our intent was to see Jake as our new police chief."

"Oh, I would so agree with that!" She vigorously chomped down on her sugar bun.

"I thought you might. But needless to say, we have a problem now. We're convinced Jake is innocent. He might not be, of course, but our gut feelings are that he would be incapable of such an action."

"He was framed," Sheryl said with a bitter twist to her mouth.

"Oh, I'm so glad to hear that you think so! It was only when Jake told us how ineffective the security was for the evidence room that we saw how it could have been done. Obviously, almost anyone with gardening knowledge could have got their hands on monkshood, but the key factor in making Jake look guilty is that the evidence from last year's murder was missing."

"That, plus him shouting to the world that somebody should kill Donniker, implying he'd like to! I heard about it several times." She took a sip of coffee, then continued, "By now, Cedar Harbor being the way it is, ninety percent of the residents have heard it, too."

"What I'm wondering is who would have had access to that room without being noticed?" I asked. "We figure, obviously, that it had to be someone who was at the party honoring him, and we're trying to put together a list. Three lists, that is. One of who attended, one of those who may have had reason to kill him, and lastly, one of people who could have gotten into the room."

"I don't know anyone who liked him," she said.

"Yes, but dislike and true hatred are two different things. Do you have any ideas?"

"I'll have to think," she mused, putting her hand to her chin. "It's such a muddle. Of course anyone who worked in the department—But I don't believe any of the employees truly hated him, unless there was something going on I don't know about."

"That's the problem. Anybody with secrets concerning the chief wouldn't talk about it now, that's for sure. But I have heard that he had business dealings on the side."

"Oh, my, yes. Sometimes I think he was on the phone half the time with wheelings and dealings. I heard him talking to

Mark Gasper, and of course to Ben Flannigan, his broker."

"Well, you're the only one we could think of who might know who could have been alone in the office long enough to sneak that key and grab the monkshood."

"They'd have needed quite a bit of time," she mused, "or know exactly where it was. You can imagine what a mess that place was! After I took over the job, I yearned to organize it, but the chief told me to forget it, it was okay the way it had always been, and besides, I wouldn't have time. Unfortunately, he was right about that. You wouldn't believe the reports that have to be made on every subject that comes to our attention. Fortunately, the chief didn't want anything to do with reports. From what I saw of his attention to detail, I was better off doing them myself. He often did stay late though, after I'd left. I was never sure what he did or who was there.

"Not that he worked extended hours, you understand. He seldom arrived before ten in the morning. I'll need to think," she said, "but if I come up with anything, I'll be sure to let you know." Glancing at her watch, she swallowed the last of her coffee and wrapped the unfinished bun in a paper napkin to take with her. Mine was long gone, which probably explained the difference between her angular shape and my admittedly rounded one. "I'd better go. Thanks for the coffee. I'll be in touch."

She took my hand, and we shook, almost triumphantly. "We'll do it!" I said. "I'm so glad you're on our side."

On my way to the Donniker house that afternoon, I considered how I'd approach Lucille. Obviously, not with a hit-list of questions. The best thing might be just to get to know her better, to try to ascertain exactly what sort of person she was. For instance, was she only shy or did she consider herself better than the rest of us in Cedar Harbor? Had her marriage been happy? After all, family members were generally the first to be suspected, I'd always heard.

I keep a supply of baked goods in my freezer, so with trepidation and a loaf of banana bread I'd taken out earlier, I knocked on her front door. The house was located on a side street, and I didn't ever remember being by it; I'd had to look up the address. It was one of those that sprang up when Cedar Harbor first began to be a bedroom community instead of a summer beach destination. That is, it was nondescript. No individuality.

Cyrus's and mine were of the same generation, but we'd each added our own touches, as had the owner before Cyrus. In our cases it was primarily in our landscaping, but Cyrus had recently installed a magnificent front door with a beaded-glass oval window. My own pink house with deep-rose colored front door stood out because of its paint job, I had to admit.

This door was a drab, brown contractor-type, and the house what I considered a dirty beige. The yard had not been planted by anyone with imagination. Standard foundation evergreens, now much too overgrown, circled the house and obscured windows. An unhealthy lawn and a lone, sad maple tree completed the effect. A gardener did not live here.

In a moment, Lucille answered my ring. She looked the same as always; her salt-and-pepper hair in a knot at her nape framed a face with a prominent nose and chin. Her eyes, behind dark-rimmed glasses, were also gray. With barely a hint of a smile she stepped back, saying, "Please do come in."

I glanced around curiously as she led me into the living room. The Donniker wedding portrait rested on an end table. Billy was actually slim and almost handsome in his tux, and beside him Lucille, with curly dark hair, looked radiant as she clutched his arm.

"What a handsome couple you were," I commented.

ers in those days."

ace brightened a smidgen. Obviously, this had been a
oject for me to choose. "And did you succeed?" I asked.

indeed. The Seattle library has an excellent section on
ect. Actually, that's where I met William."

vas checking genealogy?" I asked incredulously.

no. He was after something about police work. I don't
member what. But we got to talking, and he seemed
d in my research. And . . ." She spread her hands. ". . .
rom there. We were married rather quickly after that, I
admit. I wasn't having any success finding work I'd be
d in, and William seemed a good choice for mate. A
sical specimen, and obviously an upright individual."

speechless. Nothing about love, I thought. It sounded
'd picked him as a worthy addition to her distinguished
ee. Wow!

s a little older than he," she added. "I suppose I can
ace in my research. There's never an end once one
especially now that so much is available on the Internet.

ny dear," she still clutched my hand, "don't you worry
that they have the wrong person in jail. I know you
trumental in helping William during that distressing
year, but . . ." She chuckled weakly. ". . . just try to
police to do their job . . ." She paused significantly.
William always did."

ed my teeth and looked at her in astonishment. Was she
at dense about the man? Or did she just want the whole
go away so she could concentrate on the one thing in
seemed to have meaning to her?

never going to be friends with this woman, I was sure.
l I could do to retain my composure enough to make
vells and leave.

She didn't respond, only said, "If you'll excuse me, I'll get the coffee."

"Oh, here," I said, offering the banana bread. "You can keep it, or . . ."

"Why, thank you. I'll slice some now. That would be good with our drinks." And she disappeared.

I avoided a recliner that looked as if it might have been the chief's favorite chair, instead choosing the end of the couch where a coffee table waited to serve its purpose. Coffee wouldn't have been my first choice, but I certainly wasn't going to say anything. There were a few noises from what I knew would be the kitchen, and I took the opportunity to look around.

Framed photos were everywhere. No landscapes or drawings. Even over the fireplace, a series of what appeared to be really old photos were arranged to indicate relationships, I assumed. The highest, in two small oval-shaped frames, were of a dour-looking man and woman staring glumly ahead. So many very old pictures look like that. I understand it's because the subjects had to hold still for so long in order for the camera to catch the image.

Ribbons led to a single picture of a couple, marginally more cheerful, who were, I assumed, the next generation. These folks had apparently been more prolific. More ribbons led to their progeny: three couples, one single man and a single woman. This family tree had to be Lucille's, considering that at least two had the same chin and nose.

"You have some wonderful old photos," I commented as she came into the room carrying a tray with two steaming cups and a plate with the sliced banana bread.

"It's a very distinguished line, I'm proud to say, and I'm fortunate that my family preserved these pictures. I even have tintypes and daguerreotypes tucked away for safekeeping. Genealogy is my hobby, you know."

Well, of course I didn't know that, but I said, "How lucky you are to have all that family history. My own family had too many dead ends. They tended to have few children who either didn't marry or didn't have children. I'm afraid my branch is going to be the same," I added sadly. "I have one daughter, and she's recently divorced." I didn't mention the sad news we'd received years ago that she'd be unable to carry a baby. "How about you?" I asked. "I guess I don't know if you and the chief had children."

Her face saddened. "One of my biggest regrets," she said. "It just wasn't meant to happen."

To change the subject, obviously unpleasant to her, I brought up the story of Roberta's rescue from a canoe by the chief way back when. "And she's always been grateful," I added. "She felt he saved her life. He was young. Don't I remember he joined the force right out of high school?"

"Yes, indeed. He told me he'd always wanted to be a policeman."

I kept my mouth shut at that one. The Billy I knew in sixth grade had not been an advocate of law and order.

"He had a short stint with a small police force up in the mountains before I met him," she said, "but he always wanted to live in Cedar Harbor, and returned as quickly as there was an opportunity."

"I never had reason to see much of him as an adult," I said, wondering how she viewed the man who was so generally disliked by the rest of us.

"Well, he was so busy with his work," she said. "He belonged to many organizations, was even a national officer of one of the police groups. Civic works were so important to him.

"He was a fine man," she said softly. "I'm so glad his murderer has been caught." Her expression was odd. Satisfied, perhaps, but something else lay underneath.

"Oh, but," I blurted, "do you honestly done something so vile? I mean, you m reasonably well. There are many of us who that he's been framed."

"Framed? But how could that be? Who the monkshood from the evidence room always been jealous, you know. Consta undermine William's authority." She appea my suggestion. And then, to my horror, sl chief from somewhere in her bosom and b dear, now I'm really upset."

"I'm so sorry!" I set down my cup and t was icy cold. "That was clumsy of me."

I'd really put my foot into it this time. B her surreptitiously, something in her man me. Was it the way she held her head or, crocodile tears? Or was I being mean-spiri I've been accused of that before, although r knew me well.

"I'd better leave," I offered, standing.

"No, no." She still clutched my hand, a beside her. "I'm so glad to have company. empty these days. What am I going to do?"

"Start by drinking your coffee. And . . . bread. One so often feels better with food a think? Then you can tell me more about Where did you meet?"

"I'd just finished college in the Midwest, "and came out here hoping to find a job. Bu useless majors, in my case history. Even ther genealogy. In tracing my family tree, I'd branch who were early settlers in the Seat interested in tracking that down. And of co

CHAPTER THIRTEEN

My plans for the next day were put on hold by an early morning call. I rolled over, groaning, and reached for the phone.

"Good morning," said a cheery voice. "This is the Cedar Harbor School District. Mrs. Chelsea at the high school had a family emergency arise during the night. I truly hate to ask you, but could you possibly step in for her creative writing sections? I know Martha had you penciled in as preferring not to be called at this time, but we're really short of substitutes. We have her English One covered, but if you could come just for these two classes? Please?" she asked plaintively.

Well, what else could I do but agree? I pulled myself together and headed for the shower, mentally rearranging my responsibilities. I'd only be at the high school for the morning, so I could keep the date I'd made last evening with Marie Corrigan for three o'clock. As I stumbled around getting dressed, I wished I'd gone to bed earlier, as I surely would have had I known I'd be called. No wonder substitutes sometimes become burned out by these early-morning summonses.

It didn't take too long into the first class for me to ascertain that these students were not the cream-of-the-crop writers, but rather were in an elective class they'd assumed would be a snap. How I itched to be in a position to give them some real assignments to challenge their creativity, but it wasn't my place as a sub to do this. However, since Mrs. Chelsea hadn't known she'd be gone, there were no lesson plans, and I needed to come up with something.

So we discussed how to start a short story, novel, or even a nonfiction piece and asked them to write a beginning of their choice.

A short ten minutes later, a young hunk strolled up to my desk. "I'm done, Mrs. Galbreath," he said. "Can I go to the library to work on my term assignment for this class?"

"Go to the library?" I asked, somewhat surprised.

"Sure. That's where most of the computers are."

A blond girl with a couple of strands of hair dangling in front of her eyes waved her hand. "Me, too," she said, eyeing the hunk who pretended to be oblivious. I quickly scanned the seating chart, although with kids this age I wasn't confident that they hadn't taken advantage of Mrs. Chelsea's absence to rearrange themselves.

"Um, Hank," I said, not recognizing his last name, "and Ellen . . ." This one I did recognize, although I couldn't be sure there weren't others in the community with the same name since I didn't know the family. Diego. The name of the golf club manager. So I asked. "Is it your father who's on the city council?"

She nodded affirmatively and I continued. "Well, Ellen, I'd prefer if you and Hank would wait until the rest are through and we discuss the work."

Hank shrugged and leaned one firm haunch on my desk. Ellen, too, sauntered up, laying her paper on my desk.

"Keep it," I said, "for the discussion."

"Oh." She flicked one lock behind her right ear. "Mrs. Chelsea always takes them home and gives them back the next day with comments."

"Well, I'm only here for this one day, so we'll do it differently, shall we?"

"Sure," she agreed pleasantly. "Umm, what do you know

about the police chief's murder?"

"Nothing more than you do, I'm sure," I said, somewhat irritated. Except—Her father was on the city council. I'd decided not to squelch any volunteered comments that might be pertinent, and it was just possible she might say something useful. I wouldn't push, but—"Why should I?" I asked.

She blinked. "Because you solved the last one, that's why."

Hank the hunk stirred. Oh dear, another term I wish hadn't fixed itself in my mind. "It was you? Hey, I hear you're a real good detective. I want to write murder mysteries. In fact . . ." He waved his paper. ". . . this is the start of one. Do you think—"

"Cool it, Hank," Ellen said. "Let's hear what she has to say."

"What can I say? I have no connection with the police department, and no, I'm not a detective. It was an unfortunate situation in which I became inadvertently involved."

"My mom and dad hope you'll catch the murderer again, even if Chief Donniker was a bastard just like that Corrigan man. Oops! Excuse me, Mrs. Galbreath." She blushed. "Well, I mean they sure didn't like him, but they don't think anyone should get away with murder."

"You're excused. But please watch your language. Oh," I said, when her statement penetrated, "I had understood your father was one of his supporters."

"Heck, no. Dad said the chief shafted him." Then, evidently realizing that perhaps she'd said too much, she closed her mouth.

Oh, dear. I wished she'd continued. How on earth was I going to find out what that had been about? At least her parents wanting the murderer to be caught was a plus on their side. But I'd still like to know what had gone on between them and Donniker. Diego's vote to promote the chief was surely related.

To my surprise, Hank's mystery beginning showed promise. At least he'd definitely started with a hook. "Sam was used to bodies, but the one splattered in front of him made him gulp down the rising vomit." It wasn't my kind of mystery, but those gory ones do sell.

Several of the others either had an instinct or had taken their lessons to heart. Perhaps I'd misjudged the class. I congratulated them and urged them to continue writing.

The second section, a smaller group, included the more serious writers, and to my relief, they were so busy working on their projects that the subject of murder didn't come up. I arrived home a little before noon and left my car in my driveway since I'd be going out later. An almost immediate knock on my front door made me jump.

I was astounded when I answered. Cyrus, holding an enormous bouquet of pink roses, was standing there.

"May I come in?" His voice was humble. "Here," he said, thrusting the flowers into my arms, "these are for you. Roses always make me think of you, and I figured you'd like this color since you painted your house a similar shade. Please?"

I'm sure my mouth was wide open, but no sound came out. I stepped backward holding the flowers, and Cyrus came in, shutting the door behind him. "I hope you like them."

"What on earth?" I managed to ask.

"Donna Rose," he said, "I am here to truly humble myself and to apologize."

I shook my head in disbelief. "I seem to recall hearing that same line from you in the not very distance past. I think, Cyrus, that our relationship, such as it was, is over."

"Don't say that! Hear me out. For not the first time in my life, I was wrong. Lamentably so. Donna Rose," he said, pulling his coat off and throwing it on the couch, "again, I made a mistake. The repair people have found that a tie rod had definitely been cut. You were right. It wasn't an accident.

She didn't respond, only said, "If you'll excuse me, I'll get the coffee."

"Oh, here," I said, offering the banana bread. "You can keep it, or . . ."

"Why, thank you. I'll slice some now. That would be good with our drinks." And she disappeared.

I avoided a recliner that looked as if it might have been the chief's favorite chair, instead choosing the end of the couch where a coffee table waited to serve its purpose. Coffee wouldn't have been my first choice, but I certainly wasn't going to say anything. There were a few noises from what I knew would be the kitchen, and I took the opportunity to look around.

Framed photos were everywhere. No landscapes or drawings. Even over the fireplace, a series of what appeared to be really old photos were arranged to indicate relationships, I assumed. The highest, in two small oval-shaped frames, were of a dour-looking man and woman staring glumly ahead. So many very old pictures look like that. I understand it's because the subjects had to hold still for so long in order for the camera to catch the image.

Ribbons led to a single picture of a couple, marginally more cheerful, who were, I assumed, the next generation. These folks had apparently been more prolific. More ribbons led to their progeny: three couples, one single man and a single woman. This family tree had to be Lucille's, considering that at least two had the same chin and nose.

"You have some wonderful old photos," I commented as she came into the room carrying a tray with two steaming cups and a plate with the sliced banana bread.

"It's a very distinguished line, I'm proud to say, and I'm fortunate that my family preserved these pictures. I even have tintypes and daguerreotypes tucked away for safekeeping. Genealogy is my hobby, you know."

Well, of course I didn't know that, but I said, "How lucky you are to have all that family history. My own family had too many dead ends. They tended to have few children who either didn't marry or didn't have children. I'm afraid my branch is going to be the same," I added sadly. "I have one daughter, and she's recently divorced." I didn't mention the sad news we'd received years ago that she'd be unable to carry a baby. "How about you?" I asked. "I guess I don't know if you and the chief had children."

Her face saddened. "One of my biggest regrets," she said. "It just wasn't meant to happen."

To change the subject, obviously unpleasant to her, I brought up the story of Roberta's rescue from a canoe by the chief way back when. "And she's always been grateful," I added. "She felt he saved her life. He was young. Don't I remember he joined the force right out of high school?"

"Yes, indeed. He told me he'd always wanted to be a policeman."

I kept my mouth shut at that one. The Billy I knew in sixth grade had not been an advocate of law and order.

"He had a short stint with a small police force up in the mountains before I met him," she said, "but he always wanted to live in Cedar Harbor, and returned as quickly as there was an opportunity."

"I never had reason to see much of him as an adult," I said, wondering how she viewed the man who was so generally disliked by the rest of us.

"Well, he was so busy with his work," she said. "He belonged to many organizations, was even a national officer of one of the police groups. Civic works were so important to him.

"He was a fine man," she said softly. "I'm so glad his murderer has been caught." Her expression was odd. Satisfied, perhaps, but something else lay underneath.

"Oh, but," I blurted, "do you honestly think Jake could have done something so vile? I mean, you must have known him reasonably well. There are many of us who think he's innocent, that he's been framed."

"Framed? But how could that be? Who else could have taken the monkshood from the evidence room? And the man has always been jealous, you know. Constantly did his best to undermine William's authority." She appeared truly appalled at my suggestion. And then, to my horror, she pulled a handkerchief from somewhere in her bosom and blotted her eyes. "Oh, dear, now I'm really upset."

"I'm so sorry!" I set down my cup and took her hand, which was icy cold. "That was clumsy of me."

I'd really put my foot into it this time. But, I decided, eyeing her surreptitiously, something in her manner didn't convince me. Was it the way she held her head or, perhaps, were those crocodile tears? Or was I being mean-spirited and judgmental? I've been accused of that before, although never by anyone who knew me well.

"I'd better leave," I offered, standing.

"No, no." She still clutched my hand, and pulled me down beside her. "I'm so glad to have company. The house seems so empty these days. What am I going to do?"

"Start by drinking your coffee. And . . . and try the banana bread. One so often feels better with food and drink, don't you think? Then you can tell me more about your life together. Where did you meet?"

"I'd just finished college in the Midwest," she said, sniffling, "and came out here hoping to find a job. But I had one of those useless majors, in my case history. Even then I was interested in genealogy. In tracing my family tree, I'd found there was a branch who were early settlers in the Seattle area, and I was interested in tracking that down. And of course we didn't have computers in those days."

Her face brightened a smidgen. Obviously, this had been a good subject for me to choose. "And did you succeed?" I asked.

"Oh, indeed. The Seattle library has an excellent section on the subject. Actually, that's where I met William."

"He was checking genealogy?" I asked incredulously.

"No, no. He was after something about police work. I don't even remember what. But we got to talking, and he seemed interested in my research. And . . ." She spread her hands. ". . . it went from there. We were married rather quickly after that, I have to admit. I wasn't having any success finding work I'd be interested in, and William seemed a good choice for mate. A fine physical specimen, and obviously an upright individual."

I was speechless. Nothing about love, I thought. It sounded as if she'd picked him as a worthy addition to her distinguished family tree. Wow!

"I was a little older than he," she added. "I suppose I can find solace in my research. There's never an end once one begins, especially now that so much is available on the Internet.

"But my dear," she still clutched my hand, "don't you worry yourself that they have the wrong person in jail. I know you were instrumental in helping William during that distressing time last year, but . . ." She chuckled weakly. ". . . just try to trust the police to do their job . . ." She paused significantly. ". . . as William always did."

I gritted my teeth and looked at her in astonishment. Was she really that dense about the man? Or did she just want the whole thing to go away so she could concentrate on the one thing in life that seemed to have meaning to her?

I was never going to be friends with this woman, I was sure. It was all I could do to retain my composure enough to make my farewells and leave.

CHAPTER THIRTEEN

My plans for the next day were put on hold by an early morning call. I rolled over, groaning, and reached for the phone.

"Good morning," said a cheery voice. "This is the Cedar Harbor School District. Mrs. Chelsea at the high school had a family emergency arise during the night. I truly hate to ask you, but could you possibly step in for her creative writing sections? I know Martha had you penciled in as preferring not to be called at this time, but we're really short of substitutes. We have her English One covered, but if you could come just for these two classes? Please?" she asked plaintively.

Well, what else could I do but agree? I pulled myself together and headed for the shower, mentally rearranging my responsibilities. I'd only be at the high school for the morning, so I could keep the date I'd made last evening with Marie Corrigan for three o'clock. As I stumbled around getting dressed, I wished I'd gone to bed earlier, as I surely would have had I known I'd be called. No wonder substitutes sometimes become burned out by these early-morning summonses.

It didn't take too long into the first class for me to ascertain that these students were not the cream-of-the-crop writers, but rather were in an elective class they'd assumed would be a snap. How I itched to be in a position to give them some real assignments to challenge their creativity, but it wasn't my place as a sub to do this. However, since Mrs. Chelsea hadn't known she'd be gone, there were no lesson plans, and I needed to come up with something.

So we discussed how to start a short story, novel, or even a nonfiction piece and asked them to write a beginning of their choice.

A short ten minutes later, a young hunk strolled up to my desk. "I'm done, Mrs. Galbreath," he said. "Can I go to the library to work on my term assignment for this class?"

"Go to the library?" I asked, somewhat surprised.

"Sure. That's where most of the computers are."

A blond girl with a couple of strands of hair dangling in front of her eyes waved her hand. "Me, too," she said, eyeing the hunk who pretended to be oblivious. I quickly scanned the seating chart, although with kids this age I wasn't confident that they hadn't taken advantage of Mrs. Chelsea's absence to rearrange themselves.

"Um, Hank," I said, not recognizing his last name, "and Ellen . . ." This one I did recognize, although I couldn't be sure there weren't others in the community with the same name since I didn't know the family. Diego. The name of the golf club manager. So I asked. "Is it your father who's on the city council?"

She nodded affirmatively and I continued. "Well, Ellen, I'd prefer if you and Hank would wait until the rest are through and we discuss the work."

Hank shrugged and leaned one firm haunch on my desk. Ellen, too, sauntered up, laying her paper on my desk.

"Keep it," I said, "for the discussion."

"Oh." She flicked one lock behind her right ear. "Mrs. Chelsea always takes them home and gives them back the next day with comments."

"Well, I'm only here for this one day, so we'll do it differently, shall we?"

"Sure," she agreed pleasantly. "Umm, what do you know

about the police chief's murder?"

"Nothing more than you do, I'm sure," I said, somewhat irritated. Except—Her father was on the city council. I'd decided not to squelch any volunteered comments that might be pertinent, and it was just possible she might say something useful. I wouldn't push, but—"Why should I?" I asked.

She blinked. "Because you solved the last one, that's why."

Hank the hunk stirred. Oh dear, another term I wish hadn't fixed itself in my mind. "It was you? Hey, I hear you're a real good detective. I want to write murder mysteries. In fact . . ." He waved his paper. ". . . this is the start of one. Do you think—"

"Cool it, Hank," Ellen said. "Let's hear what she has to say."

"What can I say? I have no connection with the police department, and no, I'm not a detective. It was an unfortunate situation in which I became inadvertently involved."

"My mom and dad hope you'll catch the murderer again, even if Chief Donniker was a bastard just like that Corrigan man. Oops! Excuse me, Mrs. Galbreath." She blushed. "Well, I mean they sure didn't like him, but they don't think anyone should get away with murder."

"You're excused. But please watch your language. Oh," I said, when her statement penetrated, "I had understood your father was one of his supporters."

"Heck, no. Dad said the chief shafted him." Then, evidently realizing that perhaps she'd said too much, she closed her mouth.

Oh, dear. I wished she'd continued. How on earth was I going to find out what that had been about? At least her parents wanting the murderer to be caught was a plus on their side. But I'd still like to know what had gone on between them and Donniker. Diego's vote to promote the chief was surely related.

To my surprise, Hank's mystery beginning showed promise. At least he'd definitely started with a hook. "Sam was used to bodies, but the one splattered in front of him made him gulp down the rising vomit." It wasn't my kind of mystery, but those gory ones do sell.

Several of the others either had an instinct or had taken their lessons to heart. Perhaps I'd misjudged the class. I congratulated them and urged them to continue writing.

The second section, a smaller group, included the more serious writers, and to my relief, they were so busy working on their projects that the subject of murder didn't come up. I arrived home a little before noon and left my car in my driveway since I'd be going out later. An almost immediate knock on my front door made me jump.

I was astounded when I answered. Cyrus, holding an enormous bouquet of pink roses, was standing there.

"May I come in?" His voice was humble. "Here," he said, thrusting the flowers into my arms, "these are for you. Roses always make me think of you, and I figured you'd like this color since you painted your house a similar shade. Please?"

I'm sure my mouth was wide open, but no sound came out. I stepped backward holding the flowers, and Cyrus came in, shutting the door behind him. "I hope you like them."

"What on earth?" I managed to ask.

"Donna Rose," he said, "I am here to truly humble myself and to apologize."

I shook my head in disbelief. "I seem to recall hearing that same line from you in the not very distance past. I think, Cyrus, that our relationship, such as it was, is over."

"Don't say that! Hear me out. For not the first time in my life, I was wrong. Lamentably so. Donna Rose," he said, pulling his coat off and throwing it on the couch, "again, I made a mistake. The repair people have found that a tie rod had definitely been cut. You were right. It wasn't an accident.

Someone meant me to crash."

I inhaled. How nice to be proven innocent. But that didn't let Cyrus off the hook. His behavior had been abominable. We'd worked together enough that he should have paid attention to what I said. And he should have been more concerned about my welfare.

I held the bouquet out toward him. "Why are so many men sure that flowers make up for anything?"

He accepted them, but tossed them carelessly on the couch on top of his coat. Taking both my hands in his, he said, "I don't blame you. I don't know why I acted like that. My car . . ." Regret flooded briefly across his face before he continued. "But Donna, I know now that the car isn't nearly as important as you are. You've become . . ."

He gazed intently into my eyes, his own blue ones sorrowful. "Please. I want you to—We've been friends in the past, and I thought had become good ones. But I've come to realize that I want more to our relationship than that. I want . . . well, this isn't the time to discuss the matter, but please rethink your position and give me another chance."

Then, first to my horror and then to my surprised pleasure, he dropped my hands and hugged me. It felt good. It wasn't the sort of hug friends give each other, but rather, intimates. I stayed there unmoving for far too long, then pushed him away and stepped back. He held his hands out beseechingly.

There was a frog in my throat, but I cleared it and managed to say, "All right. I've missed you, too, Cyrus. We'll be—friends and associates again. Just—don't push it another time, okay?"

With as pleased a grin as I'd ever seen on his face, he said, "Okay." Before I knew what was happening, he picked up his coat, hesitated a moment, and then—he leaned forward, brushed my lips with his, and left.

I don't know how long I stood there before I pulled myself

together and gathered up the flowers to put them in a vase. Had I actually just been kissed?

CHAPTER FOURTEEN

Like a robot, I snipped the tips of the rose stems, then chose a sparkly crystal vase to put them in. I filled it with water, then stuffed in the flowers with no attempt to arrange them. Setting the vase down on my table, I plunked into one of the hard chairs and sank my head into my hands.

Could Cyrus possibly mean what he implied? And what did I think of that? I couldn't focus my thoughts enough to decide.

But then it suddenly occurred to me that someone had meant Cyrus to crash! Oh, my. I had accused him of not thinking about the possible consequences of the accident, and here I'd done the same thing! Cyrus could have been killed! Well, so could I, but I hadn't even thought to be sympathetic or to raise the question of who'd done it or why. Now what?

His rather ambiguous comments about our relationship had raised a barrier between us that precluded picking up where we'd left off before the accident. Did I need to address that issue first? Did he expect me to?

I fixed a quick lunch, but afterwards I didn't remember eating it. I don't know how long I sat there, but finally I came to a conclusion. The ante had been raised. For his safety as well as my own, we needed to continue our investigation, and we needed to collaborate. I didn't even know if he or the shop had reported this sabotage to the police. I was sure he'd wait to hear from me, so I might as well get it over with. I picked up the phone.

He answered quickly, as if he'd been expecting to hear from me. "Cyrus," I began cheerfully. No, I hadn't meant to be cheerful about either issue. "Cyrus," I began again in a lower tone, "I'm sorry I didn't commiserate with you about your car and ponder the question of who apparently wanted to kill you. Have you been thinking of that?"

"Of course, Donna," he said in his so often used longsuffering tone. "It did cross my mind."

"Oh, well. You needn't be sarcastic," I answered, relieved that we seemed to have returned to our usual state of—What was it? As Roberta had called it, bickering? I preferred to think of it as skirmishing. Regardless, I sensed he also would be just as happy as I to forget or postpone the issue of our relationship.

"Sorry," he said. "I think we must assume it was in connection to our snooping and that I, not you, have hit a nerve. The question is, in whom?"

"Hmm. Without knowing what you've been doing, since you're so secretive, I haven't a clue. Might it be time for our committee to meet again? I hope we'll all have prepared the lists we said we'd make, and we could keep each other informed as to whatever we've learned." It occurred to me as I suggested this that having others at our next face-to-face encounter could help keep that barrier in place. "Let's not delay. We don't want any other 'incidents.' "

"Good idea. Shall I call the others and try to set it up for this evening? Would that work for you?"

My, he was being conciliatory. A new Cyrus.

"Yes, that would be fine. I'll put together my lists today. I did visit Lucille yesterday. What an enigmatic woman. Also, I'm to have tea with Marie Corrigan this afternoon, so I'll hope her information will be helpful. But, Cyrus, for your own good, I hope you won't be so secretive about what corners you've been poking into. It isn't safe."

"At least I might chase a few mice out of their holes so we can see them." He sounded cheerful at the prospect. He'd admitted in the past that he found investigation to be stimulating. An adrenaline rush, I suppose.

"Rats might be a better description."

"Good point. Shall we plan on seven-thirty unless you hear otherwise?"

"Absolutely." I hung up, greatly relieved. Whatever happened, I knew I did not want to return to the adversarial relationship we'd had for so long after he built that miserable fence, the Berlin Wall, between our houses during my absence at the retired teachers' convention. Every once in a while, I still resented the damage it had done to my garden, but usually I left that thought buried with the plants I'd found it necessary to dispose of.

First I completed the list I'd started of the pertinent people I remembered seeing at the chief's party. Then I began the one of those I surmised had, or might have, tangled with Donniker in the past. Mark Gasper. Ross Diego, with a question mark. The other city council members who voted for him, Geri Sataro and Ben Flannigan. The mayor, Roland Oliver, though he'd been so effusive at the party that it was possible, barely, that he'd truly held Donniker in high esteem and thus voted out of conviction. Oh, dear. There weren't that many after all. Listing the ones who simply disliked him would be easier.

Thinking a moment, I added Lucille. I had no real reason to other than the fact that family members so often turn out to be guilty. I couldn't deny that I added her name in part because of the antipathy I had felt toward her after my visit.

I hoped Cyrus had made progress investigating the business affairs of those on the list. And Marie might . . . Oh-oh, I thought after a hasty look at the clock, I'd better be going.

My faithful green clunker took some effort to start on this

chilly afternoon, and for a moment I remembered longingly my rides in Cyrus's red rocket and Alice's plush Mercedes. Yes, when Roberta was here to go with me, I'd do some research on new cars. Anything I bought now would probably do for the rest of my life, considering the relatively few miles I drive these days. The serious global warming problem has made me very aware how important it is to limit driving. Not to mention that second reason for prudence, the abominable price of gas.

Marie's home didn't appeal to me now any more than it had the first time I saw it, with its pretentious pillars and a three-car garage across the front. Perhaps it reflected Lyle's pompousness rather than her tastes, I thought as I parked on the extensive asphalt. I wondered if she still employed a maid garbed in traditional black with white apron.

That question, at least, was answered when Marie herself greeted me at the door with a friendly smile. "Come in."

She led me to a family room off the kitchen, which was much more comfortable than the living room I'd been in previously. It appeared well used. The telephone sat on a desk next to hastily stacked piles of paper. I recognized them, since I do the same thing to tidy up when someone is coming. She'd chosen a light green with touches of pale yellow as the color scheme and with the plants in front of the sliding door, it had the feel of a garden room.

"Would you like tea?" she asked. "I thought I recalled that you preferred it to coffee."

"Yes, tea's what I'd like."

"Do sit down. It will take me just a moment." The kettle was burbling softly, and Marie poured the hot water into a delicate yellow and green pot waiting alongside. Humming to herself, she put it on a waiting tray, and brought it around the divider to a table beside the couch.

"You seem much happier these days," I commented. "Oh.

140

That was inappropriate!"

"Not at all. Yes, I am. I've come to terms with my daughter's death." Her gray eyes reflected a sadness that belied her words. I must have showed my skepticism. "Truly," she continued. "By the time Jolene died, she was deeply troubled, and I don't think the future would have held much for her. Her father—Well, I can only be angry at what he did to her and how he lived his life. The world is a better place without him. I only wish I'd . . ."

"Don't," I said, placing my hand on hers. "We all have regrets. And he was totally responsible for what happened, not you. You have much to be thankful for. I'm sure Will turning out to be such a fine young man is immensely gratifying for you."

She brightened. "He has, hasn't he? Thank you for saying so. Ah, well, I won't beat around the bush. It would be lovely if we became mothers-in-law, or whatever we'd be. Shirt-tail relatives? I hope you agree."

"I do, I do. But as we know, it won't do us any good to push."

"You're absolutely right." She poured the tea, and we both sipped contentedly for a moment before she began speaking. "Also not beating around the bush, I know you want to hear what I've heard, even though it's only gossip and speculation. You and Cyrus have such a talent for looking behind the obvious and finding the answers that I do feel comfortable sharing with you." Again she paused as she sipped her tea, then handed me the plate of ginger snaps and vanilla cookies. She was obviously gathering her thoughts.

I took two cookies and waited.

"I know I didn't mingle much in the community before all this happened," she began, "but that wasn't really my nature. Lyle preferred me to focus on him. What a selfish man. So, as part of my recovery, I've become quite active as a volunteer. And in so doing, I'm much more cognizant of what's happening in Cedar Harbor.

"I attend the Historical Society regularly. Haven't seen you there recently. People commented that you used to be a regular."

I grimaced. "I did. And they kept trying to make me president. For the third time! Besides, it seemed I'd heard it all before. They needed new blood. Say, I'll bet you've been good for them."

"Oh, I've had a few ideas. We're going to sponsor an essay contest about local history for students. Thought we might uncover family stories that will add to our reservoir of knowledge, as well as encourage an interest in young people. You have noticed, I'm sure, the average age of the attendees."

I laughed. "It'd be a nice change to have someone in the audience whose hair is still its own color. Or who are there, in the case of the men. What a good idea. I'll try to come to the next meeting. Perhaps I can help facilitate arrangements with the school system."

"That would be appreciated," she said. "I've also joined the local hospital guild and volunteer in the gift shop. And I hike weekly with a Parks Department sponsored group."

"Good for you." I hoped I didn't sound too amazed at the turnaround Marie was making.

"So," she continued, "I do hear things. Most of it isn't really malicious, just women idly chatting. I'm sure you know . . ."

"Oh, indeed I do." She was being more gracious about gossip than I'd been on occasion in the past, but, as young people say, whatever.

"One of the stories was that Ross Diego had stepped over the boundary with someone's wife at a Country Club party. The husband, whoever it was—I'll try to find out—wanted to make a stink, but it was hushed up so that Ross wouldn't lose his job. I just wondered if the chief could have had anything to do with it.

"And there's talk that Ben Flannigan was in trouble for

churning accounts at his brokerage, and possibly recommending unwise stocks. Again, I don't know any details.

"Oh, yes. There was a hint—You notice I'm not naming my sources. I don't think that would be fair, but if it becomes truly crucial, I'll let you know who said these things. Anyway, someone said, and I'm not sure who this time, that Chief Donniker was having an affair."

"Oh?" I perked up. I would never have dreamed that womanizing could have been one of his myriad bad traits. Although, now that I'd spent more time with Lucille, I could see why another woman might tempt him.

"And of course, everyone's talking about Geri Sataro's son. I feel sorry for her. It must be humiliating to have one's offspring raising hell in the community as he's been doing. That's all, really," Marie said. "I hope some of this gives you some leads. It truly is impossible to think of anyone we know being desperate enough to murder."

"But someone did."

"Yes, someone did. I guess no one really knows what others are thinking. I certainly am a prime example of that, aren't I?" Her tone was bitter.

Under the circumstances she had a right to be. But what her husband had done to cause his death was past, and I hoped she was able, somehow, to put it out of her mind at least part of the time. Perhaps she was scheduling so many activities now because a busy person has less opportunity to brood.

"Tell me about Roberta. Will seems quite enamored. I don't know her well, and I'd like to remedy that."

"We'll fix that. Let's plan some activities together while she's home," I suggested. "Nothing so obvious it looks like we're matchmaking, of course."

"How about having Christmas dinner here? I have so much room, and we'd really enjoy having you. I'd cater it," she added with a chuckle, "and we could all enjoy it without the hassle. Cyrus would be welcome, too, of course."

There it was again, people considering us a couple. How, exactly, had that happened?

"That sounds good to me. However, let's wait until Roberta and Will get here and see how it goes before we decide, shall we? Now . . ." I glanced at my watch. ". . . it's time for me to go. Our 'committee' to clear Jake, such as it is, is meeting tonight."

"Good. If I hear anything else, I'll pass it on."

"Please do. I'd especially like to hear about who Billy had on the side, if you can find out. That sounds as if it could be important. What if she was the wife of someone who was capable of retaliating?"

"That I can imagine," Marie answered. "Please keep me informed."

I was disappointed to see my message light blinking when I walked into the kitchen. Had the meeting been cancelled? When I pressed the button, however, Tim Borland's voice responded, not Cyrus's. "Please call me," he said, giving his number.

Curious, I did so.

"Thanks for returning my call," Tim said. "I've enjoyed talking with you, and as I said last week, I'd like to become better acquainted. Is it possible you'd be free Monday to have lunch with me?"

I was startled enough to be relatively inarticulate. "Lunch?" I said. "Just me?"

His chuckle was deep and pleasant. "Just you and me. There doesn't seem to be a much better choice in Cedar Harbor than the Inn. I thought if you're available, perhaps at one? Would that be convenient?"

"Thank you, Tim," I said. "Yes. Yes, I am free. I'll look forward to it."

After I hung up, bemused, I began to wonder. Could it be possible that two men were interested in me? A becoming gray-haired, pushy widow? To be honest, there were a number of more obvious candidates in the community for single men to pursue, including stylish and pretty Carrie Sanderson.

I'd better keep an eye on you, Tim, I thought. You might have an ulterior motive.

I fixed a quick supper then, deliberately late, headed across the now-crisp lawn to Cyrus's house. As I knocked, I admired the new beveled-glass front door. It truly was stunning.

Cyrus loomed behind it quickly and welcomed me in. "I was afraid you weren't going to make it. You're the last to arrive."

The remark might have been a subtle admonition, but perhaps not. I'd give him the benefit of the doubt. Seated on the couch were Sue and Jake. Sheryl Adams had joined us, I saw, surprised. She looked nice tonight, with more makeup than she wore to work, and softer and more flattering clothing. A cowl-necked, peach-colored sweater brought out the color in her face. *She must think she needs to be subdued for that office,* occurred to me. Or perhaps Billy had suggested it.

"Good evening," I said to the group, but especially to Sheryl. I chose a chair next to her. "It's good you've joined us."

"Sue asked me," she explained. "I'm really glad to be included and hope I can contribute."

"Nothing like having an insider in the department. Heh, heh." Cyrus grinned.

My eyes met Jake's, and he winked.

Donna Two strolled in from the kitchen. After looking around at the possibilities, she disdained us all and sat squarely in the middle of the Persian rug, beginning a methodical post-meal clean-up.

"I've printed out copies for each of you of my lists, and I thought they could be a starting point for our discussion." Cyrus handed out sheets of paper. "Let's begin by comparing our own lists against these. Sheryl, Sue tells me she invited you here at the last minute, and that you haven't had time to prepare lists even though Donna told you about them. You can't make a list of those who attended the party honoring the chief anyway, since you weren't there. However, you can certainly make additions at any time to the one we compile of possible suspects."

I opened my purse and, pulling out my own lists, began to match up names. "I see you don't have Ross Diego or his wife as being at the party," I commented, "and neither do I. That means we can scratch him off the suspect list."

"Oh?" Sue said. "What's he been up to?"

"Let's stick to the subject," Cyrus said. He did like being in charge, but that was fine as he always did a good job, give or take some of his sarcastic comments.

"Um," I interjected, "you don't have Mark Gasper on your suspect list."

"No. He and his sister-in-law left early, remember? Before, I do believe, Jake's infamous sneezing episode."

Jake blushed but didn't say anything.

Cyrus was right, of course. I don't know how I could have forgotten that. Too bad, I thought as I crossed off his name. He'd have been a likely candidate in spite of his charm.

I noted that Tim Borland was on his list of possible culprits. I definitely wasn't going to mention our upcoming tête-à-tête.

"Donna has been visiting with women who might have information and is going to report on what she's learned. Donna?" Cyrus turned the floor over to me.

"I don't really have anything tangible, but this is what I've been told." I repeated the gossip Marie had related. "I'm particularly intrigued by the possibility our Billy was cheating on Lucille. Although, after visiting with her, I'm not too surprised.

"That was catty, and I apologize. But I did find her and their relationship to be puzzling." I explained about her seeming fanaticism for genealogy. "That's basically all I have. But I've been wondering, Cyrus," I said, "how about you? Have you informed the authorities that your car was tampered with before our little episode the other day?"

"What?" exclaimed Jake as the others made noises of dismay. "I hadn't heard about that. And I have been keeping up on things in the department. That new trainee, Sam Holderson, has been keeping me informed. What's up?"

"We had a little accident the other day on the Pipeline," Cyrus mumbled, but then said, "I did report what the shop said to the deputy and, ahem, he and I had a discussion and Donna, you don't have to worry about the little matter of the ticket."

"Ticket?" Sue said. "You were driving Cyrus's car?" She started to laugh. "I never thought . . ."

"I did hear that conversation," Sheryl said. "You handled him admirably. I almost cheered."

"Ahem," Cyrus interrupted, repeating himself. "We're getting sidetracked again. Yes, Donna was driving, quite capably I will say, when the steering went out. And yes, someone must have meant to cause me, we're assuming, to crash."

"I've been urging Cyrus to be upfront about his investigations. As we discussed when we last met, he's checking out business dealings, and he does like to be secretive. I've been trying to persuade him that being closed-mouth in this situation could be dangerous. Come on, Cyrus, 'fess up? What have you been up to?"

"I, too, have heard rumblings about Ben Flannigan's activities, and I'm checking on that. Geri Sataro's son also has a disturbing past. On the surface, he's appeared to have every advantage other than, of course, whatever trauma the divorce of his parents caused."

"Maybe his behavior caused the divorce," Sue interjected.

"Certainly possible. However, he's been in constant trouble with the authorities since he was in his mid-teens, whether that authority was a teacher or the law. He's been arrested several times, but has yet to serve time. Which makes one wonder. I won't go into details, but I think it's past time someone has a talk with Geri. I'll volunteer since she seems to have cowed you, Donna."

"Cowed isn't exactly what I would have called it, but be my guest. You would probably be better at pressuring her for information than I. It will be interesting to hear a report." Peripherally, I saw Sheryl's quick smile.

"How about the rest of you?" Cyrus asked. "Anything to share?"

"I'm not really in a position to help much," Susan said, "and I do apologize."

Jake took her hand and squeezed it. The affectionate looks they exchanged made me even more resolute to clear his name. "I haven't done very well, either. Sue and I do have a few additions to your list of those at the party, though. None that leap to the front as suspects, but I'll leave the list with you, Cyrus.

"We really need to leave," he added. "It's a school night, and we promised Sue's babysitter we wouldn't be long."

"I do have one more thing to report before you go." Cyrus glanced fleetingly at me. "I've been doing some checking on the Cincinnati connection, which Donna considers tenuous at best. However, I find this extremely interesting." He extracted several pages of copied news articles from his folder. "It seems our new publisher and owner of the *Cedar Harbor Post* left that city in some disgrace. He published a series of articles about a local politician that were based solely on innuendo, without doing the checking he should. When the truth emerged, he was requested to leave by the owners of the paper there. And it was at about the same time Donniker was there for ten days at a conference.

"There also seems to be a connection to that city by Alvin Jones, the young Iraq War veteran and horticulturalist that Donna and I have befriended."

"Alvin!" I said. "I'm ashamed that I'd put him out of my mind. Did you ever find out where he's staying? He appears to us," I explained to the others, "to have come home from Iraq with traumatic stress syndrome. I guess one would have to call him a transient."

"Transient?" Sheryl said. "What does he look like?"

I described the slight young man, not an easy job as he didn't have anything particularly distinctive about his appearance, then added, "He's always clean, usually dressed in jeans whenever we've seen him, but definitely shabby clothes."

"Oh, my," Sheryl exclaimed. "You have heard about—well, maybe not. Your description matches that of an apparent shooting victim who was found on the beach this afternoon. He was, I'm told, in almost the same place that Lyle Corrigan's body was found. He had no identification.

"You must call Sheriff Calligan immediately!"

CHAPTER FIFTEEN

"Ohmigod!" I'm not sure who said it, but it reflected all our thoughts.

"Alvin's dead?" I asked with horror.

"No," Sheryl assured us. "That is, he wasn't the last I heard. They rushed him to the hospital, of course. The wound was serious, and he was unconscious, which meant they couldn't identify him since he had no I.D. on him. They'll be very grateful if you can give them his name," she concluded.

"We can tell them if it's the Alvin we know," Cyrus said. "However, we've felt that he wasn't honest about his name—his surname, I mean. He didn't like to talk about himself or his experiences. But at least it would be a starting point. Whom should I call at this hour?" he asked Sheryl.

"The police station. Someone answers the phone all night. They can reach the right person for you, probably Sheriff Calligan."

"What did you mean, an 'apparent shooting victim'?" Cyrus asked. "Was he shot or not?"

"Yes." Sheryl scratched her head. "But there was more than that. I don't know the details. But call, please. Now."

Cyrus nodded as he reached for the phone. "Hello," he said. "I need to reach the proper authority. I understand there was a shooting victim found on the beach this afternoon who's unidentified. I believe I can help with that.

"Yes, yes," Cyrus said, and then fell silent; he was obviously on hold. I think we all stopped breathing and suspended any action until he began to talk again.

"Yes. Sheriff Calligan," he said. "This is Cyrus Bates. I understand there's been a shooting. I think I can point you in the right direction as to his identity."

The conversation was short and to the point. The fact that Alvin was a recent veteran seemed to be the most salient fact to the sheriff.

"What's his condition?" Cyrus asked. "Uh-huh. Uh-huh. I see. Will it do any good for us to call the hospital? Uh-huh."

I clutched my hands together in frustration. Finally Cyrus hung up. "He says the man was found by a couple of strollers, lying in the sand. Why anybody'd be strolling on a day like this, I don't know."

"Cyrus," I said in a threatening tone.

"Um. Yes. He was bleeding from the chest. Rather a lot of blood, I gather. They had no luck finding the bullet, which evidently passed through him. You know how much driftwood accumulates there in the winter, and there was no way to determine how far the bullet traveled.

"He also smashed the back of his head when he landed on a rock. He's in the hospital, unconscious, and the sheriff actually sounded grateful for our information. Perhaps we've underestimated him. But he did say the hospital wouldn't tell me anything because of privacy concerns. Humph. As if Alvin, if it is he, would mind. He doesn't have family or friends that we know of, certainly not in Cedar Harbor."

"I don't think there's any doubt the sheriff's capable," Sheryl said. "Just—Well, you know. Here, why don't you let me call the hospital. They know me. I might be able to find out more."

Cyrus handed her the phone, and she punched in the number, which she had obviously memorized. Babysitter or no, Jake and Sue didn't leave. We all sat still and listened while

Sheryl worked her way through bureaucracy. I had to hand it to her. As she spoke in an efficient, businesslike tone, one would think she was actually calling at the instigation of the sheriff.

Finally, after a lengthy period of listening to someone who apparently knew the answers, she thanked the person nicely and said, "We think we've found friends of the gentleman. Will they be able to visit?"

Another silence while whoever was on the other end spoke. "Thank you very much," she said, still sounding official. "We'll be in contact with you in the morning." And then she hung up.

"Here's what they know," she said. "The gun was probably aimed at his heart, but the bullet fortunately went high and only damaged his shoulder. However, when he fell, he hit his head on a rock, which is the apparent cause of his loss of consciousness, along with the blood loss and exposure, of course. They're not sure yet how much damage the injuries may have caused. It might be hours—or days—before he wakes up."

"If at all." Cyrus's tone was sour.

"If at all," Sheryl echoed, looking sidewise at Cyrus. "The intern did say that."

"I know. I'm too blunt sometimes, but we must face facts."

"I don't know much about medicine, but this was the intern on duty, and he clearly knew what he was talking about. Anyway, he said there would be no visitors allowed, probably for several days at least, while they watch him. His condition is grave."

"How sad," Sue said. "We must all do what we can to help the poor man."

"Of course," Cyrus said. "First thing in the morning, I'll get busy confirming whether or not he's our Alvin, and if there's anything I can do to locate some family members. At the least, someone should be there for him when he wakes up."

If he does. I couldn't get that thought out of my mind. Poor Alvin. Just another unfortunate event in a life that didn't appear to have much going for it at best. I really had become fond of him in the short time we'd known him. "Why on earth would anyone shoot him?"

Cyrus sighed. "If we knew the answer to that," he said, "I suspect we'd know who killed Chief Donniker."

"His fingerprints should be on record as a member of the military," Jake pointed out. "Or, more simply, if he has any kind of a record at all. If he does, there's a system called AFIS, which stands for Automated Fingerprint Identification System, that can come up with answers in an hour or two. Pretty remarkable how things have changed.

"Come on, Susan," he said, helping her on with her puffy down jacket, then putting on his own. "Let's get that babysitter home. You will call us all when there's any news, won't you, Cyrus?"

"Certainly."

Sheryl also was ready to go. I hustled and put on my own coat so as to leave with her. We said our goodbyes, with Cyrus promising specifically again to phone in the morning. We walked to the curb where Sheryl's small blue car was parked.

"Thanks so much for your help," I said to her as she climbed in. "We wouldn't have gotten anywhere without you."

Wryly, she answered, "I'd say it's my pleasure, but nothing like this is ever a pleasure, is it? Sometimes I wonder why I took this job. I see so much distress and unhappiness."

"I'm sure you do," I answered, "but where would we be without people like you—and Jake—and even the Sheriff Calligans of the world? Maybe that's why he seems so hard and unsympathetic. Maybe it's his defense?"

Sheryl look at me with one eyebrow cocked. "You're a good person, Donna. So is Cyrus. What would we do without people like you?" She climbed into her car, which also started without objection. I'd have to ask her what she was driving and how she liked it, I decided. But later. Much later.

She hesitated until I reached my front door, then waved and departed.

CHAPTER SIXTEEN

Another restless night faced me, I realized as I lay in bed. So much to think about. Of biggest concern was Alvin's fate. I didn't have much doubt that the poor soul lying in the hospital was he. How many young men were floating around Cedar Harbor who wouldn't have been recognized by aide car people, police or hospital workers who had participated in his rescue?

Surely Cyrus could convince someone to let him view the man for positive identification. At least as positive as we could be, with neither of us believing he'd been honest about his name. What was his story? I hoped we'd find out, regardless of the outcome. How horrible if he were to die and be buried, with no one who had known him in the past ever finding out? A frisson of dismay shook me. Stop being morbid, I told myself. Think positive.

If nothing else, no one I knew was in a better position than Cyrus to prod the military for an identification, if necessary. After all, he'd done that sort of work when he was in the navy, and he surely knew the ropes.

I was pleased at how well Sue and Jake seemed to be holding themselves together. That was good. However, Cyrus's news about Tim created a real dilemma for me. How I wished I could consult with Cyrus about what to say on Monday. But no. No, I couldn't. I could imagine his reaction if I told him I was meeting Tim Borland for lunch. His blue eyes would turn steely and his face rigid, as he spat out the words, "Donna, are you out of your mind?"

Was I? No, I did not think so. After all, we were meeting in a public place, and I had no intention of departing with him afterward. In fact, the situation was so awkward that I might not even get lunch! How was I going to broach the subject of his reasons for leaving Cincinnati?

I mulled over the news that had been revealed in the damning clippings. The evidence seemed to be incontrovertible. But evidence of what? Even if the chief had been in Cincinnati at the time this happened, so what? I mean, Tim wasn't likely to want the news spread all around Cedar Harbor, but murder? I didn't see it. Besides, I should give Tim a chance to tell his side of it.

All right. I wouldn't hit him with it the minute we met. We'd have a civilized lunch before I brought up the question. I would, however, be very interested in his explanation.

I needed to go to sleep. Finally, reluctantly, I got up and took one of the sleeping pills I had stashed away. Greatly outdated, I was sure, but I'd always understood that the only detriment to taking those is that they might have lost their potency.

The pill worked. So well that I was surprised to be awakened by the ringing phone next to my bed, and open my eyes to daylight. I cleared my throat and answered.

"Good morning," Cyrus said. "Thought you'd want to know that I'm at the hospital. They let me see Alvin, and yes, it's he, I'm sorry to report. However, he looked as if he was resting peaceably. Didn't even look sick, other than the bandages."

I sighed. "It's just as well to have it confirmed, I suppose. Now what?" I tried to sound sprightly and awake. Cyrus has such a thing about rising early, and "getting the job done," as he used to remind me about watering our yards.

"Now I'll get busy and see that his fingerprints are taken and forwarded to the proper authorities. With a little prodding, I hope it won't take long. I'd better go. Would you call Jake and Susan for me? I assume Sheryl will hear at the office."

I swung my legs over the edge of the bed. "Certainly, Cyrus. And good luck."

After showering and putting on my robe, I called both Jake and Sue. Neither was home, so I left messages on their machines. There were so few days before Roberta would be here. Today I'd finish my cards. They could be mailed tomorrow, and that would be one thing I could scratch off my list.

Roberta and I must have been thinking of each other at the same time. That's happened to us often enough to be remarkable. Must be ESP or something. Anyway, when the phone rang mid-afternoon, I was so sure it would be her that I answered informally. "Hi, there."

She chuckled as she answered. "You knew it was me again, didn't you?"

"Well, of course. However, it would have been a reasonable guess since you'll be here on Wednesday. How are things going?"

"Great. Busy at work, of course. I'm trying to anticipate anything that could come up while I'm gone." She sighed. "But I'll be so glad to see you and to relax for a couple of weeks. How are things with you?"

I was silent long enough for her to inquire, "Mom? What's up?"

I hadn't kept her informed about the fact that Cyrus and I were investigating Donniker's murder and why. I decided there was no longer any point for reticence, since she'd inevitably hear all about it when she got here. I might as well forewarn her. It was long distance. Perhaps her recriminations would be more succinct than they would be in person.

So I did. I brought her up-to-date on the happenings concerning Jake. I didn't, however, tell her about the incident with Cyrus's car, and I didn't tell her about his ambiguous statements about our relationship, and I certainly didn't tell her about the fleeting kiss. There were a few things one didn't share with a child, especially when the situation was so amorphous.

To my surprise, she didn't light into me, only sighed, then said, "It doesn't do any good to give you advice, does it, Mom?"

"Well, that works two ways, doesn't it?" I said cheerfully. "I seem to remember a few times . . ."

She laughed. "Guess I inherited my independence from you. Anyway, I did want to tell you that you won't need to meet me at the airport. Will has arranged his schedule so that he's driving up from Portland Wednesday, and he'll bring me. Should be there by dinnertime."

I was pleased for two reasons. One, that her relationship with that nice young man was progressing, and two, that I wouldn't have to buck Seattle traffic, which would inevitably be horrendous at that hour.

"Good," I said. "By the way, I had tea with his mother the other day, and she suggested we all have Christmas dinner at their house. You don't have to decide now . . ."

"Sounds good to me," she said. "Well, I must go. See you Wednesday."

I finished up my cards by bedtime and bundled them to take to the post office. I was glad the next morning that I had slept better. I was ready to meet Tim. I had tea and toast for breakfast, surely enough considering the meal I'd be served at the Inn.

After glancing out the window and seeing only low, gray clouds that didn't appear to be full of moisture, I decided to walk to town. Perhaps the fresh air would help me think. Some of my best cogitating happens when I'm in my garden, and I hoped I'd have the same result today.

Consequently, I wore comfortable walking shoes, although

otherwise I dressed carefully. The temperature was hovering in the thirties, my thermometer told me, so I wore my black wool slacks with a black turtleneck and my Norwegian sweater. And, of course, my down coat and fuzzy hat.

I went early enough to send my cards and pick up my mail. Tim was waiting in the lobby of the Inn. He smiled warmly, his brown eyes as compelling as always, and took my arm. "I just got here, and our table is waiting." He escorted me forward.

I thought it best not to complain, as I so often did to Cyrus. As if I couldn't walk through the restaurant without aid! I know I'm probably being unreasonable when someone is so polite, but I've always had a hang-up about this procedure.

As before, he'd scored one of the best tables in the place. He must tip very well when he came here, I decided. It was a pleasure to again look at the water. No mountains in sight today, though. As I watched, a gull flew over the beach with something in its mouth and dropped it. It was a clam. It swooped down and extracted the meat. I smiled. Who could say birds didn't think?

I'd just read an interesting article about them. "Did you know that gulls can drink salt water as well as fresh? They have special glands to get rid of the extra salt. No wonder they can range so far over both land and sea."

"Clever little fellows, aren't they?" Tim answered. "Did you catch that one getting its lunch? He's eating the same thing I plan to!"

I smiled. "Me, too. That's one good thing about coming to a familiar restaurant, isn't it? We don't need to waste time mulling over the menu."

Alyssa was our waitress again and seemed glad to see us. I suspected it was more because of the tip she expected than seeing her old teacher, but, whatever. We ordered, again having a glass of wine. She brought it, and then we were alone.

"So," Tim asked, "what have you been up to?"

I had decided during my walk that sharing my school experiences might be a safe topic. First I told him about Hank's story beginning, and he laughed.

"If you ever run into someone you think has real talent, let me know," he said. "We could use an intern at the paper, and I like to encourage young people."

"I certainly will. But my substituting ranges over all ages. I'll keep it in mind, though. Thanks."

By now, we were on our entrees, and I switched between bites to my experiences with the snake. Tim almost choked on a clam and, sputtering, apologized. "That is so funny," he said. "Have you ever thought of writing?"

"Not me. My daughter, perhaps, someday," I said. "She was an English major, and I've always thought she has talent. But I know most parents think that of their kids."

Tim hadn't really had a chance to get a word in edgewise, but he didn't seem to mind. Finally I decided it was time to get to the point. "Have you heard about the shooting victim on the beach?" I asked. "Cyrus was able to see him at the hospital, and unfortunately, confirmed that he's our friend Alvin, who had Thanksgiving dinner with us." I watched his face carefully for a reaction but only saw shock and dismay. I honestly hadn't expected to see guilt, as Cyrus might have, and I was a little relieved until it occurred to me that, as a newspaper man, he must be able to conceal any emotions he didn't care to show.

"My God," he said, "I wish I'd had the news in time for Friday's paper! It'll hit the dailies before the *Post* comes out again."

I'm not very good at hiding my thoughts. I must have showed my reaction when I realized that his dismay was over the fact he hadn't gotten the news in his precious newspaper rather than Alvin's condition, because he flicked a glance at me before saying, "And the poor man. He seemed like a decent fellow. Is he going to live?"

"We hope so. No one is certain at this point." I repeated what we knew about his condition.

He pulled out his notebook and made notes. "I'll stop by the police station so I can get the straight facts and share it with the city papers. Make a few points that way."

"We got the information with a little subterfuge," I explained. "If you don't want to cause trouble for Sheryl Adams, the department secretary, I'd suggest you check with the deputy before you pass on any information. Perhaps a little reticence concerning what I've told you? Alvin was only found late Saturday, and yesterday they didn't know how much brain damage may have occurred."

This time he did look dismayed. "I hope none did. Wouldn't want to wish that on anyone."

"Perhaps they'll have more up-to-date info than we do. Cyrus is arranging for his fingerprints to be taken and filed for identification. We don't believe Alvin was totally honest about his name. Perhaps you noticed."

Tim nodded. "He was being evasive."

I took a deep breath. "As, I'm sorry to say, have you."

He shook his head, and started to speak.

I laid a hand on his across the table, and said, "Wait. I'll tell you what we know. Then you can explain."

He bit his lip, and his face hardened into a mask.

I continued, "For several reasons, Cyrus has felt that we should check you out. Cyrus found newspaper stories, Tim, about the debacle connected to your leaving Cincinnati."

He stared at me without answering.

"That in itself is not really important," I continued. "I mean, mistakes happen. But the Cincinnati connection keeps popping up. Are you aware that Chief Donniker was apparently there at a police officers' convention at the time all this was going on?"

He continued to stare, then took out a handkerchief and wiped his forehead. I let the silence press down on the atmosphere between us.

"All right," he finally answered. "I'll tell you about it. Yes, there were mistakes made. A junior reporter actually wrote the story about the politician. There'd been rumors for some time, and in my defense, I'll say that I was in the middle of my divorce at the time. I didn't insist he check his facts, nor did I myself check them." He shrugged. "The guy's a sleaze—the politician I mean—but the story was wrong. It was my ultimate responsibility."

"And you took the blame?"

"I did."

My respect for him rose a notch. "Okay," I said, "that leads to my next question. Did the chief know about it and did he confront you?" This question was dangerous, and I knew it. Did it sound like I was accusing him of the murder?

I softened it a little. "I don't believe such a thing would be a motive for murder, but people are going to wonder."

I could almost see his brain whirling. Finally, he spoke. "I can see I need to be upfront. Yes, Chief Donniker knew about it. He was there and read the papers. When I arrived in town, he phoned and asked me to stop by the office. I, of course, was totally stunned, as I'd had no inkling that anyone in Cedar Harbor could possibly know about the machinations of a Midwest city's politician. Shouldn't have tried to hide it, I guess, but that's one reason I had decided to cut all ties and resettle. That and the divorce. Thought I could quietly begin again in a sleepy little town where no one knew me." He smiled sardonically. "I'm not as smart as I thought I was."

"What happened at that meeting?" I asked.

"He confronted me with his knowledge. And then . . . then

he suggested that he'd be willing to keep his knowledge to himself. For a price."

I was stunned. "He *blackmailed* you?"

"Yes. He blackmailed me. I didn't allow myself to think of it that way. He just suggested that if I'd pay his way to a ten-day conference on Maui, including all fees, he'd forget he knew. He called it a donation to help Cedar Harbor's police department update, and implied I'd be doing a public service. I knew, of course, that public service had nothing to do with it. Neither my donation, of course, nor, I suspect, did public service have anything to do with his reason for going. He'd get a nice vacation."

"Tim!" I was stunned. "You're right. That was a stupid thing to do! Don't you know that blackmailers' demands often tend to escalate?"

"Well, his didn't. Hadn't before he died, anyway. I thought what I did was sufficient to keep him silent on something that, after all, was a minor sin."

A minor sin? Well, maybe in this world of embezzling, violence, even rape or murder. But again, I wasn't sure what I thought about his general ethics. Had he been completely open about what happened in the East, or had he been justifying his own culpability to himself as well as to me?

A twisted smile crossed his face. "The trip was to be in January. He never went. That's some consolation."

Suddenly, another thought popped into my mind. "Tim," I asked, "do you suppose the chief had been making a habit of this? Do you suppose he'd been blackmailing others?"

Our gazes met, as we realized the possible implications.

CHAPTER SEVENTEEN

Our luncheon date broke up very shortly after that. I was in a hurry to report to Cyrus; Tim, no doubt, was itching to follow up on Alvin's story. As we stood outside the Inn, I clutched my coat against a now chill wind and pulled on my hat.

Tim took both my hands and, looking me straight in the eye with his fabulous brown ones, said, "I'm truly sorry about this, Donna. I appreciate your being honest with me, and I hope you'll accept that I'm being honest in return. I'd really hoped . . . Well, that will have to wait. Do you think you can forgive me?"

I hesitated.

He noticed, and turned his head away. "I don't blame you. I can hardly forgive myself."

"Don't jump to conclusions. I was thinking. Yes, I appreciate your being forthright with me, and I can accept that you made a mistake. Or two."

"Thanks, Donna," he said, then glanced at his watch.

Oh, Lord. No wonder his wife divorced him, I thought.

"I'll be off. And I'll be in touch." He turned and hustled up the street in the direction of the police station.

It's nice to be dedicated to your work, but it must be extremely difficult to cope with a husband who so fiercely follows his profession that he puts his family last. Tim hadn't even asked if I needed or wanted a ride home.

I could forgive him, I guess, if everything he'd told me turned

164

out to be true. Perfection is not a human trait. But forgiving him and ever being interested in him as a man would be two different things. He'd implied he wanted more. Flattering, I guess. In his case, though, a friendly relationship would be all we'd ever have.

I also hurried, anxious to share what I'd learned with Cyrus. Blackmail. Who else might Billy have trapped in his net? It wouldn't be difficult to find prey in his work. How were we going to find out? I wondered if Lucille had any idea what he was up to?

I didn't even stop at my house, but hustled up Cyrus's walk, hoping he'd be home. A haggard Cyrus answered the door. Even his moustache looked a little disheveled. Could that be?

"Donna! What's up?"

"May I come in?" I asked pointedly. Not like him to forget that little invite.

"Certainly! This whole situation has thrown me, I'm sorry to say. Of course come in. Have you had lunch?"

"Yes. I have. I've just come from the Inn where I had lunch with Tim Borland." I stepped into Cyrus's lair.

His eyes did exactly what I'd envisioned, and he opened his mouth to speak, but I stopped him.

"Don't even start. I know exactly what you'll say. 'Donna, are you crazy?' Et cetera. No, I'm not crazy. And I have information I'm dying to share with you. So, close your trap!"

His mouth slammed shut, and he began to laugh. "You are one of a kind," he said. "Never known anyone quite as unpredictable. Okay. I presume your intent is to let me in on how this occurred and what happened?"

"Of course." I pulled off my coat and handed it to him. "Here." Then I pulled off my hat.

"Would you like some tea while I finish my lunch?"

"Delighted. Sorry to interrupt your meal. Tim and I never

did get to our drinks after eating, so I would like some tea. I do think I have the complete Tim Borland story, though, and I still don't see him as a murderer. He wasn't thrilled with my confrontation, but perhaps I shocked him into honesty. But first, what have you found out about Alvin?"

"Join me at the table, and I'll tell you," he said.

I shouldn't have been surprised, knowing Cyrus, that his table had been prepared as if for company. A gold-rimmed soup bowl and plate sat precisely on an exotic, apparently hand-woven placemat, which had to have come from some foreign land. The remains of his soup smelled enticing, even though I'd eaten. Not a canned soup, that was to be sure. He'd folded his napkin before answering the door.

There'd be more than one reason a man could be hard to live with, it occurred to me. No eating leftovers with a book propped in front, I suspected; not around Cyrus. And I wondered if he still ironed his underwear, even though I'd informed him he'd ruin the elastic that time I'd caught him do-ing his laundry.

He spoke as he prepared my tea, carefully heating the pot first. "Alvin's doing the proverbial 'as well as can be expected,' which I've always assumed meant they don't really know. At least he's not worse. And yes, Calligan has agreed to have his fingerprints taken. Perhaps already has. I do think he's a responsible officer of the law, and he's almost as curious as we are. I haven't, however, had time to do much more. Donna, have you been sleeping as badly as I?" he blurted.

"Well, not exactly," I answered. I admitted to my sleeping pill episode on Saturday, but then added, "Last night was better. I feel sure it was because I had a long phone conversation with Roberta. That can be soothing."

He didn't say anything as he laid another placemat, produced the appropriate napkin, and set the china cup, saucer and teapot in front of me. Poor Cyrus. Whenever I say something like that, I remember he has no one to confide in.

"I'll tell you what I learned," I began quickly. "Tim called Saturday to invite me to lunch. I did find myself suspecting his motives. Have to wonder if he just didn't want to know what we might have found out, since the whole world seems to know we're investigating. I wonder if anyone has told Calligan we are?

"Anyway, Alvin was a complete surprise to him, and he charged off like a bloodhound following a stinky trail. I did confront him, as I said, Cyrus. I'd have liked to consult with you before doing so, but I was so sure of what you'd say that I decided to continue on my own. It seemed like the perfect opportunity. I led up to it gradually, as tactfully as I could, and this is what he told me." I proceeded to lay out the whole tale for Cyrus as I poured my steeped tea and began to drink. "Do you agree that it sounds as if he was telling the truth?"

He nodded with obvious reluctance. "It's a plausible story. Not particularly admirable, which makes it more believable. It does open some tantalizing areas to investigate, does it not?"

"I've been thinking on my way home. Do you suppose Billy might have pulled this on Geri Sataro? At the least in regard to her vote, but also, possibly, for money? Her overwhelming wealth would surely be a temptation to a greedy police chief who probably considered himself underpaid."

"Yes, I'll make confronting her a high priority. I'll do more investigating of Flannigan's financial position also. Unfortunately, so many culpable people pass through that office . . ."

"I'll talk to Sheryl," I offered. "Do you approve of repeating all this to her?"

"Of course. That was implicit when she volunteered to help us, was it not? And yes, she could well have some suggestions. We need to act fast. I have an uneasy feeling about this.

Someone has murdered at least once and attempted murder again."

"You mean, you or Alvin?"

"Both, actually. We need to use care. Donna, do not put yourself in position—"

I held up a hand. "I've had that lecture before. The same goes for you. After all, you were the one attacked this time, not me. But you are right about using care. I, too, have that feeling, I guess of the calm before the storm.

"Cyrus . . ." I hesitated before going on. "I've never seen you look this distracted. We mustn't let this get to us. Please feel free to call me, just to talk or whatever, any time you're upset. That's what friends are for. This time I'll give *you* some advice. Why don't you maybe have a little drink? Just to relax you. Then, try to take at least a short nap. You'll feel better—more like your old self."

He managed a smile. "Thanks. You're right. And I will follow your advice. I guess what I'm doing can wait that long. Maybe I'm getting old."

"Don't say that! We all are, it's inexorable. But you didn't age overnight, and don't ever think you're deteriorating, because you're not."

A few minutes later, feeling a pang of sympathy, I hesitated at the front door. "Cyrus," I said, "take care." It was so unusual—unprecedented actually—to see this vulnerable side of a man who always appeared unflappable. I quickly hugged him before leaving.

I hadn't been in the house long when the phone rang. "Hi, Donna." It was Carrie Sanderson. "I apologize for not calling sooner. I said I'd explain why I was upset when I got to the hall for Thanksgiving, but I've been procrastinating. It's been difficult to decide what to do."

"You don't owe me an explanation, Carrie," I said. "For

heaven's sakes."

"It's not that. It's something you need to know, but I'm breaking a confidence. You know Ann Pullen, don't you?"

"Well, sure. Not well. She seems like a nice person. Bet she's a great teacher."

"I think she is," Carrie said. "You probably didn't have any reason to know that we've become friends through our church. And that morning, well, she called me in tears. What she told me was very private, and of course I planned to keep it that way. But I'm torn. Knowing that you and Cyrus are investigating the chief's death, I do feel I must tell you."

I froze, a shiver running the length of my body. "Tell me what?"

"She'd been having an affair, hard as it is to imagine, with Bill Donniker."

"What? *She's* the one? We had picked up a rumor that he was involved with someone, but she's young, pretty, smart. Whatever prompted her to settle for him?"

"I agree. That's a good question. But she insists that most people never saw the real side of Billy. She said he loved children, was good with hers. The old story. Said he was unappreciated and unloved at home. Why anyone falls for that guff, I'll never know, but then I guess you have to be a little older, like you and me, to have seen how often philanderers pull that."

"But what a risk! If they were found out, there are those who would think she should be fired. And what if she became pregnant?"

"Oh, she said at least that wasn't a worry. He'd had a vasectomy."

"Ohmigod! I wonder if—I don't know if—does Lucille know?"

"We never discussed that. Is it important?"

"It puts a new light on things, that's for sure," I said.

"Thanks, Carrie, for confiding in me. I'll tell Cyrus, but we won't let it go further unless there's a compelling reason. We may need to talk to her, however. There's a murderer out there. We need to know everything about Billy."

"That's what I decided. I'm glad I called you. How are things going?"

I told her about Alvin. "You see, Carrie, obviously the murderer won't hesitate to kill again."

"I'm so sorry to hear about Alvin. Hope he'll be okay."

"We all do."

After we hung up, I thought about Billy and all the years I'd known him. Was it possible what he'd needed all along was love? I didn't know anything about his family. Perhaps his misbehaving in school had been a case of a lonely boy reaching out for attention? It happens all the time. He was particularly unlovable, but could I, as his teacher, have made a difference? The thought made me deeply sad. I'd always tried to do my best, recognizing that the best isn't necessarily enough. I remembered, though, some instances where I had made a difference. Guess it goes back again to the fact that none of us is perfect. I just hoped, in my years of teaching, that most of the time I had been effective.

I sighed, then dialed the number of the police station. I was lucky enough to get Sheryl. "Any further news about Alvin?" I asked.

"Not yet. The doctors are going to be busy with medical procedures most of the afternoon, but when they clear us to send someone, our new trainee, Officer Holderson, is going over to take his prints." She obviously turned aside to talk to someone, then came back. "Sorry. Sheriff Calligan needed to speak to me."

"I won't keep you," I said. "Could we meet tomorrow morning again during your break? I have a fair amount of news."

"That would be good. Ten-thirty again?"

We agreed ten-thirty would be fine, and I hung up.

I spent the rest of the afternoon on needed tasks, including setting up the guest room, Roberta's old room, for her arrival. It no longer held the belongings of a small child, but there were reminders of her everywhere: posters of rock stars, trophies from swimming, a group picture of the gang she'd hung out with in high school. It seemed such a short time ago that she was a teenager and still living at home. I clutched the picture to me for a moment, then set it back on her dresser before I put fresh sheets on the bed and towels in the bathroom. A light dusting took care of the housekeeping.

Just before dinner, Cyrus called. It was a relief to hear his voice sounding normal. "Donna, I just returned from a little chat with Geri Sataro, and thought I'd share what she had to say."

"Helpful, I hope."

"Yes, although all I was able to do was confirm some of our suspicions. She stonewalled me, just as she did you, but, ahem, I've had some experience with people like that in my line of work. Finally I applied a little pressure. 'Geri,' I reminded her, 'we're dealing with a murderer. One who not only killed Chief Donniker, but has attempted twice more.' That piqued her curiosity. She hadn't heard about Alvin, and of course she hadn't heard about our little episode, as I imagine we both kept quiet about that. Then I hit the punch line. I said, 'We know that the chief was blackmailing people. Were you one of them?' She didn't answer for a bit, then capitulated. 'Yes,' she admitted, obviously with great reluctance, 'You might say, I was.' "

"Oh, boy," I commented. "I'll bet that was painful for her."

"I'm sure it was. No one wants to admit one's own failings, or for that matter, those of a child. But she opened up to the extent of admitting that she'd been persuaded to change her vote on the city council in exchange for the chief's letting her son off from the charges against him. Her son, by the way, has a name. Lionel. Junior."

"Lionel Sataro, Junior. What do you want to bet he was Buddy, or something like that when he was a kid?"

"Indeed," Cyrus said. "Anyway, I didn't press the question of whether money entered in to the agreement or not. It seemed relatively unimportant. We confirmed that Donniker was blackmailing another person, and that he was honored and given a raise because of it instead of being fired, as he should have been."

"Every time I develop some sympathy for the man, I hear another cruddy thing he's done. Well, I have news, too," I said. "I've been told that Ann Pullen was the woman Billy was seeing." I explained what I'd learned, and my promise to go no further with it unless necessary.

"It does show another dimension of his character, does it not?" Cyrus commented. "Before we hang up, I want to thank you for your support this afternoon. It meant a great deal to me. I'm not sure what came over me."

"We all have our moments, Cyrus, and I'm glad I could help. As I said, 'Any time.' Oops, my dinger just went off. My dinner's ready. Talk to you tomorrow?"

"Absolutely."

I took my food out of the microwave and tried to concentrate on the TV news while I ate, but it was pretty much hopeless. I had so much to think about. Lucille. What intriguing news it was about the vasectomy. I thought about the possible scenarios. Had she always known and married him anyway? I shook my head. Not possible, with her obsession for extending her "distinguished" family line. Was that what precipitated Billy's taking a mistress, because she withheld sex when she did find out? But maybe she never did. I sure wouldn't want to be the one to tell her, that much I knew. And when? When had Billy had the surgery?

Finally, I decided to give her call. Not to be blunt about the matter, of course, but only . . . well, only to snoop a little, I admitted. We were never going to be bosom buddies anyway.

She answered on the first ring. "Lucille," I said, "just checking on how things are going with you. Everything okay?"

She sounded surprised. "Okay? Certainly." I thought I sensed an implied, "Why not?" and my dislike of the woman solidified.

"Um, I'm glad to hear that. I've been hearing some complimentary things about your husband lately. You must miss him. People comment on how fond he was of children."

"Of course! I believe I told you that's why he devoted so much time to helping others."

I took a deep breath. This conversation was going nowhere. What I was going to say would disturb her and I felt guilty. But, how else was I going to get her to open up? "Lucille," I said, "Cyrus and I are still doing a little checking . . ."

"Donna. I also remember emphatically telling you that I'm completely satisfied with the job the police have done. How they let that—that criminal out on bail is more than I can believe. Please don't waste your time. And, if you'll excuse me . . ."

"Of course. I apologize. Just wanted to say I was thinking of you."

The silence on the other end told me she'd hung up. When, I didn't know, nor whether she heard my apology. Oh, well, I thought, shrugging and turning the TV back on.

I watched a couple of favorite programs. *Antiques Roadshow* always entertains me. So many things I possess, or used to have, are now worth real money. I was surprised to learn that children's toys didn't need to be one hundred years old to be valuable.

Finally, I went to bed, still mulling over the things Cyrus and I were uncovering.

I was in the deepest of sleep when something woke me. Was that a crash? Confused, I shook my head, then got up to investigate. As I did so, I was aware of the sound of a car revving up, shifting, and leaving abruptly.

Turning lights on as I went, I was appalled when I reached my living room. Glittering shards of glass on the floor lay in front of the large window facing the street. The window that now was a shattered mess. I threw my hand over my mouth as I saw what had caused the damage.

A rock, one wrapped with a paper, which I had no doubt contained a message, had landed in the middle of the room.

Oh, Lord! I'd read enough mysteries to know I shouldn't touch it. Instead, I reached for the phone to call Cyrus.

CHAPTER EIGHTEEN

I was shaking by the time Cyrus arrived. He took one look at the mess, then gathered me in his arms and stroked my hair. "Looks like we did chase the rat out of his hole, doesn't it?"

That was for sure.

"Have you called 911?" he asked.

"No. My first thought—I wanted you here."

He released me, smiling a little. I realized he was, no question about it, looking me up and down.

I glanced at myself. I was standing there in my nightie! A winter one, thank goodness, but one of a soft jersey that showed much more than I wanted.

"Oh no!" I crossed my hands over my breasts and bolted toward my bedroom for a robe. Behind me, I could hear Cyrus chuckling as he found the phone that I'd left lying on an end table and dialed.

When I hurried back to the living room, I saw that Cyrus, too, was dressed in pajamas. At least he'd put on a dark robe and it almost looked like he'd combed his hair, but it normally looked like that.

His conversation with the authorities was brief. "Cyrus," I said after he hung up, "do you realize what they're going to think? We're both dressed for bed. I mean . . ."

"I don't think it would shock them as much as you think. But I'll make sure to explain."

Very shortly, a police car pulled up in front, lights on but no siren. Thank goodness, I thought. The incident was bad enough without the whole neighborhood being awakened. And they'd all be peering out and undoubtedly see Cyrus leave eventually, dressed as he was. What a stupid thing to be worrying about. Perhaps my mind was unwilling to focus on the real problem, that someone malevolent had thrown a rock through my front window.

The officers were sheriff's deputies, not our local police. Cyrus let the two men in, saying, "I live next door, and Mrs. Galbreath called me." He nodded in my direction.

"Mrs. Galbreath?" the taller man asked, and as I nodded, he touched the brim of his hat and introduced himself. "Deputy Cohen." Glancing around, he continued, "Tell me what happened."

I was still shaking, I realized, as I began to speak. My voice came out funny. "I don't know a lot. I was awakened by the crash, and came out to see what it was. What time is it, by the way?"

Glancing at his watch, he said, "Three a.m."

"Oh. Well, I was in a deep sleep . . ."

Cyrus raised an eyebrow, and I knew he was having trouble restraining himself from telling me to get to the point. "That's really all I know, Deputy. I came out and saw the mess."

The other officer had a notebook out and was writing down what I said, as well as apparently making a sketch.

"Any reason you can think of that someone would do this?"

"Well, uh, perhaps because Cyrus—Mr. Bates—and I have been doing a little research in the community about . . ." My voice trailed off as I realized Cyrus was frowning. But what else could I say? I couldn't act completely innocent when we were quite sure of the reason for the attack. Pretending innocence would probably raise their suspicions, even if I were a good enough actor to pull it off.

Deputy Cohen raised his eyebrows as he prompted, "About what, Mrs. Galbreath?"

"Well, about Chief Donniker's murder." My voice sounded weak, even to me, and Cohen's eyebrows went even higher, almost reaching his Smokey Bear hat.

"I see," he said. "Have you touched anything?"

"No! I knew enough not to do that. But it would appear there's a note. Can we learn now what it says? It could be important."

The glance he shot me clearly showed his annoyance, but all he said was, "Did you hear anything else?"

"Yes. I'd almost forgotten. A car outside took off with a roar. It had to be a stick shift, from the sound. Maybe something sporty?"

The other officer made note of this.

"Okay," Cohen relented. "We'll want the lab to go over the note, but let's see what it says." He pulled on gloves, then carefully lifted the rock, about the size of a grapefruit, and peeled away the paper. "How about, 'Mind your own business'?"

"About what we'd expect," Cyrus said. "Mrs. Galbreath is obviously distressed. Could we cut this short and continue in the morning, if we promise to leave everything the way it is?"

Cohen nodded. "We can go along with that. I feel sure Sheriff Calligan is going to want to talk to you. But your window—I don't think it would be wise to stay here alone, Mrs. Galbreath."

"She won't," Cyrus said.

The officers left shortly after that, promising that someone would check the house regularly during the night. Their visit hadn't gone completely unnoticed. Lights were on at two of the houses across the street.

"Thanks for getting rid of them," I said. "I'll be okay. I'll go right to bed, and you can head on home—"

"No, you don't. You won't get rid of me that easily. Do you

really think I'd abandon you now, in a house completely open to intruders? To use that phrase that seems to be common between us these days, 'Your house or mine?' I am not going to leave you alone."

"Cyrus! We can't. The neighbors . . ."

"To hell with what the neighbors think. Have you ever really worried about that before? I certainly haven't. It's just a question of where we're going to sleep tonight."

I had to laugh. "Which would look worse, you strolling out in the morning in your night clothes, or . . . On reflection, if I go to your house, at least I can take some clothes with me tonight and appear fully dressed. I guess I should do that. You do have a bed for me?"

"I always keep the guest room fully ready for occupancy, even though," he admitted, "it hasn't been used often." There it was again, the Boy Scout in Cyrus. I seriously doubted that room had ever been used for its stated purpose, but "Be prepared" was certainly a motto Cyrus lived by.

"Okay, make yourself comfortable." I waved my hand toward the leather chair he always favored. I knew my tone was ironic.

It didn't take me long to prepare my small overnight case. I carefully locked the front door, which seemed superfluous, and put my keys in my purse. The lights across the street had all been turned out, I was relieved to see.

Donna Two strolled out of the guest room as we approached it. "Oh-oh," Cyrus said, "I've tried to discourage her from taking her naps here, but she's stubborn, as I've commented before—"

"Never mind. Like me. That's fine," I said, switching to baby-talk tone as I caressed the soft fur on her stretching back. "You're welcome to spend the night with me any time."

I regretted the statement when I saw Cyrus's lips twitch. I didn't dignify the issue by commenting.

"There should be everything you need in here. The bathroom's there." He pointed to the open door. "And it's stocked with toothpaste and new brushes and everything else I could think of that a guest might need."

"In the morning—"

He interrupted me. "Let's not worry about anything until then. Let's sleep as late as we can. I feel sure I'll be up before you are, but ignore me. You need the rest. This has been quite a day, hasn't it?"

"Amen. But what I was going to say is that I have an appointment at ten-thirty with Sheryl at the bakery that I'd really like to keep."

"We'll play it by ear," he answered. "Donna Two, are you coming with me? She usually sleeps with me."

Donna Two ignored him, rubbed against my leg, spraying white hair, and jumped back to settle on the impression she'd left on the bed. We both laughed. "There's that mind of her own. Do you care if she stays?" Cyrus asked.

"Of course not. I'd like her company."

"Well, you'll need to leave your door open. Her litter box is in the utility room, and she usually snacks a time or two during the night."

"We'll get along just fine, won't we?" I said, scratching her ears.

Cyrus half-saluted, then left. My eyelids were growing heavy. It would be a relief, I realized, to be away from my house, certainly until the window was fixed.

I awoke feeling much better until I looked at my watch. Ten o'clock! "Oh, shoot," I said, leaping out of bed and slipping into my robe. The house was completely quiet. Cyrus wouldn't be asleep, that I was sure of, so odds were that he was over at my place. I went to the phone.

A minute later, I said, "Sheryl, I'll have to cancel our meeting. I just woke up."

"I'm not surprised. I understand you had quite a night. Sheriff Calligan is at your house now. I gather that you're not?"

"No, Cyrus insisted I take advantage of his guest room rather than stay there." I almost said I'd slept like the dead, but thought that rather inappropriate. "How about lunch instead? I'll get dressed and go face the fireworks, and I'll surely be hungry. Perhaps Cyrus can join us?"

We agreed that I'd call if we weren't going to be able to make it. Putting the phone down, I saw an envelope with my name on it propped up against the vase of flowers on the table. Flowers. That reminded me. In the hope of comforting him when he woke up, we must see that some were delivered to Alvin. It was the least we could do, considering his love of gardens.

Removing the sheet from inside the envelope, I read, "Didn't want to wake you when the sheriff arrived. Please excuse me for taking your keys out of your purse. There's hot coffee in my maker."

Gratefully, I went to the counter and filled the cup set next to his drip maker. How thoughtful. Correctly, he knew I'd need a jolt of caffeine before facing Calligan. I carried it with me into the bedroom, where I took the necessities out of my little suitcase and headed for the bathroom. The sheriff could wait while I showered.

When I was dressed and ready, I refilled the cup, then walked across the lawn. There were two police vehicles there, one parked in my driveway.

Sheriff Calligan didn't even make an effort to be solicitous when I walked in the open front door. He glanced at his watch, then glared at me.

"You wouldn't have been here any earlier if you'd been me," I told him. "That was quite a night."

"Good morning," Cyrus said, making a face warning me

against antagonizing the sheriff further. "I turned your heat off when we got in. Hope you had a good rest?"

"I did. Thanks for having the coffee available."

"Did you remember to cancel your appointment for this morning?" he prompted.

I nodded. "Changed it to lunch. You're invited too."

"Good."

"Missus Galbreath," the sheriff hissed, "I've already had the story of the meddling you two have been doing. Not only did you create the situation that caused this mess, but you may have jeopardized our police investigation."

"What investigation?" I retorted. "You're so sure Jake did it that you're not looking elsewhere."

"And how do you know what the department is doing?" he asked sarcastically. "May I remind you that impeding a police investigation is a crime?"

I clamped my lips together. My big mouth had gotten me into trouble before. He was a jerk, even if people did think he was a competent policeman. He'd need to improve his social skills if he were to have any hopes for promotion.

"Please remember the stress that Mrs. Galbreath has been under," Cyrus interjected. "This has been a very difficult situation."

A grumbling sound emanated from the sheriff's throat before he swallowed and spoke. "We're just about done here," he said. "Mr. Bates has made arrangements for your window to be fixed. Do not, I repeat, do not continue your so-called 'investigating.' "

He picked up a briefcase from a chair, then turned toward me one last time. With his gray eyes flashing, he pointed a finger at my chest, almost jabbing me, then opened his mouth. He shut it with a snap, and whirled toward the door, his face with an almost purple tint. The door slammed behind him.

Cyrus and my eyes met, and then we both cracked up.

Beyond Cyrus, I could see the other officer bite his lip in an effort not to laugh.

Undoubtedly, we weren't the only ones who found Sheriff Calligan a difficult man.

CHAPTER NINETEEN

Sheryl was waiting for us this time when Cyrus and I walked into the bakery. "I'm anxious to hear what you two have found out," she said as we sat down and took off our coats, spreading them on the backs of our chairs. Her cheeks were pink, and she appeared quite animated. "I've already ordered."

"Then you'll excuse us for a moment while we do the same?" Cyrus asked.

"Of course."

We both chose sandwiches, since the bread here was exceptionally good. Mine was an all veggie combination; Cyrus chose ham and cheese.

We again settled at the table, and Sheryl began the conversation. "I am sorry to have to tell you that the fingerprinting of Alvin was a failure. The first batch of prints was defective. Our new man isn't very experienced at taking them yet, and they need to be perfect for AFIS. So the deputy sent one of his men this morning to do the job. We received word back just before I came. They have absolutely no record of the owner of the prints. All this tells us is that he has never been in trouble with the law. They don't keep those taken for things such as working in a school."

"Since we know he was in the military," Cyrus said, "they'll be on record there. I'll get on it immediately, and I'll pressure my sources to hurry the information."

"That'll be good," I said. "I have the gut feeling you were

talking about earlier, Cyrus, that Alvin's identity's the key to the whole thing. I surely hope they're keeping an eye on him in the hospital?" I addressed this question to Sheryl.

She nodded. "He's under guard. As I've said before, Sheriff Calligan does his job. In his own way, but I do think he's efficient, though inflexible. Another thing he's done is send men out to interview your neighbors, Donna. Someone may have seen the car, or even the person who threw the rock. A surprising number of people are insomniacs. If they find out anything, I'll let you know. Although, if the sheriff catches me, it'll be worth my job."

"Oh, that's not right," I said.

She shrugged. "I'm not sure I care. I find I'm quite enjoying helping you two. Much more exciting than filling out reports on what someone else has done. Makes me think about changing careers."

"And doing what?" I asked. "Are you thinking about police work?"

"Would that be such a crazy idea, do you think? I'm not too old to go back to school. Beats the idea of being stuck in a job I don't like for the rest of my life."

"Remember that police work would have some of the disadvantages you mentioned earlier," Cyrus said. "The people and problems you'd have to deal with."

"Yes, but I'd be doing something about them. I'm also thinking about social work of some kind, dealing with kids, maybe. Anyway, thanks, you two, for opening my eyes. I'm exploring possibilities already."

"Go for it." I gave her the thumbs-up gesture. "I was just talking to a student along those lines the other day."

Turning to Cyrus, I said, "Before I forget, let's stop at the florist on the way home and order flowers for Alvin. Surely they'd be a comfort, considering his background when and if he wakes up. Speaking of Alvin . . ." I turned back to Sheryl. ". . . any news on his condition this morning?"

"Actually, yes. It seems he's stirring restlessly and they think that's a good sign. Flowers would be nice, I'm sure. But tell me. Have you two come up with anything more in your investigating?"

Cyrus took the lead, as always. "Several things," he said. "As we agreed, this must be confidential, but I approached Geri Sataro. It seems that Donniker was blackmailing her regarding her son's arrest. She changed her vote on the question of retaining him as Chief in return for Lionel's release without charge."

"Oh, that so doesn't surprise me," Sheryl said. "They're on my list of people who were in the office after hours. I had to complete the paperwork on his release the next morning when I came to work, and I admit I was surprised and said so."

"The chief told me that he'd felt there wasn't enough evidence to charge him, and that anyway, he was sympathetic because it was just a youthful indiscretion. I remember looking at him skeptically, but he wouldn't meet my eyes. How about that? No wonder he was murdered! I don't mean the Sataros did it, but how many other people was he blackmailing?"

"Actually, at least one other that we know of. Tim Borland." Cyrus explained that situation. "Was he ever in the office?"

"We know he was at least once," I interjected. "Remember when he said he hadn't met Jake, but then Jake reminded him that they'd met at the police station?"

We looked at each other in silence. Then, I asked, "But how would any of these people know about the monkshood?"

"Good question," Cyrus said.

"Oh, but if you were around the chief as much as I was, you'd know how he liked to brag. He made it sound like he'd single-handedly solved that crime and apprehended the murderer. I think it's entirely possible that while he was inflating his ego, he'd go so far as show the monkshood to someone."

The waitress brought our sandwiches and drinks at that point, and we concentrated on our food for a bit.

Then Sheryl asked, "Have you had any luck in finding out who he was having an affair with?"

"We have," Cyrus told her. "But we promised to keep it confidential unless absolutely necessary. The story could totally ruin the woman's life. Not that we don't trust you, Sheryl . . ."

"I understand. A promise is a promise. And I'm asking you to keep a secret for me, too. My talking about what's going on at the station."

I glanced nervously around before saying, "I don't see anyone here who's likely to report to Calligan that we're meeting, but perhaps in the future it would be wise not to get together in a public place."

"You're right, Donna," Cyrus said. "Should have thought about that."

Sheryl glanced at her watch. "I can't remain much longer anyway, so I'll hurry with what I have to say. I do realize now that I likely heard the chief speaking on the phone to whoever he was having an affair with. And from remarks he made, I'm pretty positive that she, too, had been in the office."

"Oh, wow," I said. "We aren't exactly narrowing the field, are we? Who else is on your list?"

"Well, Ross Diego, but you've eliminated him." She looked at us questioningly, but we didn't enlighten her on his indiscretion either. "And Ben Flannigan."

"I'm still checking him out," Cyrus said. "Don't think I'd want to use him as my broker, but I haven't found anything so far that strictly speaking would be illegal."

"By the way," Sheryl said, "have you seen the Seattle paper this morning? It has the story about Alvin. Of course there wasn't a lot to say, just that an unidentified man had been found on our beach, and that he's listed in grave condition."

"It was inevitable, but it's just as well that the word gets out that his condition is so serious. He'd be safer, I would think," Cyrus pointed out.

Sheryl was wrapping half her sandwich in paper again and preparing to leave. "I'd better get back," she said, "but I'll call you with any news."

"And we'll keep you informed, also," Cyrus promised.

Cyrus and I walked up the street to the florist, where the scents and colors inside raised my spirits like flowers always do. I enlisted the aid of the owner of Floral Delights, Cynthia Owens. She was in the middle of making an arrangement that would be lovely, I could see, but too traditional for what I wanted for Alvin. It was mostly the browns and oranges of fall chrysanthemums. Cyrus stood by the door, hands in pockets, emanating impatience.

"I'd like a bouquet for a friend in the hospital," I explained. "But it needs to be special. He's a horticulturist, and I'd like to choose flowers that he'd especially appreciate."

Her face brightened. Obviously, that would be more challenging than what she was doing. "Do you have color preferences?" she asked.

"Umm, something soothing. Not primary colors I think. How about some of that rose and yellow alstroemeria over there, and maybe some of those hot pink carnations?"

She nodded in approval, and reached into her cooler. "Let's see. Some of these fuchsia-colored gerberas would be nice, maybe, and how about some misty? This limonium appears white, but there's a hint of lavender."

Behind me, I heard a low, impatient growl.

"Perfect. And—"

"Donna," Cyrus interrupted as he came up beside me. "We need to hurry. I need to get on the fingerprints."

"Yes, yes. I know, Cyrus, we're almost finished." As Cynthia grouped the flowers, I asked him, "What do you think?"

"Lovely, just fine." He blinked, then looked at them more carefully. "Actually, I think they'll be perfect for Alvin." He pulled out his credit card. "Let's complete this transaction."

Cynthia shot me a sympathetic glance, but reached for his card. We gave her the information about where to send them, and we departed. I, at least, was satisfied.

Cyrus hustled me to his car. "It's four-thirty in the East," he informed me. "If we hurry, I may be able to catch the people I need in their offices before they go home."

"Oh. I didn't think about the time difference, Cyrus. I do apologize. You should have gone on without waiting for me."

"Didn't want to be rude," he said. "But I won't stop at your house. I assume you can walk there from mine?"

Dumb question, since I did so regularly. However, "Certainly," was all I said.

Nervously, I watched each intersection we came to. At best, Cyrus didn't worry about incoming traffic. Today . . .

"Look out!" I screamed, as a car coming from the right swerved to miss us.

"I saw him," Cyrus's voice was calm, and he didn't slow down one smidgen.

"If a policeman saw that little maneuver, we'd really have been delayed," I chided.

"But none did," he answered. "Trust me. And, please. Don't yell when I'm driving. It's distracting."

I gulped, swallowed, hung on, and didn't speak again until I was out of the car. To his retreating back, I called, "You'll let me know what you find, won't you?"

He gave a backward wave and disappeared into his house. Inside my own, I hung up my coat and then flopped down on the couch. Stress seemed to accompany my every move these days.

I certainly hadn't expected to fall asleep, but I was awakened by the ringing phone. After blinking a couple of times to orient myself, I jumped up and grabbed the phone.

"That was quick," I said, assuming it was Cyrus. A silence greeted me, and then Sheryl's voice spoke.

"I'm assuming you were expecting another call?" she asked.

"Oh. Yes. I'm sorry, Sheryl. I guess I'd fallen asleep."

"Oh. I'm the one who should apologize for waking you. Especially after the night you just had. But I have news, and I snuck away to a pay phone to let you know. The survey of your neighborhood had results. Rather startling, I think."

"Oh? Tell me."

"It seems someone named Rodenberger has a dog who's been having a digestive upset, and he—Mr. Rodenberger, that is—was awakened a little before three by his dog's whining. He put on his bathrobe and took the dog out on a leash, to be sure it didn't take off."

"Yes, yes." Anticipation was gnawing at me.

"Oh, well. He saw your intruder. Didn't hear the breaking glass because he hadn't put in his hearing aids, but he was startled enough to take note of the man he saw leap into the car. He also saw enough of the license plate so that the sheriff was able to get an identification.

"It turns out . . ." Her voice was gleeful. ". . . that it's registered to one Lionel Sataro. Not at a Cedar Harbor address, but with a name like that, there's no doubt it was Geri Sataro's son. Sheriff Calligan has issued a warrant for his arrest."

"Oh, boy," I said, my mind whirling. "I'll get back to you."

Cyrus's phone was frustratingly busy. I'd assumed he'd be making contact with his sources by computer, but perhaps I was wrong. Or perhaps he'd found someone he really needed to talk to.

I tried every five minutes until I got him. "Cyrus," I said, "Sheryl called with news. They've identified my intruder as little boy Sataro. Guess there's no doubt."

"Outstanding," he said. "How'd that come about?"

I explained, picturing the small hairless creature I'd seen fairly often in daylight on the wrong end of a leash held by my neighbor down the street, Alex Rodenberger.

"Well, that does . . ." I heard a quick intake of breath. ". . . open a can of worms, does it not? And what are we going to do with this information?"

"Whatever we do, we'll have to be careful so as not to implicate Sheryl."

"Of course, Donna. That's a given. Let me think. Oh, by the way, I reached an old friend in D.C., and he's putting the wheels into motion. Think we should have results in the morning."

"In the morning," I repeated. "Well. Tomorrow's likely to be quite a day. Roberta and Will are getting here in the late afternoon. We may know who Alvin is by the then. And Lionel? What do you suppose his explanation will be? I still can't see all this mayhem taking place because he's angry we've investigated his mother. But what on earth could his motivation be?"

"I haven't any idea." Cyrus sounded grim. "But if he disappears into the court system, we're not likely to find out. He'll make excuses, and his mother will probably pull a few strings as she's done in the past. I'd sure like to talk to him first. And Donna, if someone else is behind his actions, and I'm beginning to have no doubt that there is someone else, Lionel could be in danger."

"Oh, Lord, Cyrus, what'll we do?"

CHAPTER TWENTY

"I think," Cyrus said in a musing tone, "that I'll give Mrs. Sataro a call."

"I'd like to listen in," I said. "How about—"

"I'll be right over. Do it from your house. Then we can discuss our next move immediately."

So, in just a couple of minutes, Cyrus was dialing my phone while I waited impatiently. Fortunately, Geri was home.

"Mrs. Sataro?" he queried. "This is Cyrus Bates. Sorry to bother you again. Are you aware that someone threw a rock through the front window of my neighbor's house during the middle of last night with a message?"

Cyrus turned up the speaker. Handy gadget. I'd rarely used the feature, but it was perfect for this situation.

"Why, no," she said. "Should I be?"

Holding up crossed fingers, and smirking at me, he replied, "I think so. Another neighbor has told us that he was walking his dog at the time. It would appear that the culprit was your son."

Oh-oh. I'd better pay a visit on Mr. Rodenberger so that Cyrus couldn't be proved a liar.

There was a silence on the other end of the line. I'd never heard any sign of perturbation in her voice, but when she finally spoke, it was obvious that this news rattled her. "And what was this message?"

"Crudely written on plain paper were the words, 'Mind your

own business.' "

"Oh."

Cyrus held his impatience for another long moment, and then spoke. "We have assumed that he is annoyed because I have been poking around in your affairs as part of the investigation Mrs. Galbreath and I have been conducting into the murder of Police Chief Donniker."

"My son isn't a murderer, if that's what you're implying!" Her voice was shrill. To my surprise, she didn't even raise the question of Cyrus's snooping.

"I'm not implying anything. The fact that you were blackmailed into voting for the chief doesn't seem to be of sufficient impact to motivate such a deed. We have, actually, ascertained that you were not the only victim of the chief. Do you have any ideas about why your son would do such a thing?"

"None whatsoever," came the feeble answer. "I seldom understand my son's behavior."

"He might be acting on another's behalf. And if he is, Mrs. Sataro, it has occurred to us that he could be in real danger. There have been two more murder attempts. The person behind all this is serious. If you have even the slightest suspicion of who that someone might be, at the very least I suggest you warn your son. I'd like to talk to him, but—"

"I don't know where he is," she interrupted. "After—Well, recently he moved to a new place. I don't know where it is, except that it's near Cedar Harbor. And no. I have no idea what he's up to, and I seldom have in the past. He's been a problem most of his life."

"I'm aware of that."

"Then you know that he's never done anything that was more than a misdemeanor."

"He's never been charged for more than that, I know, but I

imagine you or your husband have acted in his behalf in the past."

A long sigh came across the line. Then she said, "I appreciate your calling, Mr. Bates. Yes, it's time he took responsibility for his own actions. I've tried to convince my ex-husband of that many times, and then, when push came to shove, I did the same thing. It won't happen in the future, I promise you."

"We want there to be a future," Cyrus said somberly.

"Again, thank you. I'll do my best to locate him."

"Phew," I said, when he hung up. "I feel sorry for her. All her millions must mean very little in the face of the news you gave her. She does sound like a sensible woman. I can even understand her attempt to keep him out of trouble. It must be extremely difficult when one's offspring acts so stupidly." I pictured Roberta's innocent, smiling face, and gave silent thanks for my good luck. "I wonder if there are other Sataro children?"

I should have known he'd have the answer. "A daughter," he said. "Married to a professor, I understand. With one small child."

"Isn't anything secret anymore?" I asked in dismay.

Cyrus smiled sympathetically. " 'Fraid not, Donna. That's the way the world is today. The Internet is a great blessing, but also a curse. If there weren't so many evil people out there—predators, those who think it's fun to attack others' computers, greedy cheats—the world would be a better place."

"They've always been there, I guess," I said humbly. "I just didn't realize quite how much is going on in, what-do-you-call-it? Cyberspace?"

He frowned. "I find it incredible that a woman as intelligent as you insists on avoiding a medium that provides so much information at the touch of one's fingertips. So much business is conducted that way now, too. You need to keep up."

Stunned, I stared at him.

He looked chagrined. "Sorry about that, Donna. It really isn't my business."

"As if you ever let that bother you." I chuckled. Weakly. "Perhaps you're right, Cyrus. Maybe I've just been stubborn, and I'm not sure why. I've procrastinated partly because I see people get so addicted to their computers, but perhaps learning all that technology at my age fazes me."

He snorted. "Your age, indeed. If you decide to go with it, I'm here to be your tutor."

"I'll think about it. Thanks. But do sit down," I suggested. "You make me nervous pacing like that. Have you any suggestions what else we might do?"

He sat, put his elbows on his knees, and rubbed his face. "I dislike saying, 'I don't know.' Let's hope the sheriff is doing better than we are. He does have more resources. Otherwise, wait to hear about the fingerprints, I guess. And maybe, pray. If you think that will help."

We had never discussed our personal beliefs, but this didn't seem the time for such a discussion. I was surprised at Cyrus's air of hopelessness, and I truly didn't know what to say.

"I'm hoping we'll have an answer as to Alvin's identity from Washington early tomorrow morning. In the meantime, I'd suggest we both get some rest. As you said, tomorrow is likely to be quite a day."

"I'd love to see Alvin," I said.

"So would I. I feel as if my meddling got him into this situation."

"I don't think that's so, Cyrus. He came to Cedar Harbor for a reason, don't you think? Anything you or I could have done was unlikely to change the outcome."

He stood, then suggested, "Why don't we try to visit him in the morning? I'll see if I can get permission. And of course, if I receive news of his identity, somewhat reluctantly I'll need to share it first with the sheriff. But then—Let's wait and see."

We agreed that we'd be ready for action at nine in the morning.

It was earlier than nine when an imperative knock sounded on my door. I peered out the front window; then, confirming that it was Cyrus on my doorstep, I let him in.

His expression was a mixture of triumph and consternation. "You're not going to believe what I found out," he said. "Just talked to my friend in D.C., and he's e-mailing confirmation.

"Alvin's full name is William Alvin Donniker. And get this; it's William Alvin Donniker, Junior."

CHAPTER TWENTY-ONE

"Our first stop will have to be the police station," Cyrus said. "Let's go."

I grabbed my coat and purse and headed out the door. His car was waiting at the curb. When Cyrus decides to move, he moves. In more ways than one. As he accelerated, I shut my eyes. I was quite sure his driving would be more than I could stand this morning. Quickly, far too quickly, we were parking at the police station.

The deputy was behind his desk, thank goodness, and Sheryl stood when she saw us. One look at our faces, and she deferred to Calligan.

"We have news," Cyrus said imperatively, and Calligan, his eyebrows reacting to Cyrus's tone, immediately stood and came to the desk. "What's up?"

"I've just received word from my contact in Washington that Alvin's fingerprints have been identified. His name is William Alvin Donniker, Junior. Here's a copy of the e-mail."

A stunned silence was broken only by a gasp from Sheryl's direction. Then, whirling, Calligan reached for his hat. "I assume you've gone nowhere else with this information?" He looked at us sternly.

"Came straight here," Cyrus answered.

"Good. Sheryl," he said without looking at her, "I'm headed to the Donniker home. You two . . ." He pointed vigorously at us. ". . . you are following directions to stay out of this?"

"Of course. One thing," Cyrus interjected, "could you arrange permission for us to look in on Alvin? I'm assuming he's still unconscious. We just feel an obligation as friends. We've sent flowers."

"That could be arranged," Calligan said. "I appreciate your coming to me with this info. Sheryl," he said as he went out the door, "call the hospital and tell them these two have my permission to see the patient."

"Yes, sir!" Sheryl said snappily, saluting in the direction of his departing back.

Turning to us, she said, "Well, that is stunning, isn't it? Wow! Did Lucille know? Did the chief know?"

"If we had those answers, I suspect we'd know who the murderer was," Cyrus said. "And why he did it."

I'd been thinking on the way over. When I wasn't hanging on. "It sure appears that Lucille killed her husband, doesn't it? I mean, she must have been absolutely furious when she found out about Alvin, especially since the chief was unable to impregnate her."

"You're jumping to conclusions, Donna. Did she find out? It isn't as if she can be arrested just because Alvin's on the scene. All she has to do is deny knowledge. How could it be proved otherwise?"

"If she didn't know, then we'd be back to the other people who had reason to hate him, wouldn't we?" Sheryl said.

I had a thought. "That includes Jake as far as Calligan's concerned. Or do you think he's softened on that subject?"

Sheryl shrugged. "He doesn't confide in me. Well. Let me call the hospital, and then you can visit him."

"Among other things, I want to check on the security there," Cyrus said. "Alvin's recovery is crucial. We'd want him to heal regardless, but he surely has the answers we need."

Sheryl was already dialing. In a moment she was speaking to

the person on the other end. "Sheriff Calligan has authorized two visitors for the shooting victim," she said, giving our names in that very official tone she was able to produce. "How is he this morning?"

"Uh-huh. Good! I'm glad to hear that. These folks are the ones who sent the flowers. They'll be there shortly, I'm sure."

"Good news," she said as she hung up. "They think he's coming around. And," she said grinning, "your flowers appeared to help. He definitely stirred, and even opened his eyes briefly when the scent permeated the room. I thought about telling them you could provide identification, but then it occurred to me that the deputy might not appreciate that."

Cyrus nodded in approval. "The fewer people who know who he is at this point, the better." He grinned slyly at me. "Tim Borland would give his first-born for this information."

I looked him straight in the eye. "But he's not going to get it, is he? At least until Calligan chooses to divulge it. Somehow, I doubt he'd pick the local newspaper to do so, but I could be wrong."

"Shall we go?" He started to take my arm, but instead reached for the door. Cyrus *was* trainable, it appeared.

I know I'm not alone in finding hospitals depressing. They've come a long way, with cheerier colors, even wallpaper in some rooms and the staff no long forced to wear white. Didn't I remember that white was the color of mourning in the Orient? Maybe the people who design medical facilities have been told that.

Still, anxious-faced visitors, the smells of disinfectants, the urgent look on the face of a doctor who strode by, were enough to accelerate my heartbeat and make me wish to be elsewhere.

We were directed to Alvin's room, where we were relieved to see a guard perched on a chair outside. "The local police phoned ahead that we had permission to visit the patient," Cyrus told him. "Donna Galbreath and Cyrus Bates."

The man nodded, made a notation on the pad in his lap, and waved us in. The first thing I noticed as Cyrus opened the door was the scent of the bouquet, subtle, not overwhelming. My gaze turned immediately toward the bed, and my heart jumped.

The top of Alvin's head was encased in bandages, and his face underneath was as pale as the sheets. The body under the covers appeared so slight. Wires ran to monitors and tubes to his body. I gulped, approached the bed and took his free hand. Behind me, I sensed Cyrus moving a chair so I could sit next to the bed.

"We're here, Alvin," I said, stroking his hand. "Your friends Cyrus and Donna. We're so glad you're improving."

On the way over, we'd discussed the theory that people who are unconscious actually can hear what's said to them, so we'd agreed to speak to him as if he truly could.

"Ahem." Cyrus cleared his throat. His face showed his concern as he leaned forward and punched Alvin lightly on the shoulder. "We're prepared to do anything we can to help you, old man. We think we're close to finding out who did this to you. If only you could speak."

"Cyrus! I think his hand just moved. I think he did hear you! Keep talking."

"We know who you are, you know. We think Chief Donniker had to have been your father. Were you ever able to talk to him? Did he know about you? Did his wife know?"

Slowly, slowly, the lids on Alvin's gray-green eyes lifted.

"His eyes," I said. "They look exactly like those eyes that used to stare back at me from his father in the sixth grade. Alvin! Can you truly hear us?"

The lids drooped, then closed.

"Oh, my," I said. "We should tell the nurse."

Cyrus pushed the summons button. The woman appeared quickly.

"Your patient just opened his eyes," Cyrus reported.

"And moved his hand," I told her, excitedly.

"That *is* good news," the middle-aged, dark-skinned woman said. "Let me check."

We both moved back from the bed while she did so.

"Keep it up for a while, would you? His blood pressure's better than it was. I've seen lots of these head injuries. When they start making this sort of response, it usually means they'll regain consciousness. Of course," she said, hesitating, "they don't always have all their faculties, but it's one step at a time, isn't it?"

"Naturally we'll stay," I answered.

"Are you the folks who sent the flowers? They really seemed to cause a reaction. What a nice thing to do."

"May we move them even closer for a while?" I asked. "We'll put them back."

She nodded, her brown curls bouncing. "Good idea. Stay perhaps another twenty minutes? We don't want to stress him."

We agreed. She seemed truly compassionate, even if she referred to him as "a head injury," but I knew that was typical of medical personnel. Cyrus carried the vase over and perched on the side of the bed.

"I picked out these flowers just for you, Alvin," I said. "The carnations are especially fragrant. I don't think you've seen them, but there's alstromeria, and gerberas, and . . ."

We spent the next twenty minutes alternating talking to him. I was amazed at how gentle and caring Cyrus was. He must have had a lot of experience while his son was dying of AIDS. I certainly shouldn't have fussed about not liking hospitals. He'd most likely had a lengthy exposure to them, and probably bore the responsibility and devastation by himself if I'd interpreted what he'd said about his wife correctly.

Alvin showed no further sign of responding though, so, after the suggested twenty minutes, we reluctantly returned the flowers to the chest of drawers and left after I kissed Alvin lightly on the cheek and Cyrus squeezed his hand.

"Well," Cyrus said.

"Well," I responded. We walked out to his car.

"Could I interest you in lunch at the Inn?" Cyrus asked. "It might . . . well, make us feel better."

"Thanks a lot," I said, "but I really do have too much to do with Roberta arriving this afternoon. I'm planning a nice dinner. That reminds me! Would you have time to stop at the grocery? I wanted to pick up a few fresh things."

"Of course. I, too, could use a restocking. Tend to forget those things when we're involved in more exciting events."

So a few minutes later we pulled up in the parking lot of Mason's. I never fail to relive the frightening encounter I'd had with a murderer at their Dumpster. Glancing quickly behind the supermarket, I saw that the big blue thing was still there, and I shuddered.

Cyrus noticed, and smiled sympathetically. "Just look on it as a monument to your bravery," he suggested. "And your triumph."

In spite of what he said, I noticed that he was thoughtful enough to park where we could no longer see it.

As usual, when I go in the store, I ended up with far more than I'd intended. There are always sales that make it seem worthwhile. The mustard I like was two-for-one as was the no-salt catsup alongside. They joined the fresh produce and milk in my basket.

Cyrus, too, had a full basket when we met in front of the checkout. We paid, then loaded our bags in the trunk of his little red car. I made a circuit of it, inspecting the repairs that had been made after our unfortunate crash.

"They did a good job, didn't they?" I commented, patting the hood. "I'm so glad. I do feel bad about the accident, Cyrus. Perhaps if you'd been behind the wheel, you could have averted it."

"No. I couldn't. And thank you, Donna. The shop said that it would have happened no matter who was driving, and I am the one whose behavior was inexcusable that day. May we put it completely out of our minds and pretend it never happened?"

I held out my hand, and we shook. "Agreed," I said. "Except, of course, for wanting to catch whoever did it."

"Considering the rock through your window, my money would be on Lionel. But we will see. I hope."

We were silent as we both retreated into our own thoughts. Suddenly something occurred to me. "Cyrus." I turned toward him. "Where on earth does Lionel fit into this picture? He might be angry at us for investigating his mother, but there isn't a reason in the world for him to want to kill Alvin. Is there?"

Cyrus blinked. "This isn't the first time we've been on the same wavelength, Donna. I've been thinking along the same lines. The only connection I've been able to come up with is Lucille. Is she blackmailing Lionel too? Was what he got arrested for a more serious crime than we've been led to think, and the chief told her about it? Let's face it, we don't know if she was aware of his blackmailing activities, but I can see him gloating. Especially if he drank. Do you know?"

"I've never heard people comment that he had a problem, but he certainly seemed the type. Perhaps only at home after work."

"If he did, does Lucille have the goods to pressure Lionel into helping her?"

"Helping her with what? Throwing rocks at my window and sabotaging your car? Or are you thinking about shooting Alvin?

Or even . . ." The thought came to me. ". . . murdering Billy? Either Lucille or Lionel could conceivably have stolen the monkshood from the evidence room."

"But doing so implies a preconceived plan. As far as we know, Lionel would have had only the one opportunity, the night he was arrested. Could he have been angry enough to take the monkshood on impulse?"

"I could see that if the chief was making much bigger demands than Geri Sataro admitted. Real money, perhaps?"

"But then we're back to the question of how Alvin enters into that picture? I don't see it."

We mulled that over for a bit, then Cyrus spoke with force. "Lionel must know what's going on," he said. "And we're back to the original premise, that Lucille could have blackmailed him into more criminal activities for her benefit."

"What benefit?"

He grimaced. "Here we are," he said unnecessarily as he swung into my driveway. "Donna, I think we need to locate that young man. Whatever the solution is, he could be dangerous—or in danger. If Lucille is behind all this and she thinks Alvin's not going to live, then only Lionel would be able to come up with the truth."

"Or Alvin. If he revives."

"Yes, but I'm surmising that she thinks he's on death's door, thanks to that article in the paper. In the meantime others could be in danger, including you and me, I would think. Hand me the telephone from my glove compartment, will you? We need to point out some of this to the sheriff, even though he won't appreciate it."

Wordlessly, I handed him the phone. He must have programmed the police station number into it, in his typical organized fashion, because he only punched one number.

"Sheryl," he said, "may I speak to the sheriff?"

"He hasn't come back from the Donniker house. What's up?" The phone was near enough that I could hear what she was saying.

"We've come to the conclusion that he needs to find Lionel Sataro, and yes, I know. He won't appreciate our interference, but we'll take that chance."

"I'll try to reach him," she said. "Hold on."

Again, I could feel the tension filling the air in the car as we waited. Cyrus drummed the steering wheel with his hand, as he does, and I reached over and put my own on his, hoping to calm him.

Finally, the sheriff evidently answered. Sheryl repeated our request to speak to him, and she added, "They have an idea that needs investigating. Uh-huh. Uh-huh. Shall I tell them you'll call when you're available?"

"He's stonewalling us," Cyrus muttered under his breath. Then, louder, he said, "Please give him my cell phone number and urge him to return our call."

After she did so, he asked, "What's his excuse?"

"Actually, it's a pretty good one. There's been a monstrous accident on I-5, involving a number of cars and an oil tanker, and other deputies are off searching for a lost child."

"Humph! Well, thanks for trying. We'll get back to you."

Hanging up, he said, "I don't have Geri's number on this phone," he said. "May I call her from your house?"

"Of course. But open your trunk, please, before my ice cream melts."

Gallantly, Cyrus carried most of my groceries inside. I hustled my perishables into the refrigerator while Cyrus hurriedly perused the phone book. "Ah," he said, "here it is."

Fortunately, she was home. "Mrs. Sataro," he was soon saying, "I don't want to alarm you, but we feel that it's imperative that we reach your son. Do you—have you—found out anything about how to contact him?"

I set out the things I needed on the counter as I listened to the speaker phone.

"He's rented a condo in that new Kamiak Hills complex south of town, but I don't know which one. Is he—is he in more trouble?"

"We're trying to prevent trouble," Cyrus assured her.

I whispered urgently, "Ask her what Lionel's car looks like."

He did so, and then finished with, "We'll get back to you."

His eyes were bright as he looked at me. "Donna, you constantly amaze me. I certainly should have thought of that. He has a silver Porsche. We're a good pair, aren't we? Now, if he's home, I'll at least have a shot at finding which condo is his. I don't think she'd have been as forthcoming if she were involved. Let's go."

I looked at him helplessly. "Cyrus, I can't. Roberta should be here in less than two hours, and I need to do . . ."

"I'll go. You get ready for Roberta."

He turned and dashed through the door.

"Don't forget your frozen things," I called after him.

"I won't. It's cold enough. They'll be okay."

"And phone me. So I won't worry."

"I will," he called just before he slammed the car door. As I turned back toward my dinner preparations, I felt a rising glow. "Good partners?" Compliments like that from Cyrus were rare.

Chapter Twenty-Two

Quickly, I assembled the ingredients for lasagna, one of Roberta's favorites. I put the noodles on to boil, then crumbled the ground beef, onions and garlic into a frying pan. As they did their thing, I took down my favorite bowl, a wooden one that had belonged to my mother, and put together the salad.

I almost forgot the avocado. I needed to force myself to concentrate. I can make mistakes if I don't, and I really wanted a nice dinner for our first one together in some time. Still, it was impossible to forget the situation in which Cyrus and I, yet again, had become involved.

Why did we do this? Well, because in the first instance, Chief Donniker had been so inept. This time, as far as I could tell, the man in charge, Sheriff Calligan, was intelligent and apparently knew his business.

But he was also, could I say, boneheaded? His certainty that Jake was the murderer seemingly was blocking his thought processes regarding other possibilities. And there was so much at stake.

Could you, I asked myself, also have a stubborn streak, as well as a nosy one? I'd certainly been accused of that in the past. However, I did prefer the term "stubborn" to the one I'd labeled the sheriff with, "boneheaded."

I grimaced. Self-analysis could be humbling, and perhaps should be. Nevertheless, I wasn't about to give up on our investigation, and neither was Cyrus.

I put the lasagna together, set the table, and glanced at my watch. It had been an hour since Cyrus left. What was he up to? Had he found Lionel? Why hadn't he called?

And if he had located Geri's son, what was going on? Was he safe? I so wished I hadn't let him charge off on his own.

I put the lasagna in the oven and set the timer to start it in two hours, which should be about right. Then I pulled a sheet of paper out of my desk, and wrote Roberta a note.

"Dear Roberta," I wrote. *"Cyrus and I do seem to have become involved in the latest investigation. Haven't time to explain. But he went off by himself. Make yourself at home, and watch the oven for me."*

I nibbled on the head of the pen for a moment, then added, *"I'm heading for the new Kamiak Hills development south of town on Beach Drive. Should the sheriff call, tell him we're searching for Lionel Sataro."*

There. The more people who knew where we were, the better.

Grabbing my purse and coat, which I hadn't even hung up, I headed out to my car. I knew vaguely where the development was, but had never even gone by it. I headed south past Marie's house, then kept on for several miles.

I was astounded when I came to the sign indicating Kamiak Hills. The complex was huge. How could so many people have moved in and not had more impact on Cedar Harbor? But then I noticed that parts of it were still under construction, and there was big sign indicating, "Homes for Sale."

Anyway, it occurred to me, the location was far enough from Cedar Harbor that it was likely most of the people would head south, toward more shopping opportunities and jobs.

The place oozed money. For some reason, the architects had chosen a Southwest theme, which seemed inappropriate to me in our rainy climate. Maybe it was supposed to make the residents feel like they were in a warmer clime. The landscape even had palm trees, and the foliage was brilliant and certainly not native. I followed signs to the condo section, seeing luxurious homes and a golf course in the distance. Small swimming pools were located in the middle of each group of condo units.

How on earth was I to find Lionel's condo? I stopped worrying about Cyrus a bit. It would not have been easy for him, either, and he may well have spent the greater part of the hour searching. It appeared each unit had a central door. Did people still post their names there, or had the problem of privacy changed all that? And would that door be locked?

I spotted a sign, "Office," and parked in front. After pushing through the swinging glass door, I went up to the desk and punched the button.

A pert blonde popped out of an inner door. "May I help you?" she asked. "Are you looking for a home or a condo?"

"Neither," I answered. "Not exactly. I need to locate a young man who has recently rented a condo here. His name in Lionel Sataro."

"Oh, I am sorry," she said, as a look of regret slid across her face. Probably because I wasn't a prospective renter. "We're not allowed to give out that information."

"It's sort of an emergency," I hedged.

"Then I suggest you phone him? You can understand, I'm sure, our reluctance to divulge that sort of information these days."

"Yes, I can." I thanked her and left. I headed back into the complex, driving slowly along the winding streets. No people were to be seen. My guess was that mostly singles lived here, and probably they were all at work.

My best bet was to spot either Lionel's silver Porsche or Cyrus's red vehicle.

I almost passed by without seeing it. The carports were

unobtrusive, and this one was in the shade. But on my right, I spotted a silver sporty-looking car. I stopped and peered at the vehicle. Yes, indeedy, it was a Porsche. But where, I wondered, was Cyrus's car?

I still had the problem of figuring out which condo was Lionel's. I walked along the exposed aggregate path to the front door of his building, which was marked J.

The main door was not locked, and I entered a small lobby which held a comfortable looking settee, a drop-leaf table, and a large, potted jade plant under a skylight. Beyond the lobby, a door on a glass wall was locked I discovered when I tried it. The elevator was on the far side. That was a problem. First, however, I needed to find out if I was in the right place.

Mailboxes lined one wall. Alongside them was a panel with buzzers for each apartment and, to my relief, last names were posted next to the buzzers. I quickly scanned the names. No Sataro.

By now my blood pressure was probably much too high. I ignored the pounding in my ears. Now what?

Going over the list more carefully, I saw that three of the units had no names next to their numbers. Most likely Lionel hadn't been here long enough to post his. Or he hadn't wanted anyone to find him. I quickly jotted down the condo numbers.

Just then a gray-haired man came into the lobby with his keys in his hand. As he inserted a key in one of the mailboxes, I said, "Excuse me. I'm trying to find a young man named Lionel Sataro who lives in this unit, I believe. Would you happen to know which one?"

He raised his eyebrows, then evidently decided I was harmless. "No, I have no idea. But we've had a couple of new occupants. What does he look like?"

I described the young, dark-haired Lionel, and the man nodded. "Think I've seen him. Probably lives on the third floor, I believe. I'm on the second, but we shared the elevator a couple of times. Will that help?"

"A good deal," I said. "Thanks a lot."

After drawing his mail out, he unlocked the inner door, and, with a questioning look, held it open for me, then held the elevator door while I joined him.

Fortunately, there wasn't time for conversation. As he got out on the second floor, he said, "Good luck in finding your young man."

"Thank you for your assistance." He had no idea how much help he'd been by getting me into the place. Two of the three unmarked apartments were on the third floor, I'd noted. That narrowed the search a bit.

If possible, my heart pounded even harder as I stepped out on the third-floor landing. I looked at my note. The unmarked apartments on this floor were 301 and 304.

Turning down the hall in the indicated direction, I immediately noticed an out-of-place element. In front of the door to one apartment, 304 I noted as I drew closer, was something white.

I reached down and picked it up, and then my heart really began to pound.

It was a white handkerchief. A white monogrammed handkerchief. The letters were CB. I'd seen identical ones before, in Cyrus's pocket when he was dressed up and in a stack next to his ironing board.

Good for Cyrus! Like the children in Hansel and Gretel, he'd left a track. But now what? I bit my lip and contemplated my next action, and finally determined I had no choice. I'd have to ring the doorbell, announce my presence and see what happened.

First, however, I put the handkerchief back on the floor, carefully covering it with my feet so it wouldn't be noticed by whoever opened the door. I'd leave the track for anyone looking for us. I hoped it would be reinforcements from the sheriff's office.

Maybe we wouldn't need reinforcements, and I'd get inside and find Cyrus and Lionel innocently discussing the situation over coffee.

But maybe not. Gritting my teeth, I pushed the buzzer.

CHAPTER TWENTY-THREE

The door cracked open, and Lionel peered out. His eyes narrowed, and he grunted. He wasn't thrilled to see me. "You had to interfere, too," he said. "Come on in."

"Oh, I don't think so," I answered. "I'm just looking for Cyrus. Is he here?"

"Come on in!" Lionel grabbed my wrist and yanked me through the doorway into a small entry hall. I could hear voices in the room beyond us. One of them was Cyrus's, and my heart leaped in relief. At least he was okay. Rubbing my wrist, I followed Lionel into the living room.

Cyrus glowered at me. Wasn't anyone glad to see me? Oh, yes. Behind him, holding a gun, was Lucille. She beamed in delight at my presence.

"Donna," Cyrus blurted, "what are you doing here?"

"Well, the same thing you are, I presume, looking for answers. Did you find any?"

"Unfortunately," Lucille said, "yes. He did find answers. I warned you, Donna, to mind your own business."

Oh-oh, I thought. At least now I knew who the murderer was. But had she revealed why she killed her husband and shot Alvin?

Trying to calm myself, I said, as if we were having a polite conversation, " 'Mind your own business.' That sounds familiar. Does that mean you were behind the message on the rock that flew through my window in the middle of the night?"

212

"Of course. But I unequivocally had told you the same thing in person. Don't you recall?"

"Umm, yes, but that also means that Lionel's been helping you, right?" Turning to him, I said, "You are aware that your car was identified by a neighbor of mine the next day?"

"No," he snapped. "I wasn't."

"Good. That means your mother didn't tell you. That's in her favor, I would think."

"Leave my mother out of this."

"Over here," Lucille ordered, gesturing at me. "Beside your friend."

I don't know why I was going to so much effort—and it was one—to appear unconcerned. I just didn't want to give this evil woman any pleasure from knowing she was frightening me, very much. As I joined Cyrus, he took my hand.

"Oh," she almost squealed, "we're more than friends. How nice! Lionel," she ordered, "you come over here beside me."

He did so, but he definitely looked conflicted. Somehow I was sure that, whatever Lionel had done, it had been coerced.

"I think it's time we disposed of these people, don't you, my friend?"

"Uh . . ." Lionel eyes widened in what I hoped was shock.

"Oh, come on," Cyrus interjected. "What makes you think you'd get away with shooting us like you did Alvin? No one heard you on the beach, but surely the neighbors here would call 911."

"You must think I'm stupid." Lucille waved the gun. "This has a silencer. Didn't you notice? It was one William confiscated from a criminal. He gave it to me for protection on the many nights he needed to be away from home."

Oh yeah, I thought. The nights he was off dallying with his lovers. And, criminal? She'd said it in a derisive tone. What did she think she was?

I refrained from commenting out loud, however. The woman was disturbed enough without disrupting her thought processes even more. What I did do was ask, "I'm in the dark. I guess you've told Cyrus, but why are you doing this? What's this all about? Why was Alvin any threat to you?"

"He wasn't," she said through gritted teeth. "Not directly. But after I killed William, his very existence would have pointed the finger at me."

"I don't see that. Why? Just because a son you didn't know about showed up? And why kill your husband in the first place?"

"Because, after all the years I devoted to him, he was choosing to divulge his relationship with Alvin. He was going to change his will and accept Alvin into the family." The words *the family,* were almost in capital letters as she spat them out. "What would everyone have thought? I insisted he not do it, and he said . . . he said he'd leave me then. He said he'd always wanted a son, and I hadn't been able to give him one."

"But why, then, did he have a vasectomy?" I burst out. Beside me, Cyrus stiffened, and I sensed his displeasure at my disclosure.

The look on Lucille's face made me realize why. Her eyes widened in horror, and spit dribbled down her chin. "Why do you say that? What makes you think . . . ?"

I'd done it now, and I might as well finish up. "Because his mistress told us so, that's why."

"He wouldn't! Just because I miscarried a damaged fetus, the doctor said . . ." Still pointing the gun at us, she held it out to Lionel. "You do it!" she said. "You do it! They've got to be disposed of! With Alvin dying, they're the only ones who could tell what we've . . ."

Lionel backed away, his expression appalled. "Not me," he said. "I may have agreed to help you with dirty tricks, but, murder? No way, lady! You're crazy."

I winced. Why on earth hadn't Lionel grabbed the gun while he had a chance?

"Then you're disposable, too! You're the only ones who can bring me down. That sheriff is convinced he's found the murderer. Make up your mind. Do you want to live or don't you?"

Lionel's eyes were clearly communicating with Cyrus, who released my hand. Suddenly, on some unseen signal between them, they both moved. Cyrus went low, yelling "Duck!" to me as he went. Lionel went high.

As the three of them tangled, I hit the floor. This was one time brute force was needed. The gun fired with a muted sound I'll never forget.

Unfortunately for Lionel, his dive forward put him into the path of the bullet. He spun backward and collapsed. Cyrus ended up on top of Lucille on the floor.

I crawled forward, frantically searching for anything I could use as a weapon.

I've heard that intense emotion can give a person superhuman strength, and that had to be what had happened to Lucille. Cyrus appeared to be winning the fight, but Lucille still clutched the gun, which was inching toward Cyrus's head.

I spotted a brass lamp on the end table. A heavy brass lamp. Still on my knees, I grabbed the lamp, pulling the plug loose, and swung. A horrifying crunch indicated I'd made contact.

The struggle was over. Lucille, with a loud exhale, sprawled beneath Cyrus, who scrambled away. Her eyes were open but unseeing, and then the lids slowly lowered.

Panting, Cyrus rose to his knees. "Donna, I—"

A crash interrupted him. Sheriff Calligan, gun drawn, burst into the living room. "What . . . ? Ohmigod!"

"What took you so long?" I asked him.

CHAPTER TWENTY-FOUR

Chaos ensued. I must have fainted, or almost done so, because the next thing I was clearly aware of was that I was sprawled in an ungainly position on the couch, my feet hanging over the edge. No one was paying attention to me, and as I listened to Cyrus making explanations to the sheriff, I was happy to keep it that way.

Solving mysteries was one thing, but had I actually caused the death of a human being? Nausea threatened to expose the fact that I wasn't truly unconscious, and I gulped to contain it.

In a surprisingly short time, aide prsonnel arrived and began checking everyone out. Lionel was the first to be loaded on a gurney and wheeled away, which was as it should be. He may have, as he put it, been behind the "dirty tricks," but I didn't think he was the truly evil person Lucille was. I had a feeling that this might be the lesson Lionel needed for reformation.

I opened my eyes when I felt a stethoscope descend on my chest. "I'm okay," I said, although I was surprised at how weak the disclaimer sounded.

"We'll just be sure," a calm voice assured me as a blood pressure cuff was put on my arm.

Behind the young man dressed in white, Cyrus's distressed face hovered. He certainly didn't need to be worried about me. That wasn't fair. "Really," I addressed him. "I just felt faint for a second."

"More than a second," Cyrus mumbled, but his expression relaxed.

"How are you?" I asked. "How's—everyone else?"

"They're both alive," Cyrus assured me.

"Thank goodness." I relaxed and let the aide person do his thing.

"I think you are all right," he confirmed. "Would you like to try sitting up?"

Relieved, I did. I was a little woozy, but I did my best to hide it. "A drink of water, maybe?"

Cyrus quickly produced it, and as I drank, I tuned in to the proceedings.

It was amazing how many persons were necessary to respond to a situation such as this. People milled around the living room, some police, some aide personnel, some not immediately identifiable.

"Roberta," I remembered aloud. "Would someone notify Roberta that we're okay?"

"Already have." Sheriff Calligan appeared before me. "Her worried call was what sent me over here, and I figured the least I could do . . . Ahem. Sorry, folks, that I didn't get back to your call sooner. We really were tied up with emergencies. However . . ." His contrite tone switched to the officious one we were used to. ". . . your interference—"

"Come on, Sheriff," Cyrus interrupted. "I explained it to you already. We truly believed that Lionel was in danger." He neglected to include the fact that we hadn't been entirely sure what Lionel's role in the whole mess had been.

The sheriff could, I realized, follow through with his threat to charge us with interfering with an investigation. This time I'd better concentrate on not angering the man more fully. Weakly, I asked, "Can I go home?"

He hesitated. "For now," he said, "but we'll need to interview you when you're feeling better. Sure you're up to going?"

"Oh, yes." I was greatly relieved. "Thank you, Sheriff."

"We have two cars here," Cyrus interceded, "and I don't think Mrs. Galbreath should drive just yet."

"We'll deliver it," Calligan answered. "I noticed your car in front, Mrs. Galbreath. If you'd give us the keys?"

"Certainly," I answered with relief. "If I can just find my purse?"

"Here it is." An officer thrust it toward me.

"Thanks." I extracted the keys and handed them to him.

Cyrus sat down beside me. "Are you sure you're up to this?"

"I've got to be," I answered. "I want out of here. Give me a hand?"

Solicitously, he took my elbow and gave me a boost. I stood still for a second before I tried to move.

Ahead of me, medical personnel were still working on Lucille. I gulped, and averted my eyes. I must have wobbled, because Cyrus put one hand around my waist and held my other hand as he whispered, "Steady now."

Curious neighbors peeked from apartment doors as we made our way to the elevator. One woman even asked, "What's going on?"

Cyrus waved in dismissal. "Not now." In a more reassuring tone, he said, "It's over. You'll read all about it in the paper, I'm sure."

When we reached the lobby, he lowered me to the settee. "Wait here," he ordered. "My car is some distance away. I parked where I couldn't be seen."

Good idea. One that hadn't occurred to me.

Soon we were parked in my driveway, and an anxious Roberta ran out to meet us. Her dark hair was disheveled and her expression frantic. "Mom, are you okay?"

Cyrus helped me out of the car, and she hugged me tightly. It felt so good. She has a distinctive smell, and I buried my face against her shoulder. "I'm fine. Thanks for calling the sheriff. It got him moving."

"Then tell me why, *why* you keep getting yourself into these situations?" She didn't let go of me, kept patting me on the back like I used to do to her when she was distressed. "The sheriff told me just a little, that Lucille Donniker and someone else were injured. What happened? And what did you have to do with it?"

That would take a little explaining. "Let's go in," I suggested. "Is dinner ready?"

"Stop being evasive! Cyrus, I assume you'll stay? There's plenty of lasagna."

"Lasagna?" he said. "Well, I do think I'll take you up on that. And perhaps I can contribute to the story. Your mother . . . well, she fainted, and I think we should get her inside."

She stepped back, still holding both my arms. "You fainted? You, Mom? Have you ever fainted in your life before?"

"Well, no, but then I don't believe I ever almost killed anyone before either."

Roberta glared at me. Then, again acting like the mother rather than the child, she ordered, "Get into the house!"

I chuckled weakly. Then, with Cyrus on one side and my daughter on the other, I made my way into the living room. I really did think I could have managed on my own, but perhaps . . . well, it was no time to be asserting how strong I really was. My behavior might be manipulative, but I sensed that showing my vulnerability right now might be wise.

I was so glad to be home. Safe. With the danger over. "You're right," I admitted. "I never want to be in that situation again. I'm not sure . . ." I glanced at Cyrus. "How did we get ourselves into this?" I asked.

His eyes lit up with humor. "It wasn't entirely Donna's fault,

Roberta. I'd like to say that at least part of it is that we both believe in justice and truth and all those good things. But," he said, now openly chuckling, "I think your mother and I share a feeling, perhaps, that . . ." He rubbed his face. "I was going to say that we're a little smarter than some of those in power, but that's not it. Maybe, we have more common sense?"

Roberta sighed, a deep, heartfelt, almost-groan. "I remember Mother wondering what she did to deserve you as a neighbor. Maybe she was right. But, now, I want to know what happened. No, wait. I'll dish up and you can tell me over dinner."

So that's what we did. Cyrus did most of the talking. I was especially grateful that I didn't have to describe my attack on Lucille.

Cyrus finished the tale by saying, "I haven't had a chance to thank you, Donna. Again, you came to the rescue. That woman truly could have killed me had you not conked her."

"Oh, I doubt that," I said. "You were stronger, and you were winning."

"Yes, but she was the one with the gun."

I didn't answer that, but Roberta put her elbows on the table and dropped her head into her cupped hands. Cyrus looked at me ruefully, and I grimaced back.

Finally she raised her head. "Why do I feel like a mother must when she's chastising her children? But if you ever do that again . . ."

We stared at each other, and then both burst into laughter.

"Yes, Mother," I said.

We only had the proverbial twelve days until Christmas, and we'd have been busy without the addition of tidying up the details of the incident in Lionel's condo with the police. In mid-morning, while Roberta and I lingered over breakfast, the phone rang.

"Good morning, Donna, this is Sheryl. How are you?"

"Just fine," I said. "Glad it's all over."

"Well, not quite," she said. "The sheriff requests your presence at the station. Cyrus has already been here and given his statement, and now it's your turn. If you're up to it."

I had the feeling that Calligan was there, from her tone, so I didn't extend the conversation. "Sure," I answered. "In half an hour?"

"That would be fine. See you at ten-thirty."

Roberta insisted on driving me. "I'll wait in the car," she said. As I entered the office, the sheriff stood and actually came around the counter to greet me. "Thanks for coming," he said. "We need a statement from you as to what happened yesterday, and how you became involved."

I glanced at him suspiciously, but his face was impassive. Was he considering charging Cyrus and me with obstructing justice? Again I resolved to watch my tongue. "Certainly, Sheriff."

He sat me down at his desk and pointed to a recorder. "We'll be taping this," he said, "and Sheryl will type your statement out for you to sign."

I noticed he didn't offer me an option in the proceedings.

"Shall we begin?" At my nod, he turned the machine on, recording the date and time. "Let's begin with the events of yesterday," he said.

The proceedings took longer than I expected. The whole thing was convoluted. I did emphasize our attempts to reach him before we tried to find Lionel, adding that he was unavailable because of major emergencies. I saw a glimmer in his eye. I hoped it was humor.

"And so," I concluded, "Mrs. Donniker appeared to be completely crazy, and she was waving that gun around and I . . ." I gulped. ". . . I did what I thought was necessary to prevent her shooting Cyrus."

He shut off the machine, and I asked, "Is she going to recover?"

"To my regret, most likely. Ahem. I shouldn't have said that, but you almost did the county a favor."

"I didn't plan to be an executioner, Sheriff," I mumbled. "That's not part of my resume."

"No. Of course not. Sorry."

"And Lionel? Will he recover?"

"He's expected to. His mother arranged for him to be transferred to Harborview by copter, and they're among the best in the world treating this sort of thing."

"Good," I said. "I don't know why, but I feel sorry for him. I think growing up rich, and probably spoiled, can be a handicap rather than a benefit. And from what I've heard, the family had a great deal of tension."

He made a rueful face. "You're a good woman, Mrs. Galbreath. But, stick to teaching in the future, okay?"

"I intend to. My daughter made me promise. Is that all?"

He stood, reached across the desk, and shook my hand. "That's all." He looked at me straight in the eye. "Thank you."

I figured that the thank-you was for more than just coming in and giving a statement, and was likely as close to an apology as I was going to get. Then I had a thought. "I assume all charges against Jake have been dropped?"

He gave a half salute and a half smile. "All taken care of."

On the way home, I thought about the sheriff. Sheryl's assessment that he was a good cop appeared to be accurate. It was possible, even, that the man might have a human side that could come out with a little practice. If I had an opportunity, I'd try to give him some of that practice.

Roberta and I immediately made plans for the next few days. "Where do you want to start?" I asked. "Shopping and lunch or Molbak's?"

"That sounds good to me," she said. "Shopping and lunch *and* Molbak's. I think you could do with a day of pleasure after what you've been through."

So we set out for the day. Roberta offered to drive, but I declined. "Traffic will be horrendous, but I'm used to it, and you still don't have a car in New York, do you?"

"No. But I like to keep in practice."

"You can, later. You'll have people to see and things to do that don't involve me. That reminds me, though. I'm seriously contemplating getting a new car. Would you want to help me look for one if we have time?"

"Oh, that would be fun. I bet Will would like to help. He knows a lot about cars, and of course I don't. Except I'd want automatic. I saw a Prius the other day that I coveted . . ."

It was so good to have her here. I surely hoped she'd end up living closer.

The next few days went swiftly. We picked out a tree and decorated it. Might as well have the tree up early, as she was leaving right after Christmas. Colorful wrapped packages accumulated underneath.

Then, one morning while we were having a leisurely breakfast, Cyrus appeared at the door. "Just had a call from the sheriff," he announced. "Alvin has gradually regained consciousness, and he was able to give a statement. Calligan didn't tell me what he'd said, but he suggested that we might want to visit him."

"Come in," I invited. "Of course! Were you thinking of going this morning?"

"Depends on you."

"Have some coffee, Cyrus," Roberta offered, getting a cup. "If you're going, perhaps I could use the car today, Mom. I talked to Trixie the other night, and we did tentatively plan lunch together this week."

Trixie had been one of her best friends in high school. Besides, I suspected Roberta wanted to do some shopping for me. She thought I hadn't noticed, but she definitely had noted a few things I'd admired during our shopping.

So an hour later, Cyrus and I walked into the hospital. The atmosphere didn't seem as threatening this time. The fact that Alvin was recovering colored my attitude. We checked with the desk, and found that he had been moved out of intensive care. "You'll find him in 508," the nurse told us.

When we peeked in the door of the room, Alvin appeared to be sleeping, but he had far fewer tubes and wires attached, the bandage on his head was much smaller, and best of all, he looked more like a human being than a corpse. We tiptoed in.

I'd picked out a nice poinsettia at Molbak's in honor of the season, a multi-colored, ruffled flower that took my fancy. We hadn't needed to be quiet, though, as his eyes slowly opened, then widened when he saw us.

"It's good to see you." His voice was tremulous, but he clearly was coherent. "I hear I have a lot to thank you folks for, beginning with the flowers you sent." He gestured toward the dresser. Someone had cared for the bouquet and it was still beautiful.

"This one's to remind you that it's almost Christmas," I said, presenting the poinsettia.

Cyrus pulled up two chairs, and we sat beside the bed.

"I assume the sheriff brought you up-to-date on what happened?" he asked.

Alvin nodded. "I'm sorry," he said weakly. "I had no idea when I came back that . . . that I shouldn't have. All I'd hoped to do was find family."

We were all quiet for a moment. What could one say? The family he found must have been a huge disappointment, if he was looking for roots. "You didn't know anything about your father?" I asked.

Again he shook his head. "Very little. My mom didn't want to talk about him. All I knew was that I'd been born in western Washington, that he'd abandoned her, so she'd moved back to a small town near Cincinnati to live with her parents. My grandparents. They wouldn't talk about him, either. And they're long gone. Mom died while I was in the army. So—when I read William Donniker's name in the paper, and that he was from Washington, I figured it likely that he was my dad. I came out here, finally nerved myself to approach him and . . ."

"And what? Was he glad to see you?"

Alvin nodded. "Very glad. He hadn't known about me, you see. He'd left my mother within weeks of their marriage."

"Marriage?" I exploded. "He'd been married before?"

He nodded. "I found out when I discovered the marriage certificate among Mom's papers. You see, my family was not what you'd call open. Whenever I asked anything about my father, Grandma's lips would tighten, and Grandpa would leave the room. I'd given up. I figured they didn't want to talk about it because I was a bastard."

He stopped, took a breath before he continued. "I convinced myself that family wasn't important, compared to . . . well, what happened to me in Iraq. Until I saw that newspaper."

Cyrus cleared his throat. "That brings up the question. When did they get a divorce?"

"I found nothing to indicate that they ever did. And she certainly kept papers. Everything, I think." He smiled fondly. "And my father told me that he hadn't filed for divorce, either. He assumed my mother would take care of it. Which means, I know—you don't have to tell me—that very likely the chief law enforcement man in Cedar Harbor was a bigamist."

CHAPTER TWENTY-FIVE

Cyrus and Roberta were up to something. There'd been whispered conversations and shopping trips together, and firm orders for me to stay out of Roberta's room.

The days had gone fast since that crucial visit with Alvin. We returned to visit him often, and when the time came for his release, Cyrus took him to his new home, a small apartment conveniently located near the center of town. Cyrus had offered his guest room but been firmly turned down.

I'd been with him the day that offer had been made. Alvin's face had shown a mixture of gratitude, reluctance and relief. "I can't move in with you, Cyrus," he'd said. "I—I need to be alone, and I imagine you're used to your solitude, too. I've been staying in the homeless shelter." He grimaced. "It's been okay and it will be again."

"Nonsense," Cyrus said. "I'm not surprised you turned me down, so I did a little research, and I've found an available studio apartment near town where you can walk to the store, the post office and beach. It will do you for the time being."

Alvin smiled ruefully. "Thanks. But I don't have enough money, and I'm not going to take yours."

"Of course you can and will!" Cyrus interrupted. "You do realize that you'll inherit from your father? I'm not sure about Lucille's position, but as your father's legal heir, you should be in good shape."

Alvin appeared stunned. "I hadn't thought of that."

"I hope," I suggested carefully, "that you'll consider staying in Cedar Harbor. You said you don't have any family left in Ohio. We'd like to be your surrogate family, if you'll have us. Starting with Christmas Day, if you're up to it physically. We're all gathering at the home of . . ." I hesitated. The connection would be lengthy to explain, and since it also concerned the unpleasant aspects of the murder of Lyle Corrigan, I thought it best not to continue along those lines.

Instead, I finished, "Well, Marie Corrigan's our hostess. She's the mother of Will Corrigan, who appears to be in a relationship with my daughter Roberta. There'll be others there who were involved in this whole thing, including the young policeman, Jake Santorini. We told you about him. He's the one we hope will be our new police chief, when this all washes out. He deserves to be." I stopped talking when I realized tears were flowing from Alvin's eyes. Cyrus gently handed him a tissue.

So it was arranged. Alvin was released on Christmas Eve day, and Cyrus picked him up along with his few belongings, which had been held at the shelter, and took him to his new home. We'd previously stocked it with necessities. Everybody who'd met Alvin pitched in, including Jake, Susan and even, to my surprise, Tim Borland.

Tim showed up at the door of Alvin's new apartment as Roberta and I were bringing in groceries. "Thought I'd like to contribute to what you folks are doing," he said. "Brought some necessities and a few luxuries. We don't do enough for our servicemen."

I noticed one sack came from the liquor store and contained wine. Alvin probably wouldn't be allowed any yet, but he might appreciate it later. "I bought him a new electric shaver," Tim said. "Figured he probably wouldn't have one."

"How thoughtful," I said. "Thank you, Tim." For a moment, I considered inviting him to join us at the Corrigans, since I was quite sure he had no family nearby, until a picture of Cyrus's very disapproving face popped into my mind. I knew what he'd think. A few minutes later, when Tim prepared to leave, I was glad I hadn't extended the invitation.

"Thought maybe I could do a little personal interest story for the paper later, after he gets settled," Tim said.

"Always the newspaper man, aren't you, Tim?" I knew my tone was acerbic.

Tim caught it, and actually looked a touch sheepish. "Guess I am that, Donna. But I'd really like to help the man. This . . ." He waved at the parcels he'd set on the small kitchen table. ". . . was not meant to be a bribe."

"I know that, Tim, I didn't mean to imply any such thing. Thanks so much. And—Merry Christmas!"

"Can I have a hug?" he asked with a grin.

"Sure. Why not?" We shared a quick embrace. Over his shoulder, I could see Roberta's amused, speculative face.

After the door closed behind him, she commented, "I think that man has a thing for you."

I laughed. "Maybe. But it won't do him any good. Come on, let's hustle home. Still a lot to do."

So on Christmas Eve, Cyrus, Roberta and I gathered together to celebrate. After our simple shrimp dinner, we moved to the tree, leaving dessert and hot drinks for later. Roberta and I'd always opened our presents Christmas Eve, at least after she outgrew Santa Claus. It had started with, "just one," and gone from there. I personally prefer the atmosphere then over that of Christmas morning. Ornaments glistened from the strings of lights on the tree, and candles burned on the table.

Roberta and my gifts to each other weren't big surprises. Most of them were things we'd each admired while we were shopping together. She hadn't bought a lot, but I knew her finances were not what they'd been before her divorce, although

I'd never asked the details.

I'd chosen several books for Cyrus I thought he'd enjoy, including *Our Inner Ape,* by De Waal. I knew he was a voracious reader and loved books that made him think. I could tell as he thumbed through my choices that he was tempted to read rather than take part in the rest of the proceedings.

I had two packages from him. "Ohhh," I exclaimed when I unwrapped the luxuriously soft scarf and hat in a deep rose shade. "I've never felt anything so soft. What are they made of?" I asked.

"Alpaca," he said. "Glad you like them."

The other, a small box, contained an exquisitely carved ivory rose pin. "It's so beautiful," I said.

"Belonged to my mother," he mumbled. "Thought it appropriate for you."

"Thank you!" I was sitting next to him, and I turned and hugged him. "What a lovely gift."

Roberta grinned. "Now the big surprise," she said, standing and gesturing. "Come on." She led me toward her room. We'd been so busy I hadn't thought about why the room had been off-limits to me.

"Oh, my!" One side had been transformed. She'd completely removed any girlhood remnants. On her otherwise bare desk sat a gleaming computer monitor flanked by the computer box and printer.

"Hope you aren't angry with us," she said, "but Cyrus and I thought it was time you joined the Twenty-first Century. I'll teach you to play solitaire and Free Cell. I know, you'll sniff in horror at the idea of games, but it's the best way to get comfortable with the mouse. Don't think you've used one much. Then Cyrus will coach you in searching the 'Net. And, Mom, we can stay in touch so much easier. We don't have to catch each other at home. You can send me a message in the middle of the night, and I'll get it as soon as I check my e-mail."

Well. I should have had a hunch, from Cyrus's comments recently. And I had to admit, they were undoubtedly right. Soon after I thanked them, I was settled in front of the thing while Roberta demonstrated its capabilities.

"Look," she said, "you can go to Google. Just click here and type in anything that you're interested in." She demonstrated, and soon I was hooked. I would have hated to admit it, but I'm sure it was obvious. Behind us, Cyrus was buried in a book, but he looked up and made a comment every once in a while.

I glanced at my watch. "Oh, my," I said. "I didn't realize it was so late. Shall we have our dessert now?" Cyrus marked his place with the bookmark I'd enclosed, and we headed for the kitchen.

"It just occurred to me," I said as we sliced pumpkin pie and put it on plates, "Didn't you and Will exchange presents?"

"Tomorrow," she said, with a slight smile. "It's a surprise."

"For us? Or for you?" I asked, but she didn't answer.

Finally, Cyrus bid us good night, Roberta and I cleaned up the kitchen, loading the dishwasher, and we headed to bed. We hugged each other. "It's so good to have you here," I said. "I'll miss you. Wish you didn't have to go back."

"So do I, Mom, but my desk'll be piled high. I've loved being here, too. Merry Christmas!"

CHAPTER TWENTY-SIX

In the morning, Cyrus arrived on our doorstep at exactly 11:30, our agreed-upon time.

"You both look spiffy," he said.

We had all dressed in our holiday finery. Eschewing red, I'd picked a dress with a black background and a floral pattern that included flowers almost exactly the shade of my new scarf and hat. Even though my raincoat, appropriate for the day, was black, I'd liked the effect. Apparently, so did Cyrus, from the look in his eyes.

Men, of course, don't have the options we women do, but from somewhere he'd produced a tie with poinsettias on it. Roberta, who wore a red dress with a gay scarf, laughed, and poked it. "Where on earth did you get that?"

"Had it for years. Save it for special occasions like this one."

We'd agreed to take my car, and I handed the keys to Roberta. We needed room for four passengers, of course, but it had also occurred to me that it would be nice to proceed more sedately than was usual with Cyrus.

Our next stop was to pick up Alvin. He wore the same outfit he'd worn on Thanksgiving, although his left arm was in a sling. I'd forgotten about the shoulder injury. "That bandage on your head makes you look quite dashing," I told him. "Like a pirate or something." Alvin carried one of the bottles of wine Tim had given him.

Marie's house was lovely. A wreath of cones hung on the

front door, which was outlined with swags of greenery. Will kissed Roberta and me, shook Alvin and Cyrus's hands, and led us into the living room.

I particularly watched Alvin's face. I knew it had to have been some time since he'd spent Christmas like this. The joy on his face as he looked at the huge decorated noble fir almost made me cry.

Carrie'd been invited too, and she rose to greet us just as Marie came in from the kitchen. Will left to answer the door, returning with Jake, Susan, and her two boys. Jake handed a large sack to Will, and whispered something. Will's face broke into a broad grin and he nodded, then disappeared into the kitchen.

It felt so good to share this day with family and friends, I thought, as voices rose and a hubbub ensued. I was a very lucky woman.

Will drew our attention by ringing a small brass bell, then reached behind him for a tray of glasses. "The day is even more special," he announced, gesturing toward Jake and Sue. "You tell them," he said.

Jake, grinning, put his arm around Susan. "I'm happy to announce that Susan's name is now Mrs. Susan Santorini! We were married two days ago."

The sack had contained champagne, and we were soon excitedly toasting the newlyweds. "And," I raised my glass, "I hope we'll soon be toasting a new Cedar Harbor police chief!"

"Hear, hear," everybody cheered.

"Thanks everybody. We hope we'll be able to stay here," Susan said. "But if not, we still owe so much to all of you. I'd like to toast the Dump Donniker committee, may he rest in peace. Without you all, I fear we wouldn't be in this position today." She kissed Jake on the cheek.

"Well," Will said, drawing Roberta to her feet, "perhaps this would be an appropriate time to make our announcement. Roberta has agreed to become my wife."

Oh, my! Oh, goodness! Roberta held out her left hand, and Will placed a large, glistening diamond on her ring finger. They kissed as everyone cheered, and then she came over and kissed me. I almost collapsed on the sofa.

Cyrus sat beside me. "Ahem, rather a special day, is it not?"

I hadn't realized I was crying happy tears until he pulled out his handkerchief, one that would always remind me of the fear I'd felt for his safety when I'd seen it lying as a beacon in that hallway in front of Lionel's apartment.

"Here," he said, solicitously patting my cheeks with the handkerchief. As Jake and Will refilled everyone's glasses, Cyrus took my hand and squeezed it.

Briefly, I thought of Lionel, still in the hospital in Seattle, I understood, and his worried mother and even Lucille. The doctors hadn't determined yet whether she'd survive, or if she did, whether there'd be brain damage. I wondered if she had known her husband was a bigamist. If she had . . . It occurred to me she wouldn't be the only woman who'd be tempted to kill her husband for that. Most, however, would manage to resist the temptation.

I swallowed. This wasn't a joyous day for everyone. Today, just for today, I was determined to shove those thoughts back deep into my brain.

But for those I loved, it was joyous indeed.

ABOUT THE AUTHOR

Norma Tadlock Johnson has now settled in a cottage overlooking soccer fields and the mountains beyond Burlington, Washington. She enjoys gardening, reading, attending concerts and plays, and travel, especially to warm places where she can snorkel. Her other books include middle-grade novels, suspense, a nonfiction about the Mountain Troops of World War II, and four romances co-written with her daughter, Janice Kay Johnson.